THE SHADOW PRINCE

THE LONGEST NIGHT IN EGYPT

THE SHADOW PRINCE
THE LONGEST NIGHT IN EGYPT

DAVID ANTHONY DURHAM

Tu Books
An imprint of LEE & LOW BOOKS INC.
New York

Copyright © 2023 by David Anthony Durham

Jacket art copyright © 2023 by Eric Wilkerson

TU BOOKS, *an imprint of* LEE & LOW BOOKS Inc.
95 Madison Avenue • New York, NY 10016
leeandlow.com

Manufactured in the United States of America
Printed on paper from responsible sources

Edited by Elise McMullen-Ciotti
Book design by Sheila Smallwood
Typesetting by ElfElm Publishing
Book production by The Kids at Our House
The text is set in Adobe Garamond Pro

Chapter opener art copyright © by Olga Che
Egyptian symbols by Good Studio

1 3 5 7 9 10 8 6 4 2
First Edition

Cataloging-in-Publication Data is on file with the Library of Congress

ISBN 9781643796093 (HC) • ISBN 9781643796130 (EBK)

To Gudrun, Maya, and Sage for all the years of dreaming up and telling stories together

FLYING HIGH

The Best Idea Ever?

I had to shout to keep the wind from snatching my words away. "ARE YOU SURE THIS IS A GOOD IDEA!?"

Above me, Prince Khufu climbed up the rungs of what had to be the tallest spire in the world. He shouted, "IT'S THE BEST IDEA EVER!"

"But . . ." I gulped. ". . . WE'RE REALLY HIGH UP!"

So high, in fact, that the city of Abydos spread out far below us. I could make out the grid pattern of streets reflecting the glow of the night sky's starlight. It would've been a great view if I was peering over the railing of the royal barge, but it was a different story hanging on for dear life to a thin metal frame that swayed in the wind.

"THE HIGHER WE GET, THE BETTER THE RIDE!" Prince Khufu shouted.

I'd figured my new job as the prince's shadow would require a lot of dangerous things from me. But I'd never imagined this. The prince hadn't seemed this adventuresome during the shadow testing. Worried and nervous was more like it. But since that was over and I'd become his shadow, he seemed a lot more confident. And mischievous.

"IT'S STILL DARK!" I protested. "THE SUN ISN'T EVEN UP!"

Khufu stopped and motioned for me to climb up to him. When I reached him he said, "It's almost sunrise. We'll get in one quick ride on the first rays of the sun. Nobody will know we haven't slept the night away like good little kids. So stop protesting. You got to do all sorts of fun stuff during the shadow testing. Now it's my turn."

"*Fun stuff*? You think fighting demons was fun? Giant scorpions, baboon brothers, the Jackal-Headed Demon that Feeds on Rottenness—"

"He nearly fed on *you*," Khufu said, with an amused smirk.

"Not to mention Ammut!"

"Why do people always say *not to mention* just before they mention something?"

"Being attacked by metal vultures, almost getting eaten by a massive slug, nearly torched by a fire-breathing monster, and having to fight Egypt's most powerful evil magician—"

"It wasn't really Teket. Just a spell version of him."

"Watching other kids die in horrible ways. You call that—"

"Nobody *really* died."

"But we didn't know that at the time!"

Khufu let go of the rungs with one hand and pointed. "I can see the glow from Lord Ra."

"Two hands, Prince!" I snapped. "Two hands, please!"

"Relax," Khufu said, "this spire was made for climbing." With that, he resumed the ascent. I took off after him.

I couldn't really say just what the spire was made for or who would want to go up it. Khufu had mumbled something about it being for atmospheric experiments, whatever that meant. All I knew was that we shouldn't be up there. Not by ourselves. Not in the dark of night. And especially not after Pharaoh Neferu had made it clear we were not to use the sunwings.

The royal family was on a big tour of Egypt. Most of the royal family, that is. Prince Rami had fallen suspiciously sick and talked his way out of going. It was pretty obvious why. The trip was all about showing Prince Khufu off to the people of Egypt. And showing me off, too, I guess. Knowing Rami, this was not stuff he wanted to be a part of. Not that I minded. He was almost as big a sourpuss as Lord Set.

Princess Sia had also stayed behind. As the youngest of the royal children, she had the ceremonial role of representing the family in the capital. She was only eight years old, but she was already making a mark on the nation. She had been the one who convinced the pharaoh to have the shadow candidates in Khufu's testing magically transported away at the moment they would have died. She'd saved a lot of lives, including Gilli's and Seret's.

Because of her, Gilli and Seret were able to come along on the trip, too! As a cadet in the Royal Guard, Seret was aboard to learn about her duties when the royal family traveled. Gilli, as a novice magician, was along to meet with some star magician named Iset. Those were the official reasons they came along, but I really think that Pharaoh Neferu and Queen Heta arranged it as a way to reward them for helping to defeat Ammut when she attacked the prince.

Khufu and I finally reached the top of the spire. We climbed out into a small round basket. Khufu unpacked the bag he had slung over his back and shoved a bundle of cloth into my chest. I accepted it and watched him snap out another garment. He shimmied into it with enthusiasm and then raised his arms. "Look," he said, a ridiculous smile on his face, "I'm a bird!"

Not exactly. He was a twelve-year-old Egyptian prince wearing a shirt made of suncloth. It fit snug to his body, except for flaps of fabric that hung between his arms and his side. Wings, so to speak. At a banquet the night before, the governor of Abydos had given all sorts of gifts to the royal family—including two brand-new sunwing suits for the princes. They'd been designed right there in Abydos. The pharaoh had thanked him politely, but after the banquet he had forbidden Khufu from using them. "Too dangerous," he'd said. "Untried technology. I can't have you risking your necks with such things."

I figured that was the end of that. But Khufu had other plans. He'd woken me in the middle of the night, a huge grin on his face and the two sunwing suits clenched in his hands. Next thing I knew, we were scaling the spire, about to do the craziest thing I'd ever heard of.

As I put on my sunwings, I said, "Your father said—"

"My father may be the pharaoh, but he's also just my dad. And"—he stretched, checking the hang of the wings—"fathers don't always know best. He stopped having fun years ago. Hey, look, the sun's rising."

He was right. Lord Ra had just begun to burn up into the sky. As the first rays touched us, I felt the sunwings hum into life. Energy ran through them, making a tinkling sound. I'd seen suncloth work before, especially in the sails that powered *The Mistress of Light*. But feeling the energy rippling across my body was a very different thing.

"Cool, isn't it?" Khufu asked. He pulled two pairs of goggles from his pack. He handed one to me, and then strapped his own on. "Let's be quick, before the city wakes up."

"Too late for that," I pointed out. "The city's already awake!"

The direct rays of the sun hadn't reached the ground yet, but even the hint of it was enough for flying things to begin to hum with energy. It shouldn't have been surprising. Abydos was a busy trade and manufacturing city. It was famed for its traffic jams, and I could see why. The moment the sun made it possible, ships and barges, skiffs and transports began to rise, along with all the flying beetles and dragonflies and sunboards that went along with them.

Khufu flung a leg over the railing, got his footing on the outside, and then looked over his shoulder at me. The green glass from his goggles made his eyes look bulbous. "On the count of three."

Reluctantly, I pulled my own goggles down over my eyes. "Prince, I'm all for having fun and everything, but I really think—"

"One."

I scrabbled over the railing. "—you should reconsider."

"Two."

I had just enough time to get the railing at my back, holding on with both hands. "I mean we could get in trouble, me especially—"

"Three!"

2

A Quick Study of Falling with Style

Khufu let go, leaned forward, and dropped away from the tower like a diving hawk.

I dove after him, plummeting toward the earth at incredible speed. The wind roared in my ears. It yanked my body around. My arms and legs lashed at the air like I was swimming. But I wasn't. I was dropping like a stone—a thrashing, panicked, out-of-control stone.

Khufu pulled away below me. He fell even faster than I did. He cut through the air headfirst, with his arms pressed to his sides and his body rigid as a spear. I tried to follow his example. Then Khufu did something smart. Something I should've thought to do from the start. Trembling with the effort of it, he managed to spread his arms wide. The suncloth of his wings sparked to life. The energy they caught propelled him forward. He pulled out of free fall and shot over the city, the fastest thing I'd ever seen.

Gritting my teeth, I pried my arms away from my sides. It wasn't easy with the force of the wind pressing them flat. "Come on!" I shouted. I could make out people below me now. A few, having seen me, looked up. I could even tell where I was going to splatter, a tiled courtyard that seemed to be drawing me straight to it. With another shout, I flung my arms out. The fabric snapped taut, energized by the sun. I curved my body backward. Instead of crashing into the courtyard I skimmed just above it, stirring dust on the stones as I zipped past. I shot down an alleyway, right over a surprised—and grumpy—group of camels. In the shadows of the alley, I felt the power in the wings ebb slightly. I could've tried landing, but I was still going way too fast. I needed to get back up into the direct sunlight. I rose, caught the sun, and felt the wings jump back to full life.

Flying over the rooftops in pursuit of Khufu I got a chance to recall all I knew about these sunwings. I knew that there were two crucially important things to remember. First was that—as I'd just been reminded—they only work when the rays of the sun are directly hitting them. Second was that they didn't actually make you fly. All they did was boost whatever momentum you already had, more like energized gliding than true flying. The one thing you didn't want to do was come to a dead stop. Not in midair, at least. Other than that, it was just a matter of learning to steer with your body.

I made a quick study of that. I swooped and curved, rose and fell. I felt like some combination of a bird and a fish. Khufu had been right. This was serious fun! Thinking that, I pressed to catch up with him.

I can't say what sort of maneuvers a trained pilot might be able to pull off, but I bet they'd have nothing on us. Loops and dives. Turns and dips. We did it all. At one point, Khufu carved his way through a long line of slow-moving barges. He corkscrewed through them, laughing the whole way. He looked like he was enjoying himself as much as I was. He wove through the bustling morning traffic. He darted under one barge. Over another. He carved circles around still another. Pilots pointed at him, shouting things I couldn't quite make out. That was probably for the best. They didn't look too happy to have us buzzing around them.

"Hey," I called, slipping in beside the prince, "this is great!"

"Didn't I tell you it would be?"

"We should find someplace to land, though, so we can get back to our rooms before—"

"Catch me if you can!" He tapped me on the shoulder and then dropped.

"But . . ." I was having a hard time getting in a complete sentence with the prince this morning. I figured we should quit before we got caught, but . . . he wanted a chase, and a chase he was going to get. *Why not? Nothing's gone wrong yet.*

I should have known better than to ever think something like that.

3

A Bit of a Mess

I nearly caught Khufu by tucking my wings and screaming down on him from above. He rolled away just in time, which sent me plummeting into a market square with way too much momentum. I smashed into a stand of melons. I bounced off an elephant's side and punched through an awning that a vendor was just setting up. I screeched through the bustling crowd, making shoppers leap out of the way. I tried apologizing, but I was there one moment, gone the next.

Khufu entered the maze of tall buildings in the financial district of the city. I scorched in behind him. We zipped into the bustling floating traffic, passing luxury yachts and sleek skiffs and chauffeur-driven suntaxis. We curved around tight corners, going in and out of shadow and sunlight. Along the avenues racing into the sun, we blazed. Each move brought me a little closer.

I was sure I had him when he turned in to a dead end. Finally, he'd made a mistake! A massive, obelisk-shaped building blocked our path. Hemmed in by the buildings on either side, there was only one way to go. Up. Khufu flew straight toward the sky. The side of the obelisk slipped by, near enough to touch. Nearing the top, I reached for him, focused on tagging him. Focused *too* completely, I'm afraid.

As we sailed up beyond the point of the obelisk, a shadow appeared. The massive wedge of the largest cargo barge I'd ever seen. It blocked out the sky above us. Khufu darted to the left and flew directly into one of the sunsails on the barge's side. I went for the right but slammed headfirst into some sort of rudder thing. The impact knocked the rudder out of position, though I hardly noticed, thinking more about the pain in my head. I scrambled to hold on to something. The fabric of one of my sunwings got caught on the rudder. It ripped.

"No!" I gasped. "Khufu, I'm going to . . ."

Fall. That's what I did. I fell, flipping end over end, even more out of control than when I'd first jumped from the tower. I spread my wings, but that only made it worse. The ripped one did nothing but crackle. The energy of the undamaged one sent me twirling like a top. I couldn't even see the world below me, but I knew it was approaching fast. I was going to get splattered after all. On top of the fear and regret, and on top of kicking myself for being so stupid, I felt a pang of shame. Yazen, my mentor, would hear that I'd died doing a silly thing. Against a direct order from the pharaoh! Not only would it sadden him, but it would dishonor him, too.

Of course, I didn't just blame myself. I said, "Khufu, this is all your—"

Something slammed into me. It wasn't the ground, though. It was the prince. He clamped one arm around me, and, keeping his other wing stretched, he curved out of free fall and shot us down the busy lane between the buildings.

"Khufu! You did it. You—"

"Oh, no! No. Noooo!" the prince shouted. Like I said, I didn't get to finish many sentences that morning.

Khufu lost control. We careened down the lane,

ricocheting from one building to another. When the lane spilled into a large, thronging market square—probably the only one in the city that we hadn't already paid a visit to—we exploded into it. I crashed through a wall of clay pots. Khufu took out the legs of a whole line of stalls. The tables and everything on them toppled over. I rolled through a flock of goats, making the animals stampede. Khufu impacted with a fancy fabric stand, cloth flying everywhere.

We came to a full stop tangled in debris. I plucked tufts of goat hair from behind my ears. Khufu tried to shrug off the colorful scarves and head shawls he was wrapped in. For a moment the market was silent, but then people and animals began to rise. The grumble of complaints and accusations started.

"Fine, I'll admit it," Khufu said, fighting with a long wrap of purple silk. "Maybe this wasn't the greatest idea ever. You should've talked me out of it."

"I tried! You wouldn't listen."

"Well," he said, standing to meet the crowd converging on us from all sides, "next time be more convincing. It's part of your job, you know."

The injustice of it! I would've given him a piece of my mind right there, but I didn't have the time.

Shouting merchants, disheveled food vendors, ornery goats, spitting camels: all were letting us have it. And then the grim-faced City Watch officers arrived, buzzing in on nimble dragonflies.

I wish I could say that was the worst of it. It wasn't. Looking high in the sky above, Khufu and I watched as the massive barge we'd collided with careened off course. It leaned to one side.

"That doesn't look good. You don't think that's because of . . . us, do you?" Khufu asked.

The bundles piled high on the ship's deck began to slide off. Hundreds of them, raining down on the city. Each impact sent up a massive cloud of white dust. I realized what they were.

"Sacks of flour," I said. We watched, mouths agape, as white clouds billowed over the city.

"That's going to make a bit of a mess, isn't it?"

"So much for nobody noticing us," I mumbled.

For the first time that day, Khufu didn't disagree with me.

The Boat of a Million Years

Out in Egypt's western desert, a god was getting grumpy.

"Where is the little whelp?" Lord Set said, scowling. "She's late again, of course."

The god stood on the deck of the Night Barge, gazing out over the rolling sand dunes that stretched off in all directions, interrupted here and there by rock outcroppings. It was a lovely view, especially with the setting sun casting the dunes in rippling shadows. The Night Barge rode the air beside the sundock that it was tethered to. The dock also floated on the sun's energy and was anchored to the ground far below by a thin, shimmering rope. The ship was slim and beautiful, built of dark wood and highlighted with *touches of gold and crimson. Boat and dock bobbed with the air currents, while beneath them gaped the chasm that led down into the Duat, the Egyptian underworld and realm of the dead. It looked unfathomably deep, dark, and terrifying. It was those things, but it was also much more than that.*

Set was a distinctive god. He had the body of a human, but the head of an anteater. Or a giraffe. Or an okapi? Nobody was entirely sure. He had a snout and tiny black eyes that flared into flames when he had a wicked idea. Two wiggly tufts jutted out of his head. He was one of Egypt's oldest gods, and nobody could beat him at trouble-making, cheating, or causing mischief.

Catching sight of movement on the dunes, Set said, "Ah, there's the little whelp. At last. I don't understand what the Fiery Fart sees in her."

The "little whelp" in this case was a girl named Thea. The "Fiery Fart" was none other than the magnificent Lord Ra, the god whose divine grace infused the sun with the magic that powered Egypt, making it a rich, prosperous nation full of wonders. Set chose not to acknowledge that Lord Ra did much of anything. It annoyed him that all of Egypt adored Lord Ra—but most things annoyed Set.

His large, pointed ears swiveled in Thea's direction. He heard her softly whispering, "I'm not late. I'm not late. I'm not late. . . ."

"You are, too," Set said, though she was too far away to hear him.

Actually, she wasn't late. She was nearly *late*, which is not the same thing. Thea was Lord Ra's assistant. She ascended the stairway of the sky pier with one arm clutching papyrus rolls to her chest and the other swinging out to keep her balance. She leaped from one floating plank to the next as she climbed away from the desert floor, getting higher and higher as she went. Each time she landed, the step sank a little as it adjusted to her weight. She began to take the steps two at a time.

Set considered casting a little spell to shift one of the stairs to the side, just enough to send the girl tumbling down into the mouth of the underworld. But that would cause problems with Lord Ra, and he'd been in enough trouble recently.

When Thea reached the barge, sweaty and out of breath, Set said, "You're late again."

Thea was twelve, slim and brown like most Egyptians, with dark, curly hair that she wore in Afro puffs, two round circles of hair on the top of her head. Metal rimmed reading glasses dangled from a gold necklace. She dressed simply in a linen shirt, a kilt, and sandals. As Egypt was pretty much always hot, she didn't need much more. She did, however, need the braces that she wore around both knees. A childhood illness had left her unable to walk very far. The braces helped. They were engraved with magical hieroglyphs. During the day, the sun powered them, making Thea as quick and nimble as any twelve-year-old. At night her proximity to Lord Ra kept them powered.

"Technically," Thea said, "I'm not late. I've cut it a bit close, but that's because Lord Ra asked me to fetch these scrolls for him. He wants to know all about Prince Khufu's shadow testing. He thinks the new shadow might be special."

"Oh, please." Set scowled. "A cheater is what he is. It was rigged from start to finish!"

Set was right about it being rigged, but he had it exactly the wrong way around. Ash hadn't cheated; Set had. He had tried to have all the candidates killed. Though he'd managed to keep this secret from the pharaoh and the gods, he didn't seem to mind grumbling about it in front of Thea. Despite Set's best efforts, the village boy Ash had triumphed and become Prince Khufu's bodyguard and closest confidant. And fortunately, none of the other candidates died. It was a great outcome, which is probably why it made Set so grumpy.

Thea raised an eyebrow and began to say something.

"I'm not interested in your thoughts," the god said. "His divine glowiness will be here any moment." The god flicked his fingers toward the west, where the sun—Lord Ra himself—was melting into the horizon. Instead of watching the beauty of the sunset, Set inspected his fingernails. "You know this is all a sham, don't you? We don't actually need Ra to be the sun. Outside of Egypt there's an entire world that doesn't give a fig about Ra, but they still have a sun. Rises and sets all by itself. Explain that, will you?"

"Well," Thea said, "when Lord Ra joins with the sun he makes it something more than it is without him. As our sun, he shines magic down onto Egypt to power our technology and enable us to work magic. It's what makes Egypt so special, isn't it?"

"Sure," Set grumbled, "that's the party line."

Thea continued, "And the Lord Ra journeys through the underworld and—"

"Lord Ra journeys through the underworld?" Set mumbled. "Hah! Ra sleeps and I do all the work! I *answer all the riddles posed at the gates, stand up to the various demons, fight with this and that goddess. I slay the serpent Apep each and every night, only to find him waiting in the same spot the next day. The things I do for Egypt. Anyway"*—he sniffed, his snout waggling—*"here he comes," Set said. "As showy as ever."*

Showy was one description. Magnificent was another. Just as the sun vanished, Lord Ra shot toward them, riding the last rays of sunlight on a vessel made purely of radiant light. It was called The Boat of a Million Years. *At its helm, Ra approached, glowing and regal, a falcon-headed being with a sun disk crown atop his head, radiating wisdom and calm. The boat made of light would come to rest in the exact same spot as the Night Barge. Then the light would fade away, leaving Ra standing in the barge for the evening's journey. It was all rather amazing.*

Or, it was amazing to anybody except for Set. As The Boat of a Million Years *approached, Set's eyes ignited into tiny, sinister flames. He whispered, very, very softly, "One day I'll refuse to put up with this. Someday—and soon—I'll make my move. . . ."*

5

Abducted!

Oh, what a mess we made! The sacks of flour kept falling, one after another after another. Before long, the cloud of flour was so thick it blocked the sun. The barges with the heaviest loads began to sink, crashing into buildings, into markets, landing on rooftops. Still more tipped their loads, leaving piles of shattered crates and all manner of things strewn across the city. A little later the wind kicked up. By nightfall the entire city of Abydos was coated in a ghostly dusting of white. The cleanup would take days.

Khufu got an earful from his father, Pharaoh Neferu, and a disapproving frown from his mother, Queen Heta. But he still got off pretty lightly. The reprimands ended in tearful hugs and relief. They were glad Khufu was alive. He promised not to do it again; they thanked the gods and mussed his hair. There are benefits to being a prince of Egypt.

I, on the other hand, had to sit through long lectures from various court officials on the proper conduct of a shadow. I tried to tell them that it had all been Khufu's idea, but that just got them going even more. "You should never blame anything on the prince!" they exclaimed. Any misdeed on his part was entirely my responsibility—which didn't seem fair at all! They said it was my job to keep the prince from even having any ideas.

Hah! I thought. *That's easier said than done.*

They stripped us of the sunwings. Pity. With a bit more practice I could've been a professional.

Fortunately, the officials in Abydos pretended they had no idea what caused all that flour to tip from the barge. Like I said, there are benefits to being a prince of Egypt. The governor even gifted Khufu a brand-new sunskiff. It was small. It could only carry about five people, but that's because it was built for speed and maneuverability. I immediately had dreams of what it would do when the sun filled its sail and it shot out into the sky, carving turns and rising and falling. I bet we'd be able to fly circles around *The Mistress* in it!

Which is why it was a bummer when Pharaoh Neferu whispered to Khufu, "Don't think you'll be taking any joyrides in this any time soon. Not after your sunwings escapade."

I was beginning to feel we were going to regret Abydos for a long time.

Late that night, after the palace had finally gone to sleep and I was alone in my room, I stood staring at myself in one of the full-length mirrors. I was still hearing all the things that Yazen would have said to me. About my responsibilities. About always being on guard. Always steering the prince in the right direction. Never forgetting the importance of my new role. Yazen was far away, but that didn't stop me from hearing him clear as day in my head.

I had just decided to get some sleep when I saw a blur of motion reflected in the mirror. Something flew through the window. The next instant scaly talons lifted me. I tried to shout, but I couldn't get any words out of my mouth. The talons gripping me somehow kept my mouth from obeying.

My attacker leaped into the air and flew. I craned

my head around to see what carried me. The birdlike shadow was black against the sky, large and frightening. We climbed up so that Abydos reeled beneath us, and then the creature banked and dove. It fell so fast I was sure it meant to dash me against the paving stones of one of the patios. Maybe that was how this demon liked his food. Pulverized. The tiles rushed up at me, smooth and hard and . . .

At the last moment the creature's wings flared. I felt myself propelled through a window into a room. From incredible speed to a complete stop in an instant. The thing released me. I fell to the floor, gasping.

In the yellow light of the oil lamps, I took in the plush surroundings. The pharaoh and queen waited for me. They sat on either side of a small table. Neferu wore a slim gold circlet instead of a formal crown. Queen Heta watched me with with eyes outlined in dark kohl. The winged being that had flown with me took up a position beside the royals. It was Lord Horus, his falcon head regal atop a body that was human-formed now.

I hopped to my feet and stood at attention.

"Forgive us the roughness of your transport here," the pharaoh said. "It was necessary that it be unseen by spying eyes. We must trust you with something important. Something that in your role as the prince's shadow you should know. But, Ash, before we can explain we must swear you to secrecy. You must tell nobody—nobody at all—what we are about to reveal. Do you swear to keep this secret?"

This all sounded a bit too serious. "Can you . . . give me a hint about what *kind* of secret it is?"

The pharaoh's face was expressionless. "No."

"I just have to swear without knowing what I'm swearing to?"

"Yes."

"Do I have a choice?"

"Not really."

Typical grown-up stuff. They make the rules; we just have to accept them. "Okay," I said. "I swear."

The pharaoh nodded. "Good. So that you understand the graveness of this, we have summoned two gods to give testimony."

Two figures stepped out of the shadows at the edge of the room. One was a hippopotamus. Clearly, it wasn't any old hippo. She stood upright on her hind legs. Her arms were long and lean, like a person's except that instead of fingernails she had cat's claws.

Her snout was pretty much standard hippo. She had a head of braided black hair that draped down past her shoulders. *That* wasn't standard hippo either. Did I mention that her skin was blue? It was Lady Taweret, protector of pregnant mothers, also known as the Lady of the Birth House. And she oversaw the training of the small blue hippos that protected the royal children when they were in the capital.

The other god was short and squat, about Gilli's height. His stubby bare legs bulged with muscles, as did his arms. He wore only a skimpy loincloth around his private parts. His head was wide, with large eyes and cat ears poking out from hair that could best be described as a mane. He had a thick, intricately braided beard. He was one of a kind: Lord Bes.

I'd never met either of them, but their statues were all over Egypt. I bowed to show my respect.

The pharaoh continued, "Ash, there is a prophecy. A prophecy that involves you. We in this room have kept it secret for years, but it's clear to us now that it's time you learn of it." He looked to his wife. "Tell him about it, my dear."

The queen began reluctantly. "The prophecy

appeared on the day my son was born. The same day you were born, Ash. Khufu had slept on the mat just beside me, always within arm's reach. I slept, so happy to have him healthy and beautiful. When I awoke, I found a papyrus note slipped inside Khufu's swaddling wraps. Nobody knew how it got there. The servants swore that nobody had entered while I slept. Lady Taweret herself had sat at the foot of my bed, and Lord Bes had stood just outside my chamber. Neither of them saw any intruder."

"And we would have," Bes declared. "Nobody gets past me when I'm on duty!"

Taweret's large nostrils flared. "Same here. Had even a mouse stirred in the room I would've known it."

"And yet the note was delivered," Heta said. "It was signed by Djedi, the lost magician." From within the folds of her evening gown, the queen drew out a small roll of papyrus. She slid it across the table to me. "Here, read this."

Carefully, I smoothed the papyrus out beneath my palms. It looked ancient, yellowed, and fragile. The glyphs were tiny but clearly written. Perfect stylus work. Textbook neatness. I began to read them.

For the ages this child,
    for the ages or forgotten.
For the ages Egypt,
    for the ages or forgotten.
To these four must he rise above,
        When Ra to darkness is consumed,
        When swimming breathless breathes,
        When in the depths the feather finds balance,
        When sits the crown doubled, heavy as souls.
By light or by dark a shadow he must cast.
Shadowless lies ruin. Demon darkness. Evermore.

6

The Prophecy

"**S**o you see, Ash," the pharaoh said, "my son's fate is connected to yours."

"Is that what I see?" I didn't mean to sound sarcastic in front of the royalty, but I didn't understand a word of that prophecy. "I'm sorry. These words would make as much sense if they were scrambled and thrown up against a wall."

Neferu ducked his head in a slow nod. "It's cryptic, this message, but the future of Egypt is encoded in its words. You faced many tests to become Khufu's shadow. It seems there are also tests for you and my son to face together. We don't know what they mean, or when they will appear. We just know that they are challenges to your—and Khufu's—fates."

"I'm sure you can see the importance of your role in this," Horus said.

"My role?"

"Yes, you are here." The god pointed his long finger toward the page. He pierced a glyph, and when he lifted it I read the lines again.

By light or by dark a shadow he must cast.

Shadowless lies ruin. Demon darkness. Evermore.

"I'm this shadow?"

"Yes," Queen Heta said. "Whatever is to become of my son, you must be at his side. You, Ash, are as important to the future of Egypt as he is."

"How can I help if I don't understand it?" I asked.

Bes scoffed. "We don't understand it either! That's the thing with prophecies. They never say anything straight."

That wasn't the answer I was looking for. "Then what am I supposed to do?"

"Only you can determine that," the queen said. "You must keep these words in your mind and recognize what's to be done when the moment presents itself."

"And you cannot speak of this to anybody," Taweret said. "Nobody at all. That's very important."

"Ash," Neferu said, "it is especially important that

you say *nothing* of this to Prince Khufu. Prophecy is a dangerous thing. If the prince knew, it would change him. He wouldn't mean for it to, but he would act differently. If his enemies learn of it they would work to decipher it and find ways to use it against him. We in this room—and Lord Thoth and Lady Isis—are the only ones that know of it."

Five gods, I thought. *A pharaoh. A queen. And a twelve-year-old boy. Who can spot the weakest link?*

"If it will change Khufu, won't it change me, too?"

"It will," Neferu said. "There is a difference, though. Khufu must become the figurehead of Egypt. You are the *protector* of the figurehead of Egypt. It's one burden on him; a different burden on you."

And I'd already sworn to take on that burden— before I even knew what it was. Not fair. A new thought formed in my mind. "Will you give me something in return?" I asked. "If . . . if it all works out. If Egypt doesn't . . . um, get demon darkness evermore and stuff."

Horus cleared his throat. "Young man—"

The queen stopped him. "What do you want?"

"To know who my parents are," I said. "You must know, or be able to find out."

The queen consulted her husband silently. He, in turn, exchanged glances with the three gods. Eventually, they all deferred to Heta to respond.

"We know," she said.

My heart thumped. They knew. They really knew!

Heta continued, "But we can't tell you. Nor can we explain why. Believe me, it pains me to say that. But everything depends on you being only Ash. On you defining yourself and becoming the person only you can be."

"When will I know I'm the person only I can be?" I asked. I mean, it did sound pretty vague!

"You'll know when the moment comes. So will we. I promise you, Ash, that when the time comes we will reveal who your parents are. You may hold me to this promise. As I will hold you to yours."

Babbel Reporting

Lord Set stood at the stern of the Night Barge, stretching. His shoulder pained him. He worked his arm around in circles. Behind him, the world was beginning to lighten with dawn. The gods had just come up from the beckoning dark of the underworld, having completed their nightly journey through its echoing caverns.

Lord Ra stepped out of his cabin. "Fatigued, Lord Set?"

Thea walked with one arm around the falcon-headed god's waist. He was always unsteady when he rose. It wasn't just fatigue. He'd also just undergone a transformation. In the underworld, he wore a ram's head with thick, curving horns. It's the type of place where you want to look extra tough. But when he emerged on the surface, he took on his falcon-headed form. That's how he appeared now.

"Well, Raaaa . . ." Set made the god's name sound like it was the name of something squishy he'd stepped on. ". . . while you slept, I piloted the barge through the world's foulest regions. Bit of work, that."

"We all have our burdens to bear," Ra said. "Even Thea here. I would not get through the night without her healing company."

Thea's main job was to look after Ra as he rested from his long day of work. Ra spent the evening talking with Thea, reading, and writing scrolls for her to deliver during the day.

Ra turned his falcon head to look down at Thea. "Thank you, Thea. I believe I can walk on my own now. I feel my glow returning." He stepped away from her. His spine lengthened, shoulders broadened. His body regained vigor with each breath he inhaled. He grew more radiant.

Set said, "Apep made a fierce attack last night. It was all I could do to fend him off."

"Really?" Ra asked. "I must have slept through that part." He looked down at Thea and winked.

To be fair, Set did do a lot each evening. It was no picnic arguing their way through the gates, answering riddles, sometimes coming to blows with demons. The Four Weary Ones, the Wailing Goddesses, the Meerkats of the Moon, the Winged Demons, just to name a few. No matter how many times they made the journey, they tried to make Ra's nightly voyage a misery. One of the demons, Apep, tried to do more than that, as Set was describing.

"The great serpent fixed me with his deadly stare . . ." Set crossed his eyes, unaware that his imitation looked comical, not deadly. ". . . and tried to overpower my mind."

"How did that go?" Ra asked.

"I lifted my spear to pierce him, but his tail lashed out. It knocked the spear from my grip and sent me sprawling. The serpent wrapped his long body around the barge. He had us in his coils. Flames shot from his eyes. His mouth billowed smoke. He reared back to strike. I leaped to my feet and found the spear again. Just as the beast struck, I drove the spear deep into his neck. I hope I didn't wake you when I crashed down. Landed on my shoulder." He grimaced as he began massaging the joint again. "You really didn't notice any of that?"

"Missed it," Ra said. The glow inside him strengthened. It was as if he was becoming the sun from the inside out. Bright light rimmed his eyes and outlined the features of his body. "But it sounds like an amazing feat, Lord Set."

Lord Ra was almost too radiant to look at now, but

Thea kept her eyes on him. She waited for the moment when he turned to her and said, "Dear Thea, thank you. Though I am a god, you ease my burdens. I am nothing without the faith of mortals."

Set rolled his eyes.

Thea called, "Have a good day, Lord Ra!"

The moment the rays of the sun touched Ra particles of his body began to speed away, sucked toward the sun. He turned into pure light as he joined with it. He would remain with it, a god and a ship and a glowing orb all at once, high in the sky throughout the long day.

"That," Thea said, "is the most amazing thing. Lord Ra is—"

"A flaming pain in the butt?" Set said. "That he is, which is not a good thing, little Thea. Not a good thing at all."

Before he could go on, something distracted them both. A messenger beetle flew in from the direction of the capital. He appeared as a dot hovering over the dry landscape, his small wings blurs beside his round body. He flew in a straight line toward them and landed on the platform beside the Night Barge.

Standing upright, the beetle was almost as tall as Thea. His shell was bright red, a sign of his order. He took off the gauze mask he wore over his insectile face to protect against the dust. It took him just a moment to find enough breath to speak.

"Babbel reporting, Messenger Beetle Second Class," he said.

Set grimaced. "Second Class?"

Babbel pounced on the question. "I'm working on getting my wings approved for Messenger Beetle First Class. That means I'll get to do stuff like this all the time. Taking messages to gods. To royalty. If I complete these last few test runs, I'll—"

"Enough!" Set snapped. "What's the message?"

Babbel looked mildly offended. He hooked one of his long antennae with a leg and rubbed it. He let it pop back upright and said, "It's from Lady Isis! She's alerting you that you will soon be summoned to the Vault of Divine Wisdom in the capital."

"For what?"

The insect bounced on his toes and managed to make it look like he was shrugging. "That wasn't part of my message. I just say what I'm told. That's it. That's all she wrote."

Set stepped closer to him. He snapped out a hand and grasped one of the beetle's thin antennae in his fist. He leered down at the messenger. "For what reason will I be summoned?"

"To—to . . ."

Set twisted the antenna, demonstrating that he could snap it whenever he wanted to.

"So that you can hear your reprimand!" the beetle blurted. "Lord Thoth and Lady Isis don't a-ap-approve of the demons you chose during the shadow testing. They think you meant the candidates harm. Ouch!"

The snap was as audible as the beetle's cry of pain. Set released the insect's antenna, broken and drooping. "Messenger, be careful where you run in the future. I wouldn't want you having another accident like the one that broke your antenna."

Set leaped from the barge onto the floating pier, where he'd parked his chariot beetle.

"Lord Set, where are you going?" Thea called.

"I have things to attend to, Thea," he said.

Set kicked his chariot beetle in the backside as he climbed into the carriage. The insect's closed eyes snapped open. He exchanged a weary glance with Babbel, and then his wings rumbled to life. Set gripped the reins and they zoomed off with fury.

After it grew quiet, the messenger sniffed and said,

"I'll be lucky if I don't get lost." When Thea looked confused, the beetle wiggled his good antenna. "No sense of direction with a busted tenny."

"I'm sorry," Thea said.

"Not your fault," Babbel muttered. He inhaled a deep breath, fired up his wings, and flew in a zigzag line quite different from how he'd arrived.

"Poor beetle," Thea whispered. "Lord Set is such a . . ." She knew what she wanted to say, but she let it go. She didn't like saying mean thoughts about anyone. Even Set.

8

A Prodigy

The next day we were back on board *The Mistress of Light*, flying high in the sky. *The Mistress* looked like a boat fit for the Great Sea, but it was even better than that. She was a sunclipper. Built of wood as light as bird bones, the ship was powered by billowing sunsails. Instead of catching the wind, the sails captured the energy of Lord Ra while he was merged with the sun. At full speed the sails shimmered and hummed. It was breathtaking to watch the world scroll by beneath.

But it was also a sad reminder that we weren't allowed to captain the new skiff. All Khufu, Gilli, Seret, and I could do was sit in it, moping, while it was tethered to the side of *The Mistress*.

Khufu looked the part of a prince with his brilliant white tunic, gleaming armbands, and bracelets. As a symbol of his new status as the likely heir to the throne, most of his head was shaved, but he did have one long lock of hair that thrust out from the side of his scalp and hung down toward his chin. He held on to the skiff's tiller, occasionally moving it as if he were steering. A prince, but a dejected one.

Gilli, on the other hand, wasn't one to stay dejected. His round face was always thoughtful, happy, and amused by the world. He sat on one of the benches, humming a tune and walking his fingers along the skiff's railing. "You know," he mused, "if you'd asked me, I'd have told you. Sunwings are trouble. Don't mess with them."

Seret lounged on the bow at the front of the skiff, looking at ease and relaxed as only a lioness could. She stretched, yawned, and flexed her claws. Like all cats, she seemed constantly impressed by how perfect her feline form was. As semi-divine, I guess she was kinda special. She said, "I'm glad you didn't involve me. I'd look rather silly in sunwings, don't you think?"

Gilli pressed on. "Me too. If you'd asked, I'd also have said—"

"I know, Gilli," Khufu groaned. "We've been lectured enough."

Pursing his lips, Gilli shrugged. Thankfully, he left it at that.

Seret fell into a conversation with Jumpra, the caracal kitten I'd saved from the rapids during Sobek's shadow testing challenge. He got cuter each day. Small, but with enormous eyes and big ears. He'd come with us on the journey and seemed to be enjoying his nightly excursions in each new town. He was a lot more confident than before. That was partially because an enormous crocodile god, Lord Sobek, wasn't tossing him into raging rapids, but I also think he liked his new life.

He couldn't speak Egyptian like Seret could, but Seret could speak caracal. It's hard to describe what caracal sounds like. It's like a vibrating meow combined with birdcalls and mixed with cuteness. Often, he'd just make one of these sounds. Gilli called them "trills."

Seret translated things the caracal said. That's how we learned his name was Jumpra. Apparently, caracal kittens get to name themselves. He was sure he was going to be able to jump right up to the sun when he got bigger.

We were a sad group sitting there, but I was glad we were all together. These were my friends. The only friends I'd ever truly had. Even though I couldn't tell them about the prophecy, it felt good to know they were with me—that they'd all help me if they could. We'd already been through some crazy adventures together. Little did I know that we were about to embark on another one.

The pharaoh's voice jolted us all to attention. "Ah, there you are!"

Pharaoh Neferu and Queen Heta strolled toward us across *The Mistress*'s deck. An entourage of ship's officers, guards, and official-looking people trailed behind.

"Well, this looks like a happy bunch!" Heta declared. With a playful smile on her face, she barely looked like the grave queen I'd made an agreement with last night. "Maybe I can cheer you up. Children, there's someone you need to meet. She boarded in Abydos. I suspect you could all learn a thing or two from her."

The queen motioned for a girl behind her to step forward. She was a bit taller than me, dressed in the light blue robes of a low-level magician. A silver stylus dangled from a string at her neck. She had dark brown skin and slim eyebrows that looked like they'd been drawn in black kohl. Her hair was cropped short, naturally curly. The most striking thing about her, though, was her eyes. They were gray: sparkling and intense.

The queen said, "This is Iset. She'll be traveling with us for a few days. She's just completed her magical training. At fourteen, she's one of the youngest ever to do so. She received the highest scores on the magician trials in nearly thirty years. Isn't that so, Iset?"

The girl nodded. "Yes, Queen Heta. I was pleased to make my family proud."

Neferu grinned. "Everyone says she's a prodigy, picks up even complicated spells just like that." He snapped his fingers. "Comes from a family of distinguished, noble magicians. Everybody is expecting great things from her."

I'd met a lot of nobles and rich officials since we started this tour around Egypt. I had come to suspect that they were really no different from the folks I'd grown up with in the village. Just like anyone, some were generous and kind and wise, some were greedy and mean and foolish. It's just that the nobles got to be those things from a position of wealth and power. Which sort of person, I wondered, was Iset?

Iset looked at me and said, "I've heard quite a bit about you, Ash. Seeing you, though . . . you're different than I expected."

That could be a compliment, but it didn't feel like one. I couldn't think of a response. Thankfully, with the focus on Iset, nobody noticed.

"This really is a lovely skiff," Iset said. "It must be wonderfully fast. You can tell by the shape of the hull and placement of the sunsail. I've never seen lines quite like it."

"You know about skiffs?" Khufu asked.

"Yes, Prince, my destiny is to be a magician, like most in my family, but I have a . . . well, a bit of a wayward older brother. He has no interest in magic. Instead, he loves skiffs. He taught me a thing or two."

"Such modesty!" Neferu said, laughing. "She competed in the Red Sea Sunskiff Races last year. Adult division. Isn't that so?"

Iset let her eyes slip away, apparently embarrassed. "I can't deny it."

"And how did you do?" the pharaoh asked, though I had the feeling he already knew the answer.

"Well, I . . . I won first place."

Khufu found that very interesting. He held his chin with the fingertips of one hand. He nibbled on his lower lip and stared off at nothing in particular. It was the same expression he always had just before proposing some dangerous idea. Which is just what he did.

"You know what would be great?" the prince asked. "If you could teach me and my friends how to sail." He turned to his parents. "I mean, she's so good at it, right? And she's such a good role model. And terribly responsible and all. Wouldn't that be great, Gilli? Seret? What we really need is a sailing tutor! Right, Ash?"

"I guess," I said.

Khufu beamed. With a wide grin and hopeful eyes, he asked, "Mom? Dad? What do you think?"

That did the trick. The queen laughed and said, "Husband, I think he may have you."

Frowning, the pharaoh conceded, "All right, but we're about to arrive in Djerty. There's a banquet in our honor. The skiff can wait until tomorrow."

Fun Times at the Kids' Table

A little later, we approached our next stop. Lord Ra dipped below the western horizon and the ship's oars—at least a hundred of them—went to work. They were slim and long, with curving scoops that gently maneuvered the ship into dock. The hull touched down just as the ship ran out of energy. Then the whole royal entourage—which included me now—poured from *The Mistress of Light* and paraded through the streets to much fanfare. Crowds gathered to greet us. They cheered and danced and tossed flower petals that the city's magicians turned into colorful birds. It was a lot of attention, and I still wasn't used to it. I was glad when we reached the banquet hall.

Khufu, Gilli, Seret, Iset, and I were seated together at a table on the honorific platform. We were at the kids' table, so to speak, and that was fine by me. Most eyes were on the high table with the pharaoh, the queen, Lord Horus, the city's governess, and their highest officials.

What wasn't fine by me was being seated right across from Iset. Every time her eyes fell on me my face flushed, and I'd look away. I'd revised my first impression of her eyes. They weren't gray. Silver was more like it. I couldn't help but want to watch her; I just didn't want her watching me watch her. I tried to concentrate on eating.

For the first three courses, the others peppered Iset with questions. But as the servants cleared the table before dessert, she said, "Ash, I understand you're to be instructed by Lord Thoth himself. Yes? How fortunate you are! You must be quite talented."

"He is," Gilli said, "but you should see his glyphs! I can barely read them." He smirked. "The weird thing is that they work. Kind of. I mean, they work, but in odd sorts of ways. Like, during the final testing battle against the spell-magician, Ash came up with some really creative spells."

Seret said, "Tell her about how you fought the giant slug monster, Ash."

"Teket sent it to eat Ash," Khufu said. "It was enormous!"

"And hungry," Gilli added.

"Oh, dear," Iset said. "But you defeated it, obviously."

"Yes, he did," Seret said dryly, "with stunningly subtle magic."

"Do tell," Iset said.

"I . . . sent some spells at it," I said, hoping that might be enough and we could move on to some other topic.

Khufu got more specific. "He fed it."

"Fed it?"

"Yep, heaps and heaps of food," Khufu said. "Rotten stuff. Moldy stuff. Just tons of food. The slug ate so much that it rolled over, started burping, eyes rolling. And then it burst. Puff! Biggest, foulest cloud of slug smoke there ever was!"

I'd been pretty proud of that in the moment, but at the table with them all laughing and smiling, it seemed embarrassing. I was sure that Iset would have come up with something better to fight it, something clever and sophisticated.

A servant set a dessert bowl of fresh, spiced cream in front of me. I focused on it. I sat there, face hot, as the others told her all about the flying battle between Teket's fire-breathing lizard and my zigzagging bat, about how the bat set me down and then flew right into the lizard-creature and died for me because of it. Or, that's how it felt to me. In truth both the bat and the flying lizard—and Teket himself—were only spells. Still, that bat was a part of me in some way. They didn't understand that, and I wasn't in a mood to explain it. I was in a mood to get up and leave, really. I was about to when Iset's voice broke into my brooding.

"You punched him?" she asked.

I looked at her. Those silver eyes watched me, smiling and smug. She was asking about Teket in the last moments of that test. The punch that saved me and made me the Shadow Prince. Again, though, what I used to be proud of now seemed second-rate.

She continued, "How very . . . unmagical. But perhaps that's how you settled things back in your village."

Okay. I was definitely *not* liking Iset at this point. I wanted to say something biting, something to embarrass her, something to turn the attention away from me. But it had to be something so casually said that nobody would notice I was having feelings. I couldn't think of anything that sounded quite right.

Fortunately, the moment was interrupted.

Center of Attention

At the high table, Pharaoh Neferu rose. The murmur of conversation throughout the room quickly stopped. "If I could have your attention for a moment, please," he said. "Queen Heta and I would like to thank the governor for this generous welcome and banquet here in Djerty. It's been our great pleasure to introduce Prince Khufu and his new shadow, Ash, to the people of Egypt. We'd be remiss this evening if I didn't mention that we've brought with us another impressive young person. Iset, please stand." Iset put one hand to her chest, as if surprised to hear her name. She stood, looking shy and embarrassed, and the pharaoh introduced her, describing her family, her performance at the academy, and her accomplishments. When he was done, he raised a goblet and said, "To Iset, may she bless Egypt with magic for many years to come."

The entire room raised their glasses and repeated the words. When I didn't, Gilli nudged me in the ribs. I raised a goblet and mumbled.

The governess of Djerty said she'd love to see Iset demonstrate her skills. "Would that it was earlier," she said, "with the sun still high in the sky to pull magic from."

It was mean of me, but I was glad it was evening. That way, Iset shouldn't have been able to show off her magic. Or so I thought. Khufu, however, had different information. He piped up and said, "I bet she could still do a spell."

Iset said, "Oh, no, I wouldn't want to be the center of attention."

Yeah, right, I thought. I was pretty sure that being the center of attention was exactly what she wanted.

Iset moved nearer to the high table. "During the day is the best time to do magic, of course. It's most powerful then, but at the academy they've been working hard on storing Ra's magical power in styluses so that they can be used after sunset. It's new technology. My stylus, for example, can hold a sun charge for several hours. Lord Thoth believes it may eventually be possible for us to store Ra's energy in lots of ways so that we can use it through the night—the same way the light beetles can glow all night."

Lord Horus squinted one eye at her. "Lord Thoth approves of this, then?"

"He does. He thinks it will be a great advancement for humanity."

"Let us hope it's not too much of an advancement," Horus said. He was calm and spoke slowly, but his voice boomed as if his beak was right beside my ear. I'd heard his war cry could drive away whole enemy armies in terror. I could believe it. "With new powers it's easy to find new ways to misuse them. Be sure, Iset, to always use your gifts for good."

"Of course she will," the queen said. "Use it for good now. Iset, entertain us with a spell!"

"Oh, yes, please do!" several of the nobles called, clapping their hands. A chorus of others joined them.

For a moment, Iset refused, saying she had no idea how to entertain such royal company. But it was all show. She protested long enough to seem modest, then agreed. "Okay, then. A very small demonstration. What should I do . . ." Her eyes scanned the room, eventually settling on the bowl of spiced cream in front of her. "Ah, I know! Spiced milk is wonderful after a good meal, but how about a variation on it? A little something I like to whip up on special occasions."

She unfastened the stylus from her necklace. She lifted the slim sliver of metal, tilted it so that it sprung to life, and began drawing a series of quick glyphs. She moved through the room, between the tables, drawing glyph after glyph. Each one crackled in the air. They didn't fade as fast as usual, and when there was a glyph hanging over every table, she drew one last glyph and paused.

"And then," Iset said, "the final touch." She slashed a closing stroke on the glyph in front of her. An icy blue light glowed at the writing tip of the stylus. Iset twirled it.

As she did so the cream in the bowl right in front of me changed consistency. It thickened and rose into a plump swirl that wasn't liquid anymore. It didn't just happen to my bowl, though. People around the room gasped in surprise as the same thing happened to all the bowls of cream.

Iset looked pleased. "I'm afraid you can't drink the

cream in its current state, but if you try it with a spoon . . ."

She had the room eating out of her hand. Everyone reached for their spoons, dug in, and began exclaiming. I did too. A dollop of the cream stuck to my spoon. It was soft and cold on my tongue and like nothing I'd ever tasted before. The sweetness of the honey and spices lingered in my mouth, even as the coolness of the frozen cream slipped down inside me. I hated to admit it, but it was *really* good.

Iset strolled back to our table, beaming as people devoured their new dessert. She set her silver eyes on me, smiled, and whispered, "I call it iced cream. I think it'll catch on."

That little trick made Iset the star of the evening. The governess even made Iset promise to teach her household magician the spell.

Khufu devoured his bowl and called for more.

I pushed my bowl across the table to him. "Here, have mine," I said. "I'm full."

11

The Aggrieved Prince

Lord Set flew over Memphis in the heat of the noonday sun. He drove his beetle-powered chariot hard. He always drove the poor beetle hard, but when he was angry, he was particularly callous. Knowing he was going to be summoned to answer questions and be reprimanded by a council of gods annoyed him like nothing else did. Though the beetle flew at full speed, Set kicked it in the rump every so often.

"Faster, you lazy insect!"

By the time he arrived in the parking area for the Vault of Divine Wisdom, the beetle was panting, wings sputtering, completely exhausted. Set hopped off his chariot without a thank-you to the beetle.

The Great Plaza was a beautiful open space of light

and color. Set passed between clear pools of water, home to flowering plants and exotic fishes. There were gardens and areas shaded by tall palm trees. Though the vault itself was reserved for the gods, the plaza was open to the public. That had always annoyed Set. Little children splashing their feet in the pools? Mothers and fathers relaxing after a long day of work? Boys and girls flying sunkites? It was all a bit too human for him.

The Vault of Divine Wisdom was a large rectangular building built of white marble. It was simple in its construction and featured only one door—the only way in or out. It was used only for the most important godly meetings. Lord Thoth had created it to be a place of deep magic, a chamber infused with spells that muted the gods' special powers. Inside, all gods were on equal footing with one another, and with humans—without access to their divine strengths or abilities. While inside, nobody had godly powers to call upon. This was to avoid repeating some of the nastier arguments of the past, which had occasionally led to fights among the attendees, with unfortunate consequences to both gods and humans alike.

"Ah," Set mumbled, "those were the good old days."

"Lord Set!" someone called.

The god turned to see Prince Rami walking away

from one of the pools with splashing footsteps. He whispered, "Here's someone who definitely needs to wash his feet."

"Prince Rami," Set said, "I'm surprised to see you. I would have thought you'd be traveling with your family on The Mistress of Light."

"Traveling? With them? No chance. I got out of it."

"How did you do that?"

"Pretended to be sick. Puked up my breakfast on the day we were supposed to leave. It wasn't hard to convince them to leave me after that. They obviously didn't want to risk me making my stupid little brother sick just as he was about to head off on his victory tour. They left me to babysit my little sister."

He motioned over his shoulder, indicating Princess Sia playing with several other children in one of the pools. She looked happy, speaking animatedly. A smiling center of attention. Only eight years old and Princess Sia was already a natural leader.

On the other hand, Set liked the cranky edge in the boy's voice. The anger and jealousy. Those were two emotions he knew how to use. "So, am I hearing that you're still aggrieved?

"Aggrieved?" Rami asked. "You mean mad that my

brother has a shadow and I don't? That he's traveling the length of Egypt and being celebrated everywhere? That everybody thinks he should become pharaoh instead of me? Stuff like that?"

"Precisely."

"Then yes, I'm aggrieved."

This was music to Set's ears. "Such injustice!"

"It's your fault, you know?" Rami exhaled an exasperated breath. "You had plenty of chances to eliminate all of Khufu's candidates during the testing. Some god you are."

"Sorry to have disappointed you," Set said, bowing his head and hiding his smirk. "I think, though, that you are still destined for the throne."

Rami scoffed. "That's news to me. Khufu gets everything he wants, and I get left behind."

"Prince, I thought you wanted to be left behind," Set pointed out.

"Yeah, but . . ." The boy pouted. "They didn't have to seem so happy about it."

Set put an arm around Rami's shoulders and pulled him into a one-armed embrace. "It's not fair. Not fair at all. Everybody knows you're the rightful heir. Firstborn and all. In the old days that's what counted, before all this

Shadow Prince stuff complicated things. But listen, I'm not done working on your behalf. I have a plan to elevate you to your rightful position."

"Really?" Rami asked, sounding genuinely surprised.

"Yes," Set said, "really and truly." He placed a finger to his snout. "Keep quiet about it. I'll tell you more soon. You have my word on that."

After he sent Rami on his way, Set strolled closer to the Vault of Divine Wisdom. He whistled through his snout and tried to look like he was out enjoying the day. Indeed, he was feeling a glimmer of possibility. There was one aspect of what he said to Rami that was true. He was developing a plan. Gazing at the vault in which he'd soon be answering questions, he began to see it. It was right there before him. A game-changing action that would get him everything he'd ever wanted.

"Yes," he said, chuckling, and then more quietly, he whispered, "I see it now. Go ahead and summon me, Isis. When you do, you'll get more than you bargained for."

12

Inappropriate Laughter

The next morning, after *The Mistress* had taken off
again, Pharaoh Neferu laid out the three rules we had
to agree to before he let Iset take us out on the skiff.
He counted them on his long fingers. "One, stay safe.
Two, don't do anything I'd disapprove of. Three, make
sure to rejoin us in Aswan before sunset. And, Ash,
you will remember your duties. Yes?"

"Yes, Pharaoh. You can count on me." Instinctively,
I checked my holstered daggers. Three of them, all
within quick reach of my hands. I also held my trusty
spear and wore my wrist gauntlets. If for any reason I
had to fight, I was ready.

Once we agreed to the pharaoh's terms, Iset took
control of the skiff. I was looking forward to her

moving on, but today she was running the show. She sat holding the tiller with Jumpra right next to her, staring at her with his big green eyes. Even he had fallen for her. I thought, *So much for feline loyalty!*

Iset first addressed Gilli and Seret, who were on the port side of the boat at the railing of *The Mistress*. "You two, slowly loosen the bow and stern lines tethering us to *The Mistress*. Get the ropes loose enough that you're almost ready to let go. *Almost.*" She turned to Khufu and me, who were on the starboard side to keep the skiff balanced. "And you two, begin to unfurl the sail. Slowly. Just enough that the sail gets charged by the sun."

When we had the sail about halfway open and it had shimmered to life, Iset said. "Okay. Now. Gilli and Seret, release the ropes and push us off."

They did. The skiff peeled away from *The Mistress*.

"Now, unfurl the rest of the sail. Quickly!"

The skiff began to turn, caught in the swirling air currents flowing along *The Mistress*'s massive hull. For a terrible moment it felt like we were about to spin out of control. But then the skiff's sail snapped fully open. It filled with energy. Instead of spinning, the skiff sped into motion, angling away from the clipper under its own speed.

"Awesome!" Khufu shouted.

Iset spent a while getting a feel for it, turning this way and that, carving it, leaning over into sweeping arcs. Each of us held tight to something, wind in our faces, the sunsail taut with Ra's magical solar power.

For a time, we flew near *The Mistress*. I'd never seen the great clipper in flight like this. It was quite a sight. While the skiff had only one small sail, the clipper had many. Each sheet of glittering fabric billowed with the force of the sun. The air all around it buzzed with insect life. Dragonflies with six-foot wingspans flew in military formations, darting to change position every now and then. Large scarab beetles wheeled about in front of the prow, dipping and rising like river dolphins before a waterborne ship. Two guard patrol boats also flanked the royal barge. They bristled with soldiers holding spears. I couldn't imagine anyone actually being a danger to *The Mistress*, but they weren't taking anything for granted.

Iset did a few maneuvers, like rising up and flying over the clipper, circling behind it. We waved to the watching faces on the deck, and then skimmed so close along the big ship's railing that we reached out and slapped onlookers' hands as we passed. Pharaoh

Neferu looked grudgingly pleased. When he and the onlookers turned to other things, we knew Iset had their approval, and we could go explore!

We sailed away from *The Mistress* over the mud huts along the shores of the Nile, out onto the wide expanse of river that poured life into Egypt. It was so wide that I could just barely see the far bank. It bustled with so much human life: barges and fishing boats and trading vessels and small skiffs. And so much animal life: schools of fish that flashed beneath the surface, pods of hippos and logjams of crocodiles, cranes and ibises and water buffalo. No wonder Egypt was the grandest civilization in the world. We had the bounty of the Nile and all the crops it allowed us to grow. And we had the energy of the sun. Both were endless gifts that renewed themselves each and every day.

With Iset coaching us, we took turns at the tiller. When it was my turn, I pulled a trick that nobody else had tried. I flew right to the Nile and splashed down in the water, sending up a spray that drenched us all. The skiff skimmed across the river's surface. I steered around other watercraft before pulling up and going airborne again.

"Nice trick, Ash!" Gilli said.

I grinned and didn't admit that it hadn't been an intentional trick. I'd just lost control for a moment. Nobody needed to know that, though.

After that, Iset steered us downstream, back to *The Mistress of Light*. She flew under the great clipper. Worker beetles crawled across the hull, busy with various jobs. A few of them glanced at us, looking grumpy to be disturbed. I blew them kisses and waved. This really was fun.

As we passed into the clipper's shadow, the skiff's sail went limp. Where it had felt so powerful and alive in the sun, the skiff suddenly seemed to die in the shadow. It tipped forward and began a sliding descent toward a rolling field.

"Hey, uh . . . ," I said, " . . . I think there's a problem."

Goatherds looked up at us. Then, realizing that we were plummeting right toward them, they took off running in different directions. Even the goats stopped munching and panicked.

"Iset, do something!" Khufu cried.

"I knew this was a bad idea," Gilli said.

Seret hunkered down beneath her bench, her claws digging deeply into the wood.

We shouted in terror. All except for Iset. She made a sound all right, but it wasn't shouts of terror.

She was laughing!

13

Sunbursting

Through her laughter Iset managed to say, "Don't... worry... We'll... be... fine... right... about... now!"

Just as she said that we fell out of *The Mistress*'s shadow. As the sun hit the sail it sparked to life again. The skiff went from being deadweight to surging forward in an instant. We skimmed just above the ground, sending goats fleeing in protest, and then we zipped back up into the sky. That's the thing about solar-powered vessels. With the sun shining on them they were awesome. Without the sun: nothing.

Iset, apparently, had planned the whole thing. "Just having a little fun," she said, grinning.

"Do you think the pharaoh and queen saw that?" Seret asked.

"Nah, we were right beneath the clipper, out of sight," Iset said.

I realized that maybe Iset was having too much fun for my liking. At least, that's what the Shadow Prince side of me knew I should think.

"What now?" Khufu asked. "We've got hours until sunset. What else can the skiff do?"

"Well," Iset said, "there's something I've been itching to try, but . . ." She hesitated. Frowned. Shook her head. "No, I shouldn't. The pharaoh and queen wouldn't approve."

Which, I knew in an instant, was exactly the wrong thing to say.

"Of course you should!" Khufu said. "I don't know what you're talking about. If you think my parents *won't* approve, I'm all for it."

I sighed. "Prince, let's not—"

"Tell us, Iset," Khufu begged. "Please?"

"All right, but I'm not saying we should do it."

"Then we should definitely do it!" Khufu said.

This kid's out of control, I thought.

Iset fingered the stylus hanging from the chain around her neck. "At the academy I learned a lot of spells, including the one for throwing sunbursts."

"Sunbursts?" Seret asked.

"Yeah, they work like the sun, but you can form a small ball of its energy and then send it toward whatever you want."

"So . . . you want to throw sunbursts?" I asked, trying to gauge whether this was as dangerous as it sounded.

"Yes. I've been wondering what would happen if I tossed one in a sunsail. If it would—"

"Supercharge the skiff?" Gilli asked.

Iset considered. "Theoretically, that's exactly what it would do."

"Okay then," Khufu said, "let's do it!"

I tried to be a voice of reason. "What if the skiff like . . . explodes or something?"

Iset shrugged. "That's possible, I guess."

"Too dangerous," I said. I crossed my arms and tried to look stern. "Khufu, remember what your father said. We have to be safe. Not do anything he'd disapprove of. Casting a spell to supercharge and maybe explode the skiff is *none* of those things. As your shadow, I have to put my foot down."

Khufu smiled and patted me on the shoulder. "Ash,

you worry too much. You should loosen up." To Iset, he said, "Don't mind Ash. Let's go sunbursting!"

I wondered if Yazen had any idea that one of the main things I'd need to protect the prince from was himself and his newfound love for crazy ideas. I doubted it. To make it worse, it all felt even more serious since I'd heard the prophecy. Protecting Khufu wasn't just about keeping him out of trouble. It could be about his life, about the future of Egypt. I wanted to grab him and tell him everything. But I couldn't. And I wasn't sure that he'd really listen to me if I tried.

"You might want to all hunker down low in the skiff and hold on to something," Iset said.

We did. Except for Jumpra, who was apparently feeling pretty confident. He perched himself right in the front of the skiff, paws wrapped around the railing. "Ah, little guy," I said, "that might not be the safest place to sit." While Jumpra couldn't speak Egyptian, it was clear he understood us just fine. That's why it was a little frustrating that he ignored me completely. He stayed there, tail twitching with excitement.

Iset unclipped the stylus from her necklace and held it lightly in her fingers. It was beautiful, so thin and shiny. Though I'd gotten to use a stylus during the shadow testing and even received one when I became Khufu's shadow, it had stayed secured in a box back in Memphis. Lord Thoth promised I'd begin my true magical training when we returned from this journey. It was dangerous, though, for me to use magic out in the real world until I had a better grasp of how to use it safely. And certainly not to do, you know, things like throwing sunbursts into skiff sails. I almost said this, but what was the use? I shook my head, slipped down beneath my bench, and wrapped my arms around it.

Iset's first stroke carved a circle in the air. Despite the brightness of the afternoon, the circle glowed a glimmering yellow-gold. As it crackled, Iset filled the center of it with a bunch of hieroglyphs. She closed it in a cartouche, and held the stylus poised for the closing stroke. She looked over her shoulder to where Khufu watched eagerly, gripping the tiller tight.

"Go on," the prince whispered. "Do it."

14

Breathless and Clinging

Just as the circle began to fade, Iset slashed in the ignition stroke. Then she, too, crouched low in the skiff.

The glyph flared to full life. The circle bloomed into a flaming ball, heat radiating off it. There was a sound in the air like a great inhalation of breath. I felt the scorching power of it. We all did. We cringed, shielding our faces. I was sure that it was going to explode.

Suddenly, the ball took flight, straight into the sail. The shimmering cloth stretched taut. The mast let out a tortured creak as the sail bowed tight with the trapped sunburst. The skiff shot forward, two or three times faster than before. It was a good thing we were all holding on!

Seret gripped the wooden benches with her long claws, her ears and whiskers pressed flat by the force of the air. Small as he was, Gilli had slid underneath the benches, jammed in with ropes and other supplies. Khufu barely managed to hold on to the tiller, which vibrated and jerked like it was about to break off. He looked terrified and excited at the same time.

Jumpra got the best of it. Or the worst, depending. His body stretched back, horizontal and flapping madly in the air. He must have sunk his claws pretty deep into the railing. They were the only things that kept him in the skiff at all!

Clinging on for dear life, I peeked over the railing. The desert beneath us scrolled by at amazing speed. The dunes blurred. As the skiff rose, we punched through thin, wet clouds. Higher and higher. Faster and faster. I began to wonder if it would end, or if we'd just fly up into the heavens and never come back down.

The glow of the sunburst sputtered out. The sail calmed. The skiff slowed. We were so far up now that everything on the world below was super tiny. Had anyone ever been this high above the earth before? Would anyone ever again?

Seret was the first to speak. "Wow," she said. "Where are we?"

"Closer to the stars," Gilli said. He pointed.

Sure enough. Even though it was day, I could see the faint glimmer of stars.

"Is anybody cold?" Khufu asked.

"And out of breath?" Iset added.

I sure was. Cold like I'd never been before. And out of breath even though I was just sitting there. As amazing as it was being here, so high above the world, I was relieved when the skiff began a slow descent. It took a lot longer than the climb up, but eventually we returned to a reasonable height, back to the warmth of the desert. We cruised along. Below us, unending sand dunes in all directions.

Jumpra finally retracted his claws from the splintered wood. He was a puff-ball of frightened fur. He crawled unsteadily over to me, keeping himself as low in the skiff as possible. He climbed into my lap and looked up at me. His green eyes looked twice as big as normal. He made a sound that was part yowling misery, part whirring locust.

Seret translated. "He says, 'Let's never do that again.'"

Smart kitten. I couldn't agree more. I was also pleased he'd remembered me and maybe wouldn't be so in love with Iset anymore. I petted him.

"Where's the Nile?" Gilli asked.

The answering silence spoke for itself. Nowhere to be seen.

"How far do you think we flew?" Khufu asked. "Are we even in Egypt anymore?"

"Yes," Iset said. "See . . ." She drew a small glyph in the air, let it glow for a moment before brushing through it with her fingers. "Egyptian magic only works in domains loyal to Ra. There is a limit to it. If you cross into lands outside Egypt, Ra's magic has no power."

"See, it's fine," Khufu said. "We're still in Egypt. Iset can toss another sunburst, and we'll be back in no time."

"Look," Seret said, gazing out over the desert. She pointed at a meandering line of dots on the sand dunes to the west. "It's a desert caravan. We must be in the Sahara, so far to the west that traders go right up across the desert instead of using the Nile." She squinted her eyes a moment, and then said, "There's a caraviper with them."

"A caraviper!" Khufu exclaimed. "Excellent! Let's go down and see."

I frowned and tried to sound adult and authoritative. "Prince, a caraviper is a rather enormous, often vicious desert serpent. And caravans can be dangerous, you know? Bandits and all. Bandits have been known to kidnap people. A prince of Egypt would be a pretty amazing catch for them."

Gilli frowned. "Yeah, I'm not sure that's true. A bandit is a bandit. The folks in a caravan? They're hardworking people moving important goods to and from various places. There's no reason to think they're bandits."

Thanks for not *helping, Gilli!*

"Exactly," Khufu said. "I second what Gilli said. Nobody is going to kidnap me." The prince took the tiller and tilted the skiff into a descending curve. "We have time for a quick visit. And then a burst from Iset, here, and we'll zip back just like we promised. Easy."

15

Have You Heard the One About . . .

Lord Set stood at the edge of a deep precipice, peering down into the depths. He couldn't see the bottom, but he knew it was down there somewhere. He leaped. Snout flapping about in the breeze, the god leaned back and did the best he could to lounge as the rock walls zipped by him. He didn't let the fact that he was quite alone stop him from monologuing.

"Who does Isis think she is?" he griped. "Summoning me to a council? Me?"

Set flipped over and fell belly-first. He crooked his arms and rested his snout on his palms.

"She's sure to lecture me. They all will. They suspect me of foul play and all that. What nerve! Yet again, she and the other gods do everything they can to hold me back.

But I'll tell you what. They can't hold a . . ." He paused, looking perplexed. "What's the phrase? Can't hold a good god down? No, that's not it. That's rubbish. In any event they can't hold me down! The surprise will be on them. Finally, I'll have what's rightly mine. I'll rule all of—"

Splat!

The bottom of the cavern took Set by surprise. One second, he was gesticulating in the air as he monologued. The next he was flat on his belly, groaning from the impact with the stone. The crash would have broken every bone in a human's body and left him pulped, but Set wasn't a human. He rose and shook the damage off with a few stretches and knee bends. He looked about in the gloom, chose a tunnel that glowed faintly red, and off he went.

"Egypt," he said, picking up his tale. "That's what I'll rule."

Set trudged on. The red glow and heat coming from the end of the tunnel grew with each step. "I'll settle all my old scores one by one. First, though, I need an accomplice. . . ."

Set had reached the end of the tunnel. He stepped into the full crimson glare of the chamber, blinking at what he saw.

The great serpent Apep lay coiled inside a vast rock

chamber. His body was so massive that he looked like a ringed mountain, one that rose and fell with his breathing. The demon's head rested partway up that mountain. Eyes closed, he almost managed to look peaceful. Almost. Each sleepy flare of his nostrils issued plumes of black smoke. His tongue slipped out of his mouth every so often, snapping like a whip before vanishing.

"I smell you," the serpent said. His voice managed to be both a low grumble and a hiss. "I smell you, but I'm having a hard time imagining why I'm smelling you. Lost, Set? Is that it? Fell down the wrong hole and got turned around?"

Set stepped forward, putting a spring in his strides. "Nothing of the sort, mighty Apep! You're just the serpent I'm looking for. I've a business proposal."

Apep opened one smoldering orange eye. "You're joking."

"Oh, indeed," Set said, grinning. "Have you heard the one about the god that got swallowed by a serpent?"

"No, but you do smell like food. Maybe a little off, but I'm not picky." The other eye opened. It glowed bloodred.

"Look," Set said, "I know as well as anyone that you and I have had a . . . difficult relationship. It's never been personal, though."

Apep lifted his massive head. His mouth cracked open, revealing the curved swords of his razor-sharp teeth. The serpent's eyes twirled circles in their sockets. "Where's your spear?"

"Never mind that." Set made a point of not looking Apep directly in the eyes. He knew their hypnotic effect all too well. If he wasn't careful, he'd end up a glazed zombie completely at the demon's mercy. "We're both trapped by our roles. Both pawns of the system. Think about it. I don't want to spear you each and every night. And you don't really mean me any harm, right? It's Ra you're after. Him and his pompous luminosity."

As he spoke, Set moved about. He tried to look casual, as if he were just pacing out his argument. Stepping over fallen rocks and around stalagmites wasn't easy, though, especially when a giant snake head was trailing him, following every move.

"I have a plan to put him out of the game for good," Set said. He leaned back against a boulder. "Together, you and I can get rid of Lord Ra. Then during the endless darkness we can take over Egypt. We'll be running the whole show in no time at all. Forget about slithering around in caves in the deep regions of the Duat. Forget about serving humans or being asked to get a spear in your

neck every night. Your agreement to my plan will be all I need to convince the others."

"The others?" Apep asked. His tongue licked out so close Set felt the wet warmth of it.

"The other demons. They'll jump at the idea! The Mistress of Anger will sign up. The Rejector of Rebels, too. All nine of the Jackal-Headed Gods. They're sure to join. That other fire-breathing serpent is in. I always forget his name . . . I bet I can even get the Four Weary Ones to get off their butts. We'll have a whole army ready to rise when we give them the sign."

"And Ammut?"

"Glad you mention dear Ammut! She will be keener than anyone—excepting myself—to be revenged. You should've seen how Thoth cheated her by aiding that whelp, the new shadow! She'll definitely be in. She'll probably want her own city and a never-ending supply of slaves to munch on in payment, but that can be arranged. The thing is, none of it can go forward without you. You, mighty Apep, are the key to everything."

"Is that so?" The serpent blew smoke through his nose. "Let's hear just what it is you want from me, then."

Set grinned and began to lay out his plan.

16

Worrying Too Much

As Khufu sailed over the dunes, I felt my pulse quicken. I didn't like the sound of the bandit thing. Or the vicious-serpent thing. Or the kidnapper thing. Sailing toward bandits with a sunskiff and a prince of Egypt didn't seem like a very good idea. And we were on our own. That made me super nervous. I gripped my spear, hoping I wouldn't need to use it.

"Khufu," I began, "remember your father's three rules? I think this breaks . . . um . . . all of them."

"You worry too much, Ash," Khufu said.

"That's my job," I said.

"Fine. You do the worrying. I'll keep things interesting."

I tried to think of something else to say. Something

to get him to see not everything was fun and games. Looking at him, though, it didn't seem like anything would get through to him. He just hummed a tune and kept steering us toward the desert strangers, his eyes alight with excitement.

I realized something I'd been feeling but not fully facing. As much as I'd grown to like Khufu, I didn't really know him that well. He already seemed different from the shy, thoughtful boy I'd met during the shadow testing. I felt trapped. I had responsibilities to protect him, but he was a prince. Even if I wanted to, I couldn't order him around.

Finally, I tried, "If you have to do this, let's at least not say who we are."

Khufu just said, "Sure, no problem."

And then, right afterward, he did exactly the opposite! He carved the sunskiff low over the caravan, shouting out his name and bringing greetings from the pharaoh and queen. The caravanners gazed up at us, looking puzzled, waving. The camels watched us, unimpressed. The caraviper—a creature several times the length of the skiff—tensed its long, muscular body and reared up, staring at us. I didn't like the look of that.

"Ash," Khufu said, "these people aren't going to hurt us. Put your spear down before you scare them. That's an order."

Reluctantly, I lowered the spear and stuffed it under a bench.

The prince touched the sunskiff down near the front of the long line of travelers. We furled the sail and climbed out as the men, women, children, and camels gathered before us. They were dusty from their travels, wearing worn tunics and simple leather sandals. A few had cloths wrapped around their heads. All of them had the dark, rich skin of people who spent all day in the sun. The enormous caraviper didn't come near, but it was still too close for my liking.

We anchored the sunskiff into the sand. On the ground, face-to-face with them, Khufu didn't look quite as confident as he had a moment ago. He looked a bit scared, actually. I realized why. To me, these people didn't look that different from the people I grew up with back in the village. As a prince, though, Khufu wouldn't have spent much time with regular folks.

I nudged him in the side and said, "Well, we're here . . . Aren't you going to say something?"

"So . . ." Khufu said, at a loss for words. "Um . . . you all aren't bandits, are you? Kidnappers? That sort of thing?"

One of the men stepped forward. He was very dark-skinned, with hair in thick locs that he wore pulled back and tied behind his head. "No, Your Highness, we are not bandits. Nor kidnappers." His accent was strong enough that Egyptian must not have been his first language. "We are Numidian traders returning from a voyage to the lands of Mali, south of the great desert. We bear trade goods bound for the northern coast."

"I knew it," Khufu said, perking up. He smirked at me and whispered, "Like I said, you worry too much." To the caravanner, he asked, "What's your name?"

The man smiled. His deeply lined face lit up wonderfully. "I have many names, but if it pleases you, you may call me Sudeen."

Khufu introduced each of us in turn. Totally *not* disguising who we were. Many of the other caravanners stepped up to introduce themselves, bowing to the prince and saying how honored they were to have Egyptian royalty grace them with a visit. I quickly lost track of their names. At first, I was on edge, watching anyone near the prince, looking for any sign that they were up to no good.

A few kids shyly approached Seret, scared of her, but not as much as they were fascinated by a talking lioness. Before long they were petting her. She even offered them rides on her back. Gilli chatted with a circle of adults, talking about the journey we'd been on. Iset showed off a few minor spells, mostly just visual tricks like making glowing flowers bloom. She also made water bubble up right out of the desert sand. That had the caravanners running for jugs and skins to scoop it up in. From their reaction, you'd think water was more valuable than gold. In the desert it probably was. They also had a lot of things to show us: precious jewels and spices, fabrics of all colors, birds that could talk, and a monkey that could do card tricks.

Despite my concerns, I had to admit that they all seemed really nice. They didn't seem to mind that we'd interrupted their travel. They crowded around us, talkative and friendly. It was like a festival had suddenly sprung up in the middle of the endless sand dunes. And we were the guests of honor. But I kept my eyes on the sun, tracking it. After what I figured was about an hour, I was about to suggest we take our leave.

Khufu had other plans. "It's been great to meet you all," he said to Sudeen. "Now, how about introducing us to that caraviper?"

17

Sweet Girl

Sudeen led us over to the caraviper. "She is my very own," he said, gazing at her proudly. "I raised her from a tiny newborn. She is called My Sweet Girl That Slithers Faster Than All Others. You may call her simply Sweet Girl."

I couldn't imagine Sweet Girl ever having been a tiny newborn. She was thicker around than a grown man was tall. She was sinuous, scale-covered muscle, so curvy that it was hard to judge her length. Bundles of supplies had been tied on her back. Near her head a wooden frame provided what looked like a carriage house, covered over with flapping sheets of colorful cloth.

Sudeen reached the serpent's side. "These are

friends, Sweet Girl. They want to give you a belly rub." The man turned to Khufu. "Isn't that right?"

Khufu's face said nothing could have been farther from his mind. The serpent studied him warily, but she lowered her head to the sand. She rolled over a little to expose a portion of the smooth plates of her underside. She watched as first Khufu, then Gilli, and then Iset and Seret gently stroked her belly. The creature half-closed her eyes. The tip of her tail thumped against the sand. That won me over. I gave her a belly rub, too.

Jumpra padded up close to the caraviper. Sweet Girl tilted her head down. For a moment, it looked like she might snap him up in one bite. Instead, though, her long, forked tongue flicked out and patted the caracal gently on the head. Jumpra trilled.

It was just one short sound, but Seret translated it. "He says that Sweet Girl is clearly a snake of distinction."

"He said all that?" Khufu asked. "It was just one sound."

Seret shrugged. "Caracals can pack a lot into one trill."

Sudeen leaned close to the viper as if she was speaking to him. I couldn't hear a thing, but he looked very serious. Finally, he nodded and turned back to us.

"Sweet Girl has decided you are all very nice. If you like, she will give you a ride."

"That would be amazing!" Khufu exclaimed.

"Climb aboard then!" Sudeen said.

As Gilli, Iset, and Seret did so, I pulled Khufu aside. I leaned close to him and said, "I don't think your parents would—"

The prince playfully elbowed me in the ribs. "Really, Ash, lighten up. I thought you'd be more fun than this. But it's like all you do now is worry."

"I'm just trying to—"

"I know. You're trying to protect me. I'm sure the time will come when I really need that. Right now, though, I want to go ride on a caraviper. Think about what this is like for me. I never got to do things like this before. Like *never*. I'm only having fun now because of you. My shadow. This is all because of you."

From the carriage atop Sweet Girl, Sudeen called, "Prince, will you be coming?"

Khufu looked at me. "Well, Shadow, can I go?"

That caught me off guard. I'd been feeling like he wasn't paying any attention to my concerns and my responsibilities. Just the fact that he acknowledged me and asked for my approval did something to me. "All right," I said. "But this is the last fun for the day. After this, we're heading straight for Aswan."

"Absolutely," Khufu said. "Thanks, Ash." He climbed up to sit with the others.

I followed and we set out on a wild, slithering trek across the sand dunes. It was like riding atop a river of muscle and smooth scales. We rose and fell over the sand's contours. Climbing up steep dunes, the serpent zigzagged so much that we swayed side to side. Sliding down the bigger dunes was the best. We picked up so much speed! Sudeen threw his hands up in the air and shouted from the joy of it. Pretty soon, we were all waving our arms and shouting and laughing.

We returned to the caravan camp and climbed down off Sweet Girl. We said our goodbyes and trudged back to the sunskiff. Once inside, we waved at the caravanners and prepared to depart. The sun was already sinking into the horizon.

"We don't have much time," Iset said, suddenly looking nervous. "But if we get up above the dunes, we should be able to catch enough of the sun's rays to draw a spell."

The skiff managed to climb out of the depression. Once above the dunes, the sail filled a little and gained some height. Iset dashed off the sunburst glyph and slashed in the closing. We all grabbed on in anticipation of the burst of speed. The spell's brief illumination filled the sail like a burst of wind. Then died. It didn't even move the skiff forward.

"Iset," Gilli said, his voice a little worried, "is this another joke?"

She tried again. The same thing happened. Again and again. She was still trying, desperate, when the prow of the skiff nosed into the sand and came to rest in the shade on the far side of a dune. The sail drooped, completely limp.

Iset looked at us with worry in her eyes. She said, "I think we have a problem."

It's Just My Nature

Down in the Duat, Lord Set stood on the deck of the Night Barge, staring into the eerie, dark cavern ahead of the ship. It was late. Many of the evening's trials and obstacles were behind them, and their journey was nearly complete. Only the biggest of the night's challenges was still at hand. The god gripped a terrible weapon. The Spear of Vengeance. Forged in the distant past by sorcerer blacksmiths, it was the heaviest, strongest, deadliest spear the world had ever known. With it, Set had fought and defeated the serpent Apep countless times. It was a demon-killing weapon. Tonight, though, Set would do what he'd only dreamed of before. This time, he was going to change everything.

He turned and trudged toward the mid-ship cabin that Lord Ra rested in, with Thea near at hand. He stepped into the doorway. There, in the dimly lit room, Lord Ra reclined on a couch, sleeping. He was in his underworld form. His head was that of a ram, dark and foreboding. Thick, black horns curled out of his forehead. It was the intimidating appearance he wore down in the realm of demons. He did not, however, frighten Lord Set.

Thea was awake. She sat at a small desk cluttered with documents. She was combing her Afro puffs and squeezing them into their round shapes as she read. She lifted her gaze from the papyrus and looked at him. "Lord Set?" she asked. "Do you need something?"

The god didn't answer. Not with words, at least. But from the beady black orbs that were his eyes sprang two tiny flames. They burned bright inside his dark silhouette.

"Lord Set," she asked, "why have we stopped? Is . . . is anything wrong?"

"Wrong?" The god's voice was low and malevolent. "Of course something is wrong. But it will be righted soon enough."

Just then, the sound they both knew well began. It started as a rumbling from far below them. It became a grinding like scaled metal on stone. The wood of the barge trembled. The writing instruments on the table nearby began to clatter. Ra stirred but didn't wake.

She cried, "The enemy is here, Lord Set! Go fight him!"

Set growled, "Yes, the enemy is here. The time has finally come."

For the briefest moment, Thea looked relieved. But the expression vanished when Set didn't turn to face Apep as he did every night. Instead, he stepped forward, bringing the spear up. He threw the weapon with all his might. Before Thea could shout a warning, the sharp point of the spear pierced deep into Ra's abdomen. The god convulsed around it. His eyes snapped open, lighting the room with two brilliant beams of light. His hands found the shaft of the weapon and clutched it. He moaned.

Set reached him in a bound. He grabbed the spear and wrenched the point upward, bringing Ra with it. He marched back out onto the deck. Ra dangled from the end of the spear. He tried to speak, but only managed one word, "Why?"

"It's just my nature," Set snarled. "This is who I am! And you, do you know who you are? You're food!" He thrust the spear high above his head.

"Noooo!" Thea yelled.

The clink of scales reverberated through the cavern as Apep came out of the dark depths in which the barge hovered. His massive nostrils flared, issuing plumes of steam. When he spoke, his voice rumbled and shook the stones loose from the cavern wall. "You've actually done it," he said. "About time."

Apep snapped his head forward. He plucked Ra from the spear and tossed him, twirling him into the air like a snack. He caught him in his great jaws and swallowed.

Just like that, Lord Ra was no more.

"Noooo!" Thea yelled.

The serpent lowered his head and fixed his simmering gaze on the girl. He burped. "She's a troublesome one. Should I eat her, too?"

Set considered the possibility, snout wrinkled and one thin eyebrow cocked. "No, Apep, I shouldn't want you to do that. Dear Thea, always such a good little girl. Nauseatingly loyal to Ra. She'll learn a thing or two about life from this encounter. Let's leave her to think on it."

The serpent looked away from her and peered a little closer at Set. "You seem to have forgotten something. From now on, I'm to be called Lord Apep. Remember? That was part of the deal."

"Done." Set bowed elaborately. "O mighty Lord Apep. The newest god of the Egyptian pantheon!"

"And I get a whole city. That was part of the deal, too."

"Of course. Take your pick. Whichever one you'd like. Rename it after yourself. Apepopolis. That's got a nice ring to it, doesn't it?"

"I could get used to it." Apep grumbled. "Anyways, I'm done here, and Ra's a tough old bird. I need to rest up while I digest him." The serpent twisted his massive head away and dropped down into the depths, his scales grinding.

Thea threw herself at Set, pounding him with her fists and shouting, "Why? Why? Why?!"

Set looked down on her, amused and not the slightest bit hurt by the battering. "Ra is gone. With him gone there's nothing to measure the turning of night into day. Time, you see, is frozen. With him gone, the dark of tonight will be eternal. With him gone, there's no human magic."

"You're . . . ending magic?"

"Not all magic. The gods will still be gods." To demonstrate this, he snapped a flame to life with his fingers and wiggled it in the air. "But with Ra gone all those clever devices—barges and machines, styluses and whatnot—will be useless. Even if other gods rally to his side, the pharaoh won't be able to withstand the onslaught of demons I'm sending against them. Imagine it, Thea, the underworld drained of the damned, the spurned, the rejected. Today, a new age begins for Egypt. The age of Lord Set! Farewell, Thea. Try not to get eaten."

With that, the god leaped over the railing and vanished.

19

The Deep Thoughts of Camels

Yeah, we had a problem. We were stuck in the desert for the night.

Sudeen invited us to share their camp and food. They built a fire of . . . um . . . dried camel poo. It sounded gross, but it burned nicely and cast a gentle light and heat. They hung a cooking pot over it. Pretty soon we had a bubbling stew that smelled so good it made my mouth water. Sweet Girl slithered around all of us to ring the camp like a protective wall. Inside it, we all sat close together, eating and chatting late into the night.

The camels settled down around us, all long legs and round knees. They kept up a constant chewing, their mouths working in strange circles. They looked like they were considering our folly and were about to make a speech about it at any moment.

Khufu must've had the same thought. "I'm glad camels can't talk," he said.

Sudeen's eyes lit up. "Oh, but they can. They most certainly can! When the world was young, they often spoke. They had opinions on many things. On everything, actually. They voiced their thoughts in language that would make an Egyptian scholar's head spin. Believe me, this was so."

One of his companions said, "No, that couldn't have been so."

Sudeen seemed to have been waiting for just that response. His face, so full of deep wrinkles, was lit by a smile as he said, "When the world was young, many animals could talk. Not just ones touched by the divine, like our guest Seret. Many other creatures could. Baboons loved to argue in loud voices. Hippos bellowed jokes to one another as they bathed in the river. Cranes debated matters of etiquette, plumage, and fishing. Elephants were the wisdom keepers of the world, who could answer any question posed to them."

He paused and looked around. His kind eyes touched face after face. "But none of them, you see, were as talkative as the camels. Camels had a very high opinion of themselves, and not much respect for the other creatures of the world. They saw the folly in other animals, and in humans. They thought it their right to tell us all about it."

"No, it couldn't have been so," one of the caravanners said.

"Ah, but it was!"

I realized that this was all some sort of game they played. A storytelling back and forth. I wondered how many other topics Sudeen could hold forth about.

"Now, there was one camel who was wiser than all the others. His name was Larad the Loquacious. You know what 'loquacious' means? It's a special type of talkative. That's what Larad was. He was also very keen in his judgment. Everyone knew it. Word of this camel's judgment spread far and wide across the land, until the crown prince heard of it."

"Which crown prince?" Khufu asked. "What country are you speaking of?"

"A faraway one. A land to the east of Egypt, over the sea. A land of desert and stone. A land built around the might of another great river, the Euphrates. In that land the prince heard of Larad and summoned him to his palace. He questioned the camel on matters of law, literature, and science. He found nobody in the entire kingdom to be sharper or more vocal in expressing himself."

Sudeen raised a hand. "Now, admittedly, Larad could be hard to be around. His was a sharp mind. His tongue was like a knife. He cut fools down to size like he was chopping fruit. The prince valued him for this. The two of them became great friends. They traveled through the desert together, talking of all manner of things. Larad often spoke of the mistakes the boy's father—the king—was making. He would name a particularly bad decision and say, 'For saying such a foolish thing, the king should be silenced forever.' He told of the follies of the prince's brothers and named their many faults, and said for each of them that this or that prince 'should be silenced forever.'"

"For one that liked to talk so much," Gilli said, "he seemed to want others to be silent an awful lot."

Sudeen smiled. "Just so. But the prince loved to hear it, and for a time all was well between the camel and his prince. Some years later, that prince became the king. His father died and he found himself on the throne. On the day of his coronation, he made many new decrees. He liked his new power and wanted every-one to bow down to him. He made a new law that everyone, on coming into his presence, must put their forehead on the ground in reverence to him. Everyone did. Everyone except for one camel."

"Larad?" Iset asked.

"Just so. Larad would have none of it. He thought the bowing was too much, and that the prince had lost his senses when the crown was set atop his head. He told him as much, in a loud voice that all the court heard. The new king liked Larad's sharp tongue when he spoke of others, but he didn't care for being cut with the same blade. Do you know what he said? He said, 'For saying such a foolish thing, that camel should be silenced forever.'

"Larad was so insulted that he shut his mouth that very instant and never said another word. He blew air through his nose. He chewed his cud. He pursed his lips and exhaled blubbery breaths through them. He spat on the ground. He did a great many things, but he vowed to never again speak another word. All camels, when they heard of it, took the same vow."

"No, it couldn't have been so," a voice said.

"Ah, but it was! Camels have been silent ever

since, though they are no less opinionated. Sometimes," Sudeen continued, "they can't help but comment on the world. They don't speak loudly, but sometimes they whisper under their breath, or find some other way to communicate their thoughts to us. If you listen closely, you just may hear them. Let us listen."

Sudeen held a hand cupped beside his ear. The whole group hushed. All listened. Even the camels stopped their slow chewing and held motionless, ears erect as if they, too, wanted to hear one of those whispers. The moment held for a long time, with nothing but the whistling of the night's breeze to be heard.

Then one of the camels farted. It was a loud, blubbery sound that lasted longer than I would've thought possible. When it ended, we all sat in a stunned silence. Embarrassed. Confused. And then . . . Sudeen threw back his head and started laughing. In no time, we were all shaking with laughter, rolling about, and holding our bellies.

When we'd gotten ahold of ourselves, Sudeen looked across the fire at me. He said softly, "Such are the deep thoughts of camels."

20

A Confession

Sudeen and the others told more silly stories. They were clearly trying to make us comfortable and ease our worry. I was glad about that. It was especially good seeing Khufu looking comfortable with these humble caravanners. He was getting a glimpse of life as other people lived it. Maybe, in a small way, the experience would give him perspectives he would never have had. That seemed like a good thing, the kind of thing that could help make him a better pharaoh.

At some point, sleep finally caught up with me.

When I awoke later it was still dark. No sign of the sun or even a lightening of the eastern horizon. The camp was quiet, sleeping forms of people and camels all around. I peeled off the blanket that someone had placed over me, rose, and walked away from the circle of bodies sleeping around the embers of the fire. I slipped through the opening in Sweet Girl's encircling wall and climbed a nearby sand dune.

Sitting on my heels, I took in the contours of the sand, highlighted and shadowed by the stars. It was beautiful in a way, but also lonely and desolate. Nothing moved out there. I hated to think that right now, far away in Aswan, the pharaoh and the queen must be worried sick about us. What would they say when we got back? How would we explain? How would *I* explain? After this, would they even want me to be Khufu's shadow? I was so deep in thought, I didn't notice someone approaching until they were right beside me.

"I guess you can't sleep either," a voice said. It was Iset. She sat down. We shared the silence for a while, and then she said softly, "Thank you."

"For what?"

"For not blaming this all on me. You could. You'd be right. It's all my fault that we're out here."

I was about to say that it wasn't any one person's fault, but she seemed to sense it and kept talking.

"No, it's on me. It's just that . . ." Iset kept her gaze

out over the dunes. In profile, I could only see one of her eyes. It glistened in the starlight, heavy with what looked like a gathering tear. "Until I was twelve, I thought I was destined to be a pilot like my brother. That's all I wanted. It's what felt right. But then at school I scored high on a test for magical potential. I'm not even sure what I did, but all of a sudden, everyone thought I should train as a magician. It was like I didn't have a choice. If I had a gift, it was my responsibility to use it. My parents were so proud. My brother, too. So, I tried. I worked as hard as I could. But I couldn't shake the feeling that someone had made a mistake. At some point they'd realize I wasn't the magician they thought I was. What would happen then?"

She let the question sit for a moment. I didn't have an answer, but I could tell she wasn't really waiting for one.

"I scored well," she continued, "but only because I worked really, really hard. While the other apprentices slept, I'd sneak away to study and practice. The others didn't know I only aced the exam because I barely slept for a year. I was miserable and tired and worried. Then, when I came aboard *The Mistress*, I wanted to impress the pharaoh and the queen. They said all those nice things about how I'm the youngest person to become a magician that anyone can remember. I loved that. I got carried away. I just wanted everyone to like me. Instead, I just made a mess of things."

So how about that? I'd come up to sit on the dunes to sulk, to worry about myself and how people would judge me. I hadn't considered that someone else might have their own story, their own fears and worries. I wasn't sure what to say, so I just leaned to the side and nudged her shoulder with mine. Somebody else, however, did know what to say.

"We do like you," a voice behind us said. I recognized it instantly. Khufu.

Gilli and Seret were there, too, just a little ways down the slope of the dune. And Jumpra appeared right beside me. *What's with sneaking up on people tonight?*

"How long have you been standing there?" I asked.

"Long enough," Khufu said. "I guess none of us could sleep."

Gilli walked up and sat down on the other side of Iset. "Don't worry. We'll find a way to explain things to the pharaoh and the queen. We're a team after all."

Seret padded up beside us, her gaze out on the

faintly starlit dunes. "Hey guys, I know we're having a moment and all, but . . ." She narrowed her eyes, squinting into the distance. ". . . there's something out there. It's coming this way."

21

The Girl in the Desert

I jumped to my feet, trying to see whatever she saw, but there was nothing but the dark dunes with soft contours of the starlight on them all the way out until the world faded to black. I'd learned not to doubt Seret's keen eyesight, though.

"Can you tell what it is?" I asked. I scarcely wanted to know the answer. What sort of things roamed the desert at night? Probably not ones I wanted to bump into.

Seret said, "I can almost make out what it is."

Squinting, I finally saw something. A vague shape moved through the dunes, small and hardly notice-able. It walked upright. I could tell that much. "There's somebody out there," I whispered.

"A girl," Seret said. "She's coming toward us. She looks very weak. Oh . . ." Seret gasped. "She's fallen." She crouched down like she was about to leap away. The muscles in her back and legs rippled. "Wake the others. Have them ready for when I return with her. She's going to need help, I think."

"You can't go out there," Khufu said. "You don't even know who she is!"

"A stranger in trouble deserves help just as much as a friend." She leaped away.

I watched her bound across the dunes, quickly growing smaller. Gilli said what I was thinking: "Seret, I hope you know what you're doing."

Back in the camp, we woke the others. We spoke so quickly, words tumbling and jumbling over each other, that Sudeen had to shush us and have us talk one at a time. Once he understood, Sudeen responded nearly as quickly as Seret had. He ordered the fire stirred back into life. He had torches lit to help Seret find her way back. Others gathered water, food, and medical supplies.

Soon, we all stood along the edge of the camp, with the rekindled fire warming our backs. We watched for the lioness and the girl, but with the bright fire behind us we couldn't see nearly as far as we could under starlight.

"Where is she?" Iset asked. "Should we go after her?"

"She will not miss this beacon," Sudeen said. "Give her a few moments more. If need be, I'll take Sweet Girl out after her."

When Seret appeared, she did so suddenly. From not being there at all, it was like she leaped right out of the night. She balanced the limp body of a girl on her back. Breathing heavily, she said, "Take her. She is alive. Bruised and hurt. Exhausted, but . . ."

". . . alive," Sudeen said. He and several others swept in, catching the girl as she slid off Seret's back.

Sudeen spoke to his companions. Several of them lifted the girl and set her on a mat. I noticed she had braces on her legs, which was confusing. What was a girl with braces on her legs doing out here alone at night? A woman covered her with a blanket and dabbed at her forehead with a wet cloth. Still others put a kettle on to make tea for her, along with heating up a soup broth. Seeing how completely out of it she seemed, I figured they might be in for a long wait before she woke up.

I was wrong.

The girl awoke as one of the caravanners slipped a pillow under her head. She bolted upright, brown eyes round with fright. "Wh . . . where am I?"

"Dear girl," Sudeen said soothingly, "you are safely among friends. Worry not."

"Worry not?" She didn't seem to understand the words. Her eyes moved from face to face. They settled on Khufu. "Wait. I'm dreaming." She shook her head. Judging by the way she winced this was enough to have convinced her that she was awake. "Is it really you, Your Highness?"

"You know me?" Khufu asked.

"Your likeness. In statues and murals."

Sudeen pressed a glass of tea into her hands. "Drink this. It will restore you. When you have strength, you can tell your tale."

The girl cupped the tea in her palms. For a moment, she seemed to take comfort from Sudeen's words and the warmth in her hands. She leaned to sip. She stopped. Her eyes grew large again. She looked up. The sight of the dark sky seemed to wake her up completely. "No, we can't waste time! Lord Ra's been eaten. We have to help him!"

"Calm yourself, child," Sudeen said. He and the other caravanners tried to soothe her, but the more they tried the more agitated she became.

"It was Set!" she shouted.

Everyone froze.

Seret placed a paw on the girl's shoulder. "What is your name?"

"Thea."

"Okay, Thea, tell us. Slowly, so that we understand—and please drink. We are listening."

None of us were prepared for the story she had to tell.

22

Again with the Grumbling

Meanwhile, in a cavern in the Duat, Lord Set stood before a throng of demons. He moved through them toward the boulder he intended to make his stage. Demons came in all shapes and sizes. Some short and stout. Others absurdly tall, with limbs that bent at strange angles. Some were furred. Some horned. Some bore resemblance to recognizable animals. Others were wholly unique—and ghastly—creatures. Fortunately, in the fetid cavern air, lit only by rippling shades of red and orange, it was hard to make them out clearly.

Set had nearly reached the boulder when a massive spider-like demon blocked his way. The god stopped and cleared his throat. No response. He tried again. Still nothing. He glanced around long enough to establish that nobody was yet paying him any attention. He stooped low and scrabbled beneath the creature's hairy belly. On the other side, he brushed stray hairs from his shoulder and regained his prim composure. He climbed up onto a boulder.

"Dear friends," he said, shouting to break through the cacophony. "Here we are again, gathered together in this sacred chamber of demonic malevolence." Set put special emphasis on malevolence. It was one of his favorite words. "You may be wondering why I've called you all here," he said. "I know, it hasn't been that long since I last called this great host to a meeting."

This was met with a chorus of grumbling growls and hoots and screeches. To a human ear it would sound incomprehensibly monstrous. But Set knew just what they were moaning about. He had expected the complaints and had his response ready.

"Quiet down! This is not like last time. I know the shadow testing thing didn't go quite as planned. I promised you young humans to feast on. I did in fact get a good number of you into the first day's test. By all appearances, one after another of you devoured the contestants."

The grumbling kicked up a notch.

"How was I to know that the rules had been changed? Instead of feasting on young flesh, they were whisked away from your jaws and safely hidden away somewhere. Nobody told me a thing, I assure you. Quite an insult, really. But . . ."

Again with the grumbling.

"Listen!" His eyes suddenly went bright orange and flared to enormous size, completely changing his appearance, making him as monstrous as any in attendance. "If you'll just LISTEN!" He finished the sentence with a shout of aggravation that reverberated through the cave. It shook stalactites free from the ceiling. A few unfortunate demons got squashed by them. Set shrugged. He had their full attention again. He snapped back to his regular appearance.

"The problem back then was that I needed to play by the rules of Isis and Horus and the pharaoh and such. This time, however, we'll be playing by my rules. I have struck a blow that changes everything, dear friends."

He went on to explain Ra's fate and the role that he and Apep played in it. Actually, he had to explain this several times. Demons weren't the brightest of creatures. But he eventually boiled it down to the essentials. Ra was no more. Time had stopped. Egypt had been cast into never-ending night. Humans would be powerless to use magic. The long night of demons had begun.

"Egypt belongs to us," he declared, "and with me ruling it, you are going to have a lot more fun."

The demons pointed out one small remaining problem: all the rest of the gods. They were as powerful as before. What was Set going to do about them? Apparently the demons weren't entirely dimwitted.

Set paced in a circle atop the boulder. He was enjoying himself now. "You clever creatures. Such an eye for the tricky details! Worry not. I have a plan for that as well. I have no doubt that all the major gods will soon be called to Memphis for a council. All I have to do is await my summons. I'll head to Memphis and take care of every-thing. The gods will not be a problem for you."

He bowed, one outstretched arm drawing circles in the air, much like he had before he abandoned Thea in the Night Barge. It was a well-practiced gesture.

"I know you still have questions, but I wouldn't want to spoil the surprise. You do your part. I'll do mine. And your part is this. Spread the word. Gather your most hideous of friends. Climb out of these depths and stand beneath the night sky and see proof that what I've claimed *is true. Make your way toward the capital. Keep to the dark. But be near. When all is ready, I will summon you to the feast with a shout so great it'll ring through the ages!"*

23

Thea's Tale

When Thea finished her tale, the group sat in stunned silence. If what she said was true, solar farms would die. Solar ships would fly no more. Magicians would find their styluses useless. And the creatures of the deep, dark places would thrive in the everlasting night.

And Set. What else did he have planned?

Thea said, "If you ever wish to see the daylight again, you must help me."

"Help you how?" Khufu asked. He explained to her how they came to be out in the desert with the caravanners. "We're stuck here ourselves. It would take weeks to get back to *The Mistress of Light*, if we were lucky enough to find it. We're out here by ourselves."

Thea went on, undeterred. "Then we'll have to do it by ourselves. We have to stop Set. You don't know him like I do. He's monologued so much about all the injustices done to him. The old scores he wants to settle. The things he would do if he ruled Egypt. It will be a nightmare if he gets away with it." She paused, her eyes jumping from face to face frantically. "You believe me, don't you? The proof is right there."

She pointed at the sky. It was as dark as ever and showed no sign that dawn would come again. Staring at it, I felt a thought taking shape somewhere in the back of my mind. I wasn't sure what it was, though. Just . . . something.

"We can't just sit here talking!" she cried. "We have to go into the underworld and find a way to save Lord Ra. If you knew Ra like I do, you'd do anything to save him. Last night, he told me what the world was like in the early days, when it was newly created. When he spoke, I could see it all for real, like I was there. I watched as the Nile first rushed into being. It carved out the valley of Egypt, flooding it with silt-rich water that fed marshes that soon teemed with fish and birds. The first crocodiles climbed up from the riverbed and stuck their snouts up into the air. I saw birds discover what their wings were for. I watched life spread across the plains in a stampede. It was incredible. He talked about how much he loved Egypt."

Khufu started, "Let's say that everything you've said is true—"

Thea smashed a fist into the sand. "It is!"

"That's what I'm saying. But if it's true, you're asking us to save Lord Ra from inside a great serpent's body? How do we do that?"

"I don't know," Thea said. "He's a god, though. He's not necessarily dead just because he was swallowed. Not yet, at least. If we're fast and smart we'll find a way. We can pilot the Night Barge ourselves and go after him. Apep will go back to his lair to digest his meal. It probably takes a while to consume a god as powerful as Lord Ra. That's where we'll find him."

"That sounds exceedingly dangerous," Iset said.

"So does piloting through the underworld," Seret added.

Thea chewed her lip as if she was thinking something through. She touched the round-rimmed glasses that hung from a chain at her neck. But then she piped up and said, "Nah, that's pretty much the easy part."

"Okay. Let me see if I got the details of this right,"

Gilli said. He squeezed his chin and pursed his lips thoughtfully. "We've got a diabolic plot concocted by a devious god intent on taking over the world. We've got another god trapped inside the belly of a gigantic demon serpent. We've got to pilot a ship through an underworld that Thea calls 'the easy part.' And then we have to face that demon serpent, who, by the way, is reported to have a roar that causes earthquakes and a hypnotic stare that renders his prey immobile, and who goes by several titles, including: the Uncreator, the Eater of Souls, the World Encircler, the Killer of Joy, just to name a few. Are those the rough details?"

Thea nodded.

We stood in an uncomfortable silence until Khufu said, "Thea, give us a moment. My friends and I need to talk about this together."

24

For Egypt

We gathered at the edge of the light cast by the campfires. Looking up at the sky, I couldn't help but remember the presence of Lord Ra in the sky above the village. Day after day that glowing orb moved slowly across the sky. Too slowly, I used to think, since I spent plenty of time training beneath it or doing work around the compound. To me, Ra had mostly been sweat and heat and sun-dried plains so bright I had to shield my eyes to see into the distance. Now, I realized just how much more he was.

"This is crazy," Seret said. "I don't know what to think."

"First," Gilli said, "we need to figure out whether we believe her or not."

"I believe her," Khufu said. "I remember her now. She was with Lord Ra when he visited my father once. I thought how strange it was that someone so young had so much responsibility. I was kind of jealous. Anyway, she is who she says she is."

"There's also this sky," Seret said, motioning toward it with her paw. "This long night . . . We wanted an explanation. Now we've got it."

Gilli exhaled. "Well, then . . . second, what do we do about it?"

Iset clenched her stylus in a fist. Her face, for the first time, wasn't composed. She looked scared. "We can't go into the Duat. It's way too dangerous. Lord Set himself was barely able to get past all the gates and all the demons. Thea wants us to do all that *and then* find the most terrifying serpent in the world and somehow save Lord Ra. Apep was able to swallow a god. What do you think he'd do to us? We need to take word back to the pharaoh and the queen. They can do something, call on the gods and sorcerers."

"But we can't use the skiff," Gilli pointed out. "Your stylus ran out of charge. And if the sun is not coming up again . . ."

"Then we walk," Iset said.

For a moment, I agreed. Khufu's parents would never want us to take him into the underworld. A thousand things down there could be the end of us. Doing what Thea wanted seemed impossible. Walking across a dark desert had its own risks, but at least if we just kept moving, we'd reach a city or town or get back to *The Mistress of Light*. We'd find help.

But, as the others kept talking, I realized something none of them did. The prophecy. A line from it jumped into my head: *When Ra to darkness is consumed* . . . Wasn't that what had just happened? Ra. Consumed. Darkness. It had to be! And that changed everything. We were the only people in the world who knew what had happened. I couldn't just pack up with the rest and go looking for help. Being the Shadow Prince was about protecting Khufu, but it was also about protecting Egypt. I must do something. Not the easiest thing. Not the safest thing. I had to face it directly. That meant . . .

"I'll go with Thea," I said.

The others dropped their conversation and stared at me.

"I'll go with Thea," I said, trying to sound more certain than I felt. I looked from face to face. "The rest of you go with Khufu and walk back across the desert. That will be the safest for the prince. If I can help Thea I will."

"Just you and Thea?" Gilli asked. "That's exceedingly—"

"It doesn't matter. I have to do this."

"Ash, you were the one who wanted to stop taking risks," Seret said. "Now you want to take like the biggest risk ever?"

"I don't *want* to," I said. "But I . . . I *have* to. There's a reason I must do this."

"What reason is that?" Seret asked.

I exhaled. "That's the thing. I have a reason, but I can't tell you. Just trust me. I would explain if I could, but I can't. I swore I wouldn't. It's a Shadow Prince thing."

Gilli frowned. "A Shadow Prince thing? That's a new one."

Khufu put his hands on my shoulders and asked, "You're serious about this?"

I nodded.

"Then I agree. If you have to go with Thea, you should. There's only one thing. I'm going with you." I started to protest, but he spoke over me. "There's no way I'm sending my shadow into the Duat alone! I know you have responsibilities, Ash, but so do I. It may feel like we're out here because we took chances and did things that we shouldn't. But what if we're *supposed* to be here? What if we're the only ones who can help? As a prince of Egypt, I can't walk away from that."

I tried to argue, but Khufu kept going.

"ANNDDD if I'm with you, though, and things get really scary, you can always use the Eye of Isis."

I paused with my mouth open. How could I have forgotten about the Eye of Isis? It was the special gift that Lady Isis drew around my eye after the shadow testing.

"When Lady Isis gave it to you, Ash, she said, 'This means that when you are protecting the prince and are in grave danger or in need of help, I will know it. I will aid you if I can.' But if you're not protecting me, it might not work. So, if you want to protect me *and* save the world, we have to do it together."

He had a point. I knew from experience that gods could be very precise about how they worded things. For all I knew, the Eye of Isis might only work on exactly the terms that she said. I'd have to be careful to pick the right moment to use it.

Gilli shrugged and said, "Okay. I'm in. I know it's dangerous and may be the last thing we do, but we've got to try. For Egypt."

"Me too," Seret said. "We all signed on to serve Egypt. Let's get started."

Iset hadn't said a word yet, but I could feel her staring at me. For the first time, I looked right back into her silver eyes. "For Egypt," she said.

INTO THE
UNDERWORLD

25

Still Second Class

Far out in the western desert, near the gaping hole into which the Night Barge normally descended to begin its journey, Lord Set waited to be summoned to the capital. The pier and its stairway planks that had floated above the hole the night before lay scattered across the sand. The waiting was a part of Set's plan. Still, he was bored and grew impatient.

He scanned the dim horizon. Nothing. Not a thing moved in the whole great expanse.

He got up and did a few deep knee bends, though he stopped abruptly when he felt a twinge in his back.

He folded pieces of papyrus into paper birds and tossed them into the air. They never got far. They veered off in one direction or another. Or just nosedived.

He paced the perimeter of the pier, muttering bits and pieces of the speech he planned to give. Things like: "The vile serpent rose up from the depths . . ." and ". . . his eyes were two swirls of chaos . . ." and "I fought with all my godly strength . . ." and "Ra stumbled upon us, mumbling and incoherent . . ." and ". . . he must've been sleepwalking . . ." and ". . . nothing I could do to save him . . ."

He tried on different expressions of emotions: fear, bravery, grief, anger, guilt. At least, he thought he was trying on different expressions. In truth he felt none of those emotions. He looked pretty much the same no matter what he was pretending to feel.

Later, stretched out on his back atop the pier, he tilted his head up to the night sky and exhaled a long, snout-waggling breath. "Would you come on already?" he asked. "Summon me to the stupid council!"

As if in answer, his godly ears picked up the faintest thrum of noise in the distance.

He snapped to his feet. His long ears pivoted around to better hear the sounds. "Yes! About time." He leaped from the pier and dashed to the edge of the chasm. He climbed down a little ways and, clinging to the stone wall, he waited.

The sputter of a messenger beetle's wings grew louder.

When they were close enough, Set climbed back up to the surface. He rose to his feet in the sand, swaying unsteadily. He trudged toward the pier as the newly arrived beetle landed on it.

"Messenger! Messenger!" he called. "I've need of you!" He reached the pier panting, patting his forehead with a handkerchief, and generally pretending to be exhausted.

The beetle had a face that would be distinctive to another beetle. Not so much to human or even godly eyes. He did, however, have one very crooked antenna, with a bandage wrapped around it. He tapped his heels crisply and said, "Babbel reporting, Messenger Beetle Second Class."

Set frowned. "Oh, you again. Still Second Class?"

Babbel did his full-shell imitation of a shrug. "It's only been a few days. I'm working on it."

"Whatever," Set said, remembering to look miserable. "I've just now climbed from the depths of the Duat. You wouldn't believe the way I've labored! And the tragic things I've seen."

Babbel's eyes traced where the god's footsteps had left the pier walking toward the chasm, and then where they returned from it. He bent down and picked up one of the papyrus birds, a crooked little thing that Set had stepped on when it didn't fly straight. He said, "Sure." He looked past Set. "Isn't there supposed to be a ship here? The Night Barge?"

"I think you're supposed to bring messages—not ask questions."

Babbel studied him with one eyebrow raised. He sighed and said, "Okay, so there's a new message. Lady Isis has pushed back the small council meeting to discuss your . . . um . . . You know, the shadow testing stuff."

Set crossed his arms and looked menacing. He'd forgotten about pretending to be tired. "Get to the point."

"That's off until later, but an emergency meeting of all the gods has been called. High priority. Drop whatever you're doing. Or whatever you're . . ." He held up the papyrus bird he was still holding. ". . . not doing. Head immediately to the capital. That's it. That's all she wrote."

This was exactly what Set had been waiting for. "And this is because?"

"Look around," Babbel said. "Everything's dark. All over Egypt. It's chaos. Nobody knows what happened. Things have ground to a standstill. The gods are troubled. People are afraid. I mean, things are crazy."

All this pleased Set so much that he closed his eyes and basked in the glow of his own devious brilliance for a long moment. When he remembered himself, he opened his eyes, cleared his throat, and said to Babbel, "You may go."

Babbel turned to leave but paused. "Hey, where's the girl who was here before?"

"Her? It's tragic, but I suspect she's quite dead at this point. Demon food." He waved vaguely in the direction of the chasm. "It got rather ugly down there."

"Oh, shame. I liked her. She was nice."

"I'm sure the demon who devoured her thought so, too."

Set strode toward his flying beetle. It had been awake and watching. It thrummed to life to avoid Set's usual kick start. It didn't help. Set kicked it anyway.

26

A Pouch Full Of . . .

I didn't know just what to expect from a journey through the Duat, but I knew one thing: I was gonna need my weapons. I checked and rechecked my knives. I drew them again, making sure I was as fast as ever. I hefted my spear and danced through a few moves, blocks, and thrusts, trying to limber up.

The caravanners provided us small bundles of food and a couple of skins of water. We slung them over our shoulders or tied them around our waists. Having done that, there wasn't much more preparation to make.

Just before we parted, Sudeen pulled me away from the others. He said, "Though we cannot make this journey with you, we wish you success at it. The fate of your nation is in your hands. That is why I want to offer you a present." He handed me a small pouch. "This is filled with memories. Do not open it until you have need of them. And do not open it too frequently, for it only contains a few."

"Memories?" I asked. Memories were things in the mind. Bits and pieces of the past—not something you put in a pouch. "I don't understand."

"When you have need of them you will understand," Sudeen answered, as if it were the most obvious thing in the world. He smiled. "Now, we must part. You on your mission; us to continue our journey home."

"Good luck," I said, fingering the pouch of supposed memories.

Sudeen touched me on the chin and said, "And to you as well. I hope I will see you again, Ash. There is much to your story that is still to be told. I hope to hear it all one day."

Sudeen rejoined his companions. He climbed the harness onto Sweet Girl's back. Once seated, he said, "Farewell, prince of Egypt and brave companions. May you succeed at your quest." He turned the giant viper, and all the caravanners stepped into motion. Some mounted on camels, some walked, some rode atop the caraviper. Sweet Girl slithered away, reluctantly glancing over her shoulder at us.

"I'm going to miss her," Gilli said.

In no time at all, the whole caravan faded into the darkness, leaving the six of us alone in a vast, eerie landscape. It might have been my mind playing tricks on me, but somehow the night didn't feel like a normal night anymore. While I knew the landscape around us was empty, I couldn't shake the feeling that there were things lurking out there. Things that might appear out of the dark at any moment.

"Well," Khufu said, "I guess it's time to go."

"Yes, we should hurry," Thea said. She still sat on the mat that had been laid out for her, with the blanket on her lap. "There's just one thing." She pulled the blanket back, revealing her legs and the braces on them. I'd forgotten all about those!

"What are those?" I asked.

She frowned and, for a moment, it looked like she wouldn't answer. Then she exhaled and explained. "When I was little, I got very sick. It started as a fever, but got worse fast, headaches and aching muscles. My body began to feel so, so heavy. It got so I could barely move. I was bedbound for weeks. I finally got better, but not all the way better. After the illness my knees weren't as strong as before. I needed crutches to walk. When Lord Ra chose me to be his attendant he had these solar braces made for me. When they're charged my legs are as strong and as fast as anybody's. And when I'm near Lord Ra they're supercharged. But after what happened with Apep and Lord Ra the charge drained out of them. They worked long enough for me to climb out of the Duat, but they gave out just before Seret found me." She hesitated. "I can walk. I mean, I've gotten stronger. It's just . . . more work for me than for you."

We stood there, all stunned as Thea's story sunk in.

Thea added, "I'm sorry. I didn't want to mention it before."

"Why not?" Gilli asked.

"I was afraid you wouldn't help me. That you'd think I couldn't lead you back there and through everything. People can be mean. Underestimate me because I'm different."

Seret crouched down beside Thea. Gently, she ran her paw over the etchings on the braces. "I think these are beautiful, and I'm glad they help you. You were super brave to do what you did and to find us."

"Also," Khufu added, "it's another reason for us to save Lord Ra."

Thea's eyes brightened. "You mean you'll still help?"

"Of course!" We all said it at once.

"There's a lot of climbing down the cavern walls to get to the Night Barge. I don't think I could do that again."

"No problem," Seret said. "Luckily for you, I've got these." She held up a paw and flexed her claws. "If you hold on to my back I'll do the climbing for you. You see, Thea, we're a team. We help each other. It used to be just the four of us, but then Iset joined the team. Now you have!"

Thea's face flushed with emotion. She looked choked up.

"Come on," I said, "let's get going."

27

A Memory?

We made slow but steady progress across the desert, backtracking over the footprints Thea had made earlier. Thea trudged along. I could tell she was putting in a lot of effort. Though the night was cool, there was a sheen of sweat on her forehead. She breathed heavily, and sometimes she had trouble pulling her feet out of the sand.

She'd said that her solar-powered braces helped a lot. That made all of us, I think, want to bring Ra back to life even more. For Thea, but also for all the people who were helped by Ra's gift to us. I hadn't even known there were sun-powered walking braces. What other things were there that I hadn't heard of? What other things hadn't been invented yet?

It was frustrating and cruel that Set would take all that away. And why? For power? There were more important things than that.

After walking for a while, we all took a rest. I sat down a little away from the others. I went to reach for my waterskin, but instead touched the memory pouch. I loosened it and held the small sack in my hand. It felt empty.

I doubted it contained anything, but I couldn't help wondering how I was supposed to use it if it did. For one thing, whose memories were in it? And why would someone's memories help me? I thought about it for a while, until I remembered something. Once I'd seen a traveling performer back at the village. The man's trick had been predicting people's futures. He had a bag he would put his hand into. He would feel around for a time, until he thought he had the right prediction, and then he would pull it out and inhale it. After that, he would speak his prophecy. I didn't know if he was ever right about any of them, but . . .

I loosened the strings on the pouch and reached in. For a moment I felt exactly what I expected to: nothing. My fingers searched all around the small space with no luck.

"Filled with memories, huh? Filled with air is more like it."

Something brushed through my fingers. I froze. Had I really felt that? It hadn't been much, just a passing touch, like when mist touches skin. I moved my hand more. There it was again. I closed my eyes and concentrated all my attention on the sense of touch in my fingers.

Yes, there was something in the bag. More than one something. It was like they were tiny, vaporous fish swimming around, sliding through my fingers. I gently cupped one. I closed my hand around it and drew it out. Staring at my closed fist, I could feel that it held something delicate and fleeting. Could I really be holding a memory? I didn't want to open my hand, because I felt sure that whatever I held would simply fade into the air if I let it go. What to do with it, then? I had an idea.

I looked around. The others were talking quietly. No witnesses to the rather strange thing I was about to do. I put my cupped hand up to my mouth and opened it just as I breathed in.

In an instant, I was someplace else.

I lay on a reed pallet in a small room. The roof above

me was woven of palm fronds set over a simple wooden frame. My room.

Yazen's face appeared. He said, "You're awake! Good. You have a visitor. He has come to say hello, and then goodbye. He leaves this day for a long, long journey."

The man lifted me. He simply slipped his hands under my armpits, hoisted me up, and set me on his crooked hip. Yazen was so big, so strong. I knew his hip, and the way his arm wrapped around my back. It was an embrace I loved. Yazen turned, and I turned with him.

A man entered the room. He wore sandy robes, with a wrap of cloth that went right around his head. He began to unwind the headdress.

"You have to say goodbye to him, Ash," Yazen said. "He should be gone already, but he says he must see you one last time."

The man finally pulled the cloth away and shook out the long knots he had for hair. He looked at me and smiled . . .

The scene vanished, and I was again sitting on the sand. It took me several long, slow moments to piece together the different aspects of the vision. Of course, it was amazing enough just to have had it. But if this were true, it was my memory. It had felt like I had really been there. I had been home again, but home as a younger, smaller version of myself. That was why Yazen could lift me up like that. I was just a baby, old enough to toddle around and say a few words. It could really have been a memory, except for one thing. The man that had come to visit me was . . .

"Sudeen," I whispered. The man in the dream had the same brown-skinned face, the same bright smile. *Sudeen? In a memory of mine?* I thought I had never seen Sudeen before meeting him and the caravanners. *How could he possibly know Yazen? Why would he have been at the compound? It doesn't make any . . .*

My thought trailed off when I heard the others call to me. I tied the drawstring of the pouch to my belt and stood up. Time to walk again.

It can't be a real memory, I concluded. Maybe the pouch wasn't really a memory pouch at all. It must hold something else. Imaginary moments. Meaningless visions. Useless stuff, obviously. A collection of memories that didn't make any sense and probably weren't memories at all!

28

The Climb

I'm not sure what I expected an entrance to the Duat to look like, but a narrow crevice in a rocky outcrop wasn't it. It was a small enough opening that I'd never have imagined the hugeness of the realm beneath it.

"Are you sure that's it?" Gilli asked.

"That's it," Thea said. "It opens up inside."

"Doesn't look like much," Seret said. She crouched close to the crevice, sniffing. "But it does *smell* like . . ."

Thea finished for her. "Like death?"

Seret sighed. "I didn't want to say it, but yeah."

"Wait." Khufu took a step back, as if he'd just realized something shocking. "Are we going to the Realm of the Dead?"

"Not exactly," Thea answered. "The route the Night Barge travels is like a tunnel through the underworld. The Duat is all around it, but we just travel through, not quite a part of it. If you want to see ghosts, you need to enter by the Osiris Gate. That takes you to the Field of Reeds—the part of the underworld reserved for the dead. I've caught glimpses of it before. It's a lot like the world of the living, from what I can see. Dead people do the same things we do here. They build houses. Raise crops. Hunt and fish. They get married and raise families. From what I can see being dead isn't that much different than being alive. You're just in a different place. Let's get moving. I'll tell you more on the way down."

I went through the crevice first. I was worried that I wouldn't be able to see anything in there, but once my head was through and my eyes adjusted there was an eerie orange light. I could make out the contours of the rock wall stretching down into the depths. I started climbing.

The others followed me. We were silent at first, each of us nervous, feeling for every hand- or foot-hold, focused. The rock was warm and a little slick. I jammed my fingers into cracks and wedged my sandals against anything that seemed like it would hold me. It was hard work. I heard occasional grunts from others. Jumpra was the most at ease out of all of us. He leaped along below us, from one tiny shelf to another. He made it look like a game.

At one point, when Iset was above me, she shouted, "Oh no!"

I looked up to see she'd lost her grip. She slid down the wall toward me so fast I didn't have time to move. Her foot slammed down on the fingers of my left hand. I cried out but couldn't move my hand with her weight on it. It hurt, but it turned out to be a good thing. My fingers made a good foothold, apparently. It slowed Iset long enough for her to get a grip on the wall again.

When she was able to lift her foot off my fingers, she said, "Sorry, did that hurt?"

"Didn't feel a thing," I said.

I was trying to be cool. It totally did hurt. But before long everything hurt. All my fingers seemed battered. My toes began to rub raw from the rocks. My arms and legs were getting tired.

"How much farther?" Gilli asked.

Thea, who had her arms wrapped around Seret's neck, answered, "A bit."

A bit? What's that mean? Thea seemed nice and all, but she could also be cagey, as I was about to learn.

After a short silence, Thea said, "So, about the Night Barge's route . . ." We all stopped climbing. "No, don't stop. There's no time. Keep moving."

Once we started down again, she continued, "Like I said, we're not going through the Realm of the Dead. The Night Barge travels through the Realm of Demons."

"That doesn't exactly sound better," Gilli said.

"It's not," Thea admitted. "I should be honest with you. Piloting the barge is scary. Real scary."

"You tell us this *now*?" Khufu asked. "We're halfway down the wall!"

"I figured that was a good time to do it. Because from here it's easier to climb down than back up to the surface. Also, with everybody climbing nobody can hit me." She said this with a light tone that made it into a joke.

Nobody laughed. We huffed, fumed, and continued our descent.

"I've made the journey many times," Thea said, "but it's always been with Ra. With Set, too. He was always unpleasant and didn't want to be there, but he had to protect the barge. And, honestly, he did."

"Until he didn't," Iset said.

"Yeah. So we don't have either of them to help. It's just us. Us and all the other things down there."

"Like what other things?" Khufu asked.

"There will be demons."

I groaned.

"Which ones?" Gilli asked. "Some are worse than others."

"It's different every night. I can't say which ones we'll come across. Some will ask us riddles. Some will try to lure us into traps. Some will attack us. Some would love to have us for a midnight snack. And right at the end there's the Keeper of Souls to get by. She's as scary as Apep."

The Keeper of Souls? Worryingly, that name didn't ring any bells. For years Yazen had taught me all about demons. Their names. Their shapes. Their deadly tricks. And their weaknesses. Problem was there were soooo many of them. Maybe more than I even realized. It was hard to keep them all straight or to remember every-thing. Unlike during the shadow testing, we wouldn't have a god watching over us. We wouldn't be able to use magical spells. And we wouldn't be magically whisked away to safety when a demon defeated us.

This time, it was for real.

Thea cried out, "Oh, look, we're at the bottom!"

29

So Easy

Set arrived in the capital trying to look tired and sad. He was actually neither, but he had to play his part perfectly if he was going to pull his plan off. He wanted to look like he'd been through a horrible ordeal. His normally crisp tunic was tattered and stained. He'd accomplished this by tearing the fabric himself and rolling around in mud on the bank of the Nile. He also walked through a field of grazing cattle without watching where he stepped. Soon enough, he was quite grimy, with feet that smelled of moist cow droppings.

He arrived late. That was also on purpose. He wanted to make sure that every god possible was inside the Vault of Divine Wisdom. In the dark of the already long night, the flowers had begun to droop. The fish were mere shadows of their normally vibrant colors. Torches burned through-out the Great Plaza and inside the vault. They cast a feeble light compared to the glow of light beetles. The smoke rising up from them clouded the air and gave the scene a sinister look. Set liked the atmosphere.

He walked slowly, intentionally giving the other gods more time to go inside the vault. Lady Bastet—in full feline form—slipped gracefully in. Lord Anubis strode with solemn determination, his jackal head tilted toward Lord Sobek's crocodile head as they talked. It was a real who's who of the gods. And there were surely loads more already waiting inside.

Unfortunately, several gods lingered near the entrance. They turned to watch Set approach. They made him a bit nervous. Other gods were not to be trifled with, and the ones watching him were some of Egypt's most formidable: Lady Isis, Lord Thoth, Lord Bes, and Lady Taweret.

With his piercing Ibis eyes, Lord Thoth took in Set's clothing and his muck-covered feet. "Lord Set, what's the meaning of this? You've been summoned to a High Council of the Gods in our most sacred chamber, yet you look like you've just bathed in a pigpen. Explain yourself."

"Not a pigpen, Lord Thoth," Set said. "I've come from the bowels of the Duat."

Lady Isis said, "Unwashed or not, it's good that you've finally arrived. We had planned to hear your testimony about events during the shadow testing. That will have to wait, though, as we have more pressing matters to discuss."

"Of those matters I know much." Set gestured toward the dark, starlit sky. "This long night . . . it's all the work of that vile serpent Apep. He hypnotized me with his swirling eyes. By force of will I broke free of the grasp he had on my mind. But it was too late. He'd already swallowed Ra. You know, he's been trying to do that for a while. Guess he finally got lucky."

Realizing he'd started to lose his solemn tone, Set cleared his throat and continued with more misery in his voice. "I didn't give in. I fought Apep on the barge. I fought him flying through the air. I pursued him through the underworld's darkest, dankest chambers. I struggled with all my might against the demon, but he escaped into the unknown." After a weighty pause, he added, "Lord Ra is lost to us."

For a few long moments, the gods standing around him said nothing.

Lord Bes broke the silence first. "Camel snot! That's what I call that story. Camel snot! Apep swallows Lord Ra, and you expect us to believe you had no hand in it?"

"I'll admit, I did have a hand in it," Set responded, "in that I failed to defend Lord Ra. I come to you disgraced." As if exhausted just by admitting it, Set hung his head, his snout limp with disappointment. Even the bony tufts beside his ears drooped. His posture was such that he looked to be offering his neck for chopping, should the other gods decide to punish him. It was a good show. But that's all it was, show. "If I could trade places with Ra I would. I'd rather Apep had swallowed me whole . . ."

"I'd rather that, too," Bes grumbled.

". . . but he cast me aside and had eyes only for Ra."

Lady Taweret crossed her long arms and said, "Strange that after all the many encounters you've had with Apep, it's only now that he defeats you."

"Strange indeed," Lady Isis agreed. "Have you any other witnesses to what transpired? What of the girl who attends Ra? Thea. Why is she not with you?"

Set sighed dejectedly. "Poor, poor Thea. In the confusion she was cast out of the barge. She perished in the depths."

Lady Taweret asked, "So nobody can confirm your story?"

"None but Apep himself." Set lifted his tiny eyes as he

added, "Of course, nobody but Apep can deny my account either."

"Quite convenient for you," Bes growled. He flexed the muscles of his human torso, and he let out a low growl from his lion head. "I have half a mind to—"

Lady Isis placed a hand on his shoulder. "No, Bes, not here," she said. "We should continue this inside, with all the gods in attendance and on the neutral ground the Vault of Divine Wisdom creates. We have many decisions to make, and we must act fast. If what Set says is true, we'll need to dispatch a rescue mission as soon as possible. Let us all go inside."

The gods murmured agreement and complimented Isis on her wisdom. As they began to file into the council chamber, Set said, "Give me a moment. I'll wash up a bit in one of those fountains."

Lord Thoth hung back long enough to say, "Yes, do that. The guards will let you in when you're ready. Be quick."

Thoth stepped through the chamber's thick doors, leaving just the two door guards. They stood motionless, legs spread wide, both hands clenched on the shafts of heavy iron spears. The guards kept their lips pressed together. They stared, stony-faced, at Set.

Set glanced around, making sure that no other gods lingered outside. Nor did he see any approaching from afar. With that, he knew the time had come.

Lightning quick, he darted forward. He grabbed both guards and knocked their heads together. They fell to the stone tiles and lay there unconscious. He slammed the vault's great doors closed. He snatched up one of the guards' iron spears. With a burst of godly strength, he slipped it through the door's ringed handle and bent it into an intricate bow. He did the same with the other spear. He added a locking spell as well.

"There," he said, when he was sure the door could not be opened from inside. "I think the council is going to go on longer than they expected. Try eternity. So much for your rescue mission."

The gods inside the room banged on the door. They pressed against it and demanded that it be opened. Bes roared with all the force of a lion. Anubis barked his rage. Isis called to Set, demanding he release them. That was all they could do, though. They were trapped. No magic could break into that chamber; no magic could break out of it. He'd rendered them as powerless as mere mortal humans.

"So easy," Set said as he strolled away. "They really do make it so easy to be me."

30

Pretty, Pretty Bats

We dropped onto a stone ledge. A few feet away, the cavern still stretched below us. I'd never appreciated the feeling of a solid surface under my feet so much. Everyone collapsed. Gilli lay on his belly, hugging the ledge. We were all grimy and sweaty. My muscles ached. My fingers were rubbed raw. But we'd done it. Here we were, in the Duat, a place I'd only ever heard of in tales. A place, really, I wasn't all that excited to be.

This was the realm of Lord Osiris, ruler of the underworld. The way he came to rule here was gruesome. Ages ago he and Set fought bitterly. Set cheated, ambushed him one day, and . . . well, Osiris . . . died. Set never wanted the god to return, so he chopped him up into pieces and spread them far and wide. Like I said, gruesome. But since Osiris was a god, his wife, Lady Isis, knew she could save him. She searched everywhere until she found all the pieces of him. She put him back together and brought him back to life—almost. There was still a part of him that was dead. Since then, he has ruled the Duat. They say the job is as big as ruling Earth—and probably scarier at times.

I thought about how mad I'd been about the sun-wings and the sunbursting in the skiff. All those reckless things I worried so much about. What I wouldn't have given to be back in that sunlit world, with only things that now seemed silly to worry about.

A little farther along the ledge, a vessel floated in the middle of the fathomless cavern. The rock walls stretched up on either side of it. The cavern also fell into nothingness, with rippling otherworldly light making everything vaguely visible, but also still dark. The Night Barge was completely still. It looked kinda sad, really. A set of oars jutted out to either side. They looked too thin to propel the boat.

The barge swayed as each of us leaped aboard. I made a point of not looking down as I jumped. Thea put us to work straightaway. She divided us into two pairs, each pair sitting side by side, gripping the same oar. I didn't love that we had to sit with our backs to the bow of the ship, which meant we couldn't see what we were rowing toward. One of us—Gilli to start—was posted at the bow as a lookout. Thea gripped the tiller at mid-ship.

"Okay," she said, when everyone was in place, "Row us to Ra!"

I'd expected rowing to be hard. Instead, it was almost effortless. The oars caught the air as if it were as thick as water but pulling through it wasn't hard. It was just that no matter how fast we tried to pull, the oars moved with a slow, patient rhythm. Gradually, the walls of the cavern slid by on either side.

"Don't look at them," Thea said. "Just ignore them."

"Ignore what?" I asked.

"The Winged Spirits."

"The Winged Spirits?" We all did exactly what Thea had just said not to do. We looked around.

"They're on the walls!" Seret cried out.

I saw them. Black shapes plastered to the stone walls. Not just shadows but . . .

One by one, as if prompted by the touch of our

eyes, the creatures jumped into the air. Bats. Bats as large as people. The air above the barge filled with them. They flew slowly, as if they didn't have to beat their wings frantically like the bats I saw every evening back at the village. Like those bats, these darted, changed direction, cut this way and that. They just did it at an easy tempo.

Jumpra scampered around the deck, tracking them with his hunter's eyes.

One of them flew up to my side of the barge and hovered, watching me.

"Hey, I said *don't* look at them!"

It was too late. I already had, and now I couldn't look away. The bat's eyes glowed an intense red. I had never seen a red so vibrant.

"They want you to look at them, but don't!" Thea said.

Why? I wondered. The bat was strangely beautiful. Big, adorable bat ears. A squiggly, wrinkled nose. Whiskers. Why had I never noticed how cute bats are? It hung in the air, as if it was smiling at me.

"Iset, grab him!" Thea called. "Grab Ash. He's transfixed!"

I heard that, but it sounded silly. I wasn't

transfixed—whatever that meant—I just needed to hang with this bat.

I opened my mouth to tell the others this but someone slammed into my back, threw their arms around me, and yanked me down. I sprawled on the floor between the rowing benches. I was tangled up, I realized, with Iset.

"Hey . . ." I started to complain, trying to wriggle free.

"No!" Iset hissed, close to my ear. "That thing's not right. It's not what it seems."

As if angered by Iset saying that, the Winged Spirit screeched. It flapped its wings hard and fast. It shot up into the air above us. I was staring at it when it flipped over.

"Ash, it's not real," Thea said. "It's not real! You have to understand that!"

The bat pulled in its very real wings. It dove, screeching, straight down at me. Suddenly, it wasn't cute at all. It was terrifying! It had a mouth full of needle-sharp teeth and it was heading right toward me.

"What do I have to say to get through to him?" Thea cried. "He's not listening! You have to distract him. Somebody, say something to distract him!"

31

And Also, Glittery Fish

Khufu sputtered, "Um ... um ..." and then shouted, "Bouncy balls!"

Seret yelled, "Barking baboons!"

Gilli screamed, "Top me up, Old Man!"

Iset said, "I can make iced cream!"

What? It was such a weird chorus of nonsense that I turned to look at them. A moment later, I felt the force of the bat slam into me. Only, just as I felt it, the weight evaporated and passed right through me. The others huddled around, asking if I was all right, checking me for damage. Once they knew I wasn't hurt, they started shouting at me for not listening.

"Ash, did you hear me when I said not to look at them?" Thea asked.

"Yeah, but they looked so cute."

"The Winged Spirits are *not* cute! They're the opposite of cute. They're just like the Glitter Fish."

"The what?"

Thea scooted across the bench to sit beside me. "Okay. The best way to handle this is for you to see for yourself. Look below us."

I peered over cautiously. Whoa! I was expecting yawning nothingness. There was that, but there were also fish. They swam through the fathomless reaches beneath the barge. They weren't in water, but that didn't seem to matter. They looked beautiful. They were all different sizes. Some long and sinuous. Some flat and thin. Some short and stout. Their scales glittered as they reflected the subterranean light. I leaned farther out.

"They're beautiful," I said.

Thea scoffed. "Keep watching."

The small fish swam in such a transfixing weave of light and motion that I didn't notice what was below them until the last moment. A larger shape surged up from the depths at incredible speed. All at once, the screen of smaller fish peeled away. The monster hidden beneath them rose. It was all mouth, filled with crooked rows and rows of knifelike teeth. They seemed to go on infinitely inside it, growing smaller into the distance like it was bigger on the inside than it was on the outside. As frightening as it was, I couldn't move. I just waited there as that horrible mouth got nearer and nearer and—

Thea yanked me back. The leviathan snapped its mouth shut on the air where I had been. It rose up for some time, its scaly hugeness dwarfing the barge. And then it lost its substance. Its scales and fins faded. Its entire massive body became vapor. It vanished.

"What just happened?" I panted.

"You almost got eaten by a thing that only half exists." Thea pushed me back toward the oars. "Like the bats, the fish are just phantoms. They're real, but they can only hurt you if you believe they can. And if you look at them too long you can't help but believe. So, if you want to survive down here you really need to learn to listen better. When I say something like 'Don't look at them,' do yourself a favor and *don't look at them*!"

Message received, I thought. Listen to Thea. We all

got the message, except for Jumpra. He still tiptoed along the railing, tail flicking each time a Winged Spirit flew near him. I guess they didn't have the same effect on caracals.

We got back to rowing. We worked in silence, each of us realizing that we were in a really different, dangerous dimension. Was anything down here what it seemed? How would I even know what's dangerous and what's not in a world like this? And if we did get through this *easy part,* how were we going to deal with the hard part?

"Can I ask a question?" I asked as I rowed. "How, exactly, are we going to defeat Apep? I've got my spear and knives, but I'm thinking they won't do much against the Lord of Chaos."

"There's an access tunnel to Apep's den just beyond the final gate," Thea said. "We'll surprise him. You're right, though, not just any weapon can harm Apep. Fortunately, we've got the Spear of Vengeance."

She took one hand off the tiller long enough to point. The spear lay cradled in a holder near the prow. It was a long, impressive-looking weapon, with a treacherous barbed point. It looked cool, but it was so large I wasn't sure I'd be able to lift it.

"It's magical," Thea said. "I'm betting that if we just stick Apep with it we can convince him to cough Lord Ra up."

"You're confident of that?" Gilli asked. "Seems like an odd cause and effect. Stick him. He spits up a god?"

"Anyway . . ." Thea gripped the tiller with both hands again. "We've got more immediate things to think about. The gates. Each of them is controlled by different demons. We have to get past all of them."

Seret dug her claws into her oar as she pulled. "What are these demons like? How do we get past them?"

"See for yourself," Thea said grimly. "We're approaching the first gate."

32

The Four Weary Ones

"**W**e've got demons!" Gilli called from the prow of the ship.

"Okay, everyone," Thea said. She gripped the oar tighter. "It's important that you be as quiet as you can."

"Why?" Khufu asked. "What's going to be there?"

Thea put her finger to her lips. "Shhh. Go take a look."

We released our oars and joined Gilli. The barge kept moving, slowing as it rounded a bend in the cavern. Sure enough. Demons. I wasn't sure if I should be horrified or relieved by the sight of them.

The case for being horrified was pretty solid: four giant demons. They were basically human-shaped, but they were huge, each of them with large fists and long legs with knobbly knees. Their bare feet were so massive they could have squished any of us to a pulp with just a heel. Enormous clubs leaned up against the stone wall. Just one blow from one of those tree trunks would splinter the Night Barge to pieces.

Considering all that, what was there to be relieved about? Well, the fact that . . .

"They're asleep," Iset whispered.

The four demons snoozed in a tangle of limbs. They sprawled over an enormous pile of rubble. Not exactly an appealing bed, but they didn't seem to mind. One of them slept with his mouth hanging open. Another snored so loudly the sound echoed off the cavern walls. Another tried to change position, grunted, and then settled back to stillness. One mumbled to himself, sounding vaguely like he was singing a song. Despite all the noise they were making, they were all fast asleep.

"They're the Four Weary Ones," Thea whispered. "They're always tired, but they get very angry if they get woken up. So let's be very, very quiet. We may just get off easy here."

"I thought there was supposed to be a gate," Iset said.

"That pile of rubble they're sleeping on?" Thea answered. "That used to be the gate. Over the centuries they knocked it down. But it's still called a gate because the Four Weary Ones still guard it. Now, let's be *really* quiet."

We rowed with slow, careful strokes. The Night Barge moved forward again. My pulse pounded. I could feel it in the palms of my hands where they gripped the oars.

Though there was no actual gate to pass through, the cavern closed in tight at the spot where the giants slept. The first one—the snoring one—was near enough that I could smell his demon breath. Not pleasant. Not pleasant at all. I would've pinched my nose closed if I could have let go of the oar. Instead, I held my breath and kept to the slow, steady rhythm of the oars. He gradually slipped behind us.

The next giant was even closer. His face was turned right toward us. Beneath his closed eyelids, his enormous eyes slid around, jumping from thing to thing like he was having an action-packed dream. All he had to do was open one eye. I was sure he was going to do exactly that. He murmured something, and then suddenly chomped his teeth together and growled.

Without meaning to, both Iset and I stopped rowing. Khufu and Seret, on the other side, didn't. With all the power coming from just one side, the barge began to turn. Toward the sleeping demons! When I realized what was happening, I started to pull again, but Seret yanked the oar out of my hands. It was too close to the third demon, almost touching him. She moved it so that it lay flush with the ship's hull. This kept it from touching the demon, but it didn't do anything to stop the vessel's turning momentum.

My eyes shot up to Thea. She strained at the tiller, pulling with all the might she could muster to correct the turn. The railing of the barge skimmed along just beside the third sleeping giant. It followed the long stretch of one leg, so near that I heard the giant's curly hairs scrape along the hull. With all the hushed silence that faint sound seemed incredibly loud.

Thea took one hand off the tiller long enough to wave at Khufu and Seret. They got the message: backward row. They tried that, but neither knew how to do it and the oar just flailed in the air.

Thea changed her message: stop rowing! That they could do.

The next few moments were excruciating. The

barge continued its slow turn. We brushed past the third giant's enormous foot. Oh, the bunions on that foot! And the state of his toenails! Yikes.

And then we were past them. Only when the giants were some distance behind us did we start to relax.

"This may not be that hard, after all," Khufu said. For the first time since we'd come down into the underworld, he looked at ease. "Abandoned gates. Sleeping demons. Piece of cake."

"I'll drink to that!" Gilli said. He lifted his water-skin and poured a stream of water into his mouth.

"Hey," Seret said, "go easy. That's got to last for all of us."

Gilli kept drinking.

I was about to ask for a swig myself, but I saw something that made the words stick in my mouth. A black shape crawled up and over the railing behind Gilli. It moved slowly, stepping onto the deck and rising to full height. It was a woman. She had long, chaotic hair that hid her face. She wore a dark, tattered gown of some sort and carried a long sliver of metal in her hand.

A sword.

33

The Wailing Goddesses

Time slowed. The woman shuffled forward while Gilli went on drinking. She took halting, unsteady steps. She jerked and flexed her hand carrying the sword like she couldn't wait to use it. She was just behind Gilli. She reached up with her free hand and cleared the screen of hair from her face. Her skin was blue-white, stretched around eyes that sparkled like polished black stones. My blood ran cold. Khufu, Seret, Iset, and Thea were all frozen in fear.

Gilli, still clueless, lowered the waterskin and saw our gaping expressions. "Why are you looking at me like that? I didn't drink all of it. There's plenty. Here." He stretched forward to hand me the waterskin just as the demon sliced her sword through the air where his head had just been.

She let out an earsplitting keening. It was a horrible noise, like a thousand cats howling in pain all at once. Gilli spun around. The demon raised her sword again and slashed. Gilli dropped the waterskin and ducked. The blade missed. The woman screeched all the louder. Unfortunately, another screech answered her from behind me.

I spun around. A bony, blue-white hand grasped the railing and another black-draped demon-woman leaped on board. I realized who they were. If I wasn't mistaken these were—

"Oh no, it's the Wailing Goddesses!" Thea shouted. "Don't let them cut you!"

The hooded demon-woman shuffled toward me, cutting the air to ribbons in front of her. Two more landed with thuds near the front of the barge.

I had to be careful. There was more to it than just avoiding being sliced and diced by rusty old swords. With the Wailing Goddesses, if one of their swords drew blood, all their swords would drip with it. And I mean gush. It would make the barge a slippery mess, impossible to keep your footing on. And more than a little gross, too.

I scurried away from a goddess sliding toward me with her sword. Her blade cut through the air so close to my nose that I smelled the rusty metal. I tried to stay near Khufu to protect him, but he didn't make it easy. He darted, dove, and jumped as much as anyone.

Except for Jumpra. He was a screeching, terrified puff-ball moving faster than I'd ever seen him. He *did not* like Wailing Goddesses.

For a time, I did nothing but dodge, bouncing from one corner of the barge to the other, trading places with others in the confusion. We couldn't do that forever, though. My spear was down by the rowing benches, but I had my trusty knives. All I needed to do was get a good shot at one. If they would just hold still long enough! But I had to be careful. If I threw a knife and missed, I'd never get the weapon back.

Seret stood toe to toe with a goddess, slashing with her claws as the demon slashed back. Seret was quick, but she barely managed to avoid the curved blade.

Another goddess chased Iset into the Night Barge's cabin. But Iset dove through the window and back out onto the ship's deck, landing on her hands and neatly rolling up to her feet. She slammed the cabin door shut. The demon inside raged around the enclosed space.

Gilli was underneath the rowers' seats with a Wailing Goddess standing above him. She stabbed her sword down between the seats as he rolled from under one bench to another. She would've caught him eventually, but Thea managed to use the handle of the tiller to swipe the goddess's legs out from under her. The goddess went down, tangled and thrashing in her robes.

I spun around just in time to see the screeching form of a Wailing Goddess rushing toward me, her robes flapping and her teeth bared. I reached for a dagger, but one of her bony hands shot forward and grabbed my wrist before I even touched the handle. With my other hand, I grasped for another dagger. Again, though, her free hand snapped shut on that wrist, too. Her grip was like iron. She lifted my arms above my head, then clamped both of my wrists into the grip of one hand. She lifted me off the deck. I squirmed, twisted, kicked. I tried to pry her fingers loose. No luck. Wow, was she strong!

She pulled me close to her face. Her black eyes

stared into mine. Her lips stretched into a grin, exposing gleaming white teeth. With her free hand, she plucked one of my daggers from its sheath. She waved it in front of my nose. And then, with a flick of her wrist, she tossed it over her shoulder into the cavern's abyss. She did the same to my second and third daggers. I could only watch them flip end over end as they fell out of sight. Gone forever.

She cackled madly. She lifted me even higher and unsheathed her sword, waving it in front of me, teasing. And then, drawing back her sword arm, she swung the blade toward me. Clearly, she was hoping to cut me in half. I had other plans.

I pulled up my legs and scrunched into a ball. The sword cut through the air just beneath me. I twisted around and uncoiled a roundhouse kick to the goddess's side. She dropped me.

I bolted away. Any hopes I had of getting my spear were quickly dashed. One of the goddesses had planted herself right above it, like she was guarding it.

Running along the railing with a goddess trailing me, I tried to form a plan. The fact that the goddesses' swords gushed blood might be super gruesome and scary, but Yazen had said it was also a weakness of sorts.

It would make the floor slippery for them, too. If you dodged them long enough, they were likely to slip, trip, and get tangled up in their long gowns.

Easy, right? Well . . . to get things flowing, one of them needed to cut a victim. I didn't want myself or anybody else to get diced with long blades, but I had to do something. I was the prince's shadow, after all. If anybody needed to sacrifice themselves, it was me. Maybe if I could get a goddess to cut me just a little bit . . .

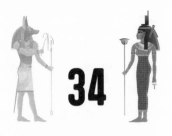

34

The Flood

I ran out of railing. I jumped back to the deck and ducked the goddess's strike, one that came way too close. I got wrapped up in the folds of her long dress. The fabric smelled foul, dead, rotten. I flailed to get free.

When I did, I sprawled out across the deck. I landed with the waterskin that Gilli had dropped right in front of my nose. I grabbed it and spun around. The goddess was waiting for me, her sword hand raised high. As she struck, I did the only thing I could think of. I shoved the waterskin at her. The sword punctured the skin. Water gushed at the goddess's face. She fell back, screaming. She shook her head furiously, and then raked her wet hair out of her face. Some of it stayed plastered there, but she glared at me through it. I think she was a little bit aggravated with me.

She came forward again, her black eyes fixed on me. Her mouth opened in a grisly, garbled song. Trapped against the stern railing, I couldn't see any way out. Her free hand shot out and clamped on to my neck. I tried to kick or punch her, but with her long arm holding me I couldn't reach. She raised the sword. I closed my eyes, not wanting to watch the blade cut down.

Something hit my face, but it wasn't the cold slice of metal.

It was a drop of water. Followed a moment later by another, and then by a steady stream. Blinking, I looked at the goddess. She held the knife poised to strike but had paused to look at it. She even stopped wailing. The water spilled from the blade in a steadily increasing flow. The same thing was happening with the other three goddesses. They all stopped their attack and watched water pour from their knives. A lot of water!

She cut into water instead of blood! I thought. That means their knives will flow with . . .

Things were about to get seriously wet. I squirmed

out of the goddess's grip. I managed a leg swipe that knocked her legs out from under her. With her down, I turned toward the others and yelled, "Grab on to something!"

I got to a railing just before a deluge of water burst upon us. Instantly, the deck of the barge was awash with a foaming torrent.

The goddesses began wailing again, but this time it was with fright. They all lost their footing and went down, swirling around the deck, legs and arms flailing. As the flood poured off the barge and disappeared into the depths, it took the four goddesses with it.

Seret retracted her claws from the deck. Gilli peeked out from under the benches. Khufu and Thea untangled themselves from the railing they had clung to. Jumpra appeared, looking completely calm. He began licking himself dry.

"Wow," Khufu said. "I thought we were done for."

"That was clever thinking, Ash," Thea said.

Clever thinking? She thought I'd planned the whole water thing. I shrugged, smiled, and said, "Thanks?"

"Does this mean we've passed through a gate?" Gilli asked.

"Well, not exactly," Thea said. "There are more gates, yes, but each is different. Some aren't even gates at all. Like everything in Egypt, it's complicated. It's not just the gates we have to worry about. In between them there are plenty of dangers. The Winged Demons. The Glitter Fish. The Wailing Goddesses. They're not gates. They're just . . . demons doing what they do. You never know who might show up."

"Great," Khufu said, in a tone that meant the opposite of great. "So you can't predict what might jump out at us."

"Exactly." Thea let that sit a moment, then perked up. "Anyway, we won't have to deal with the Wailing Goddesses anytime soon! Onward to save Lord Ra!"

"Um," Seret said, "we do have a new problem, though." She stepped on the deflated waterskin to indicate it. "Now we don't have any water."

Thea bit her lower lip as she thought about that. "I know where we can get some. There's only one place down here that—"

Thump! Something massive plummeted down just beside the barge. Whatever it was fell down into the chasm's depths, but the force of its passing was great enough to make the barge rock.

Gilli said, "What was that?"

Thea pointed at something in the cavern behind us. "Look! The Four Weary Ones are awake!"

The commotion must have woken the giant demons. They were up and angry. They stood atop their mound of rubble, hurling boulders at us.

"Row!" Thea yelled. "Row like crazy!"

We dove for the rowing benches, grabbed our oars, and pulled with everything we had. Boulders rained down around us. They fell thwomping through the air. Some of them bounced off the cavern walls and ricocheted down, twirling in unpredictable directions.

Finally, we rounded a buttress of rock. We couldn't see them anymore, and they couldn't see us. But one of the giants threw one last boulder. It smashed into the cavern wall beside us. A big slab of rock peeled off the wall and slid down just next to the barge. When it passed, the suction of it on the air made the barge tip. I slid across the bench and stared over the railing into the unending abyss.

Seret sank her claws into my shoulder and held me in place. "Sorry," she said, once the barge righted again. "You looked like you were about to take a swim."

The slab of stone disappeared into the depths, but

another, smaller stone spiraled from it toward the barge. It crashed into the barge and punched right through the hull! We peered through the hole at the depths below. The barge dipped.

"We're sinking!" Thea shouted.

"How can we be sinking?" Iset asked. "We're not even on water!"

"I don't make the rules," Thea yelled. "Start rowing again!"

How a ship that wasn't floating on water could sink I couldn't explain either, but Thea was right. It was as if invisible, gaseous water poured in through the hole in the hull. The barge got sluggish. The rowing got harder, too. The oars moved even slower than before, and they were heavier now.

The barge ground to a halt beside a rock shelf, and we all climbed out to survey the damage. The Night Barge leaned to one side. The gaping hole in the hull looked even worse now that we could see it from a different angle. As we watched, the barge slipped farther down. I was no expert on magical boats that floated on air in the Duat, but it was pretty clear that—

"She's sinking," Gilli said.

35

Servants of the Prince

Lord Set walked through the streets of Memphis, grinning from ear to ear. The city wasn't in complete disarray yet, but the questions of frightened people echoed through the streets. There was a growing realization that something was wrong, that surely Lord Ra should have risen hours ago. The night sky above was sinister in its silent, unending darkness. It twinkled with just enough starlight to cast the world below in faint hues of white and blue, with shadows everywhere. With any stored solar power depleted, the city couldn't rely on solar torches and light beetles. Instead, people were lighting torches and building fires, turning the stars' blue light into a hellish red and yellow glow, and filling the air with thick black smoke.

"Just like in the old days," Set mused, "when humans

crouched around fires, afraid of the dark and all the things hidden in it."

He passed many houses with families huddling inside, terrified as they watched him stroll by. He greeted them. "Fine night, isn't it? There's nothing like the smell of burning things in the evening, eh?"

A few brave souls called to him, asking for news. For help. For the reassurance a benevolent god could offer. Set was not a benevolent god. He gave them none of these things. He did enjoy hearing them beg, though. "Soon," he whispered, "they'll understand that big changes are here. Soon, they'll be worshipping me properly."

He entered the royal palace gardens. Guards rushed into formation to halt his progress. He glared at them until they withered beneath the hot, vile touch of his gaze. They backed away.

"As well they should," he said. "This is my palace now."

Once in the family's private quarters, Set followed his nose toward his target. It was an easy scent to follow. The smell of a certain prince's unwashed feet. That, and the smell of fear.

As he turned into the hallway that led to Prince Rami's bedroom, a voice shouted, "Halt!"

It was so sharp and forceful that Set stumbled to a

stop. He could see down the whole hallway. It was empty, with just statues and plant vases lining it. He hesitated a moment, taking in the silence. "Must have come from outside," Set decided. "Godly hearing can be a burden."

He started forward again.

"I said, 'Halt!'" A figure stepped out from behind one of the vases.

Set blinked. "A tiny blue hippo?"

Indeed, it was a diminutive hippo. A bright blue one. He stood on his hind legs, with his arms crossed and a severe scowl on his snout.

"And who, pray tell, are you?" Set asked.

"A Servant of the Prince! He's not receiving visitors."

Set scoffed. "And you think you can stop me?"

"No," the hippo said, "but I figure we can."

On that cue, other blue hippos stepped out from behind the statues and vases. All of them just as small. Just as blue. And just as stern.

"Do you know who I am?" Set asked them.

Chuckling, one of the hippos said, with an exaggeratedly snively voice, "Do you know who I am?"

The others laughed. A few tried their own imitations.

Set growled. "You insult me? I could exile you to the lowest depths of the Duat for that!"

This was met with more imitations. Elaborations. Sillier and sillier threats delivered in Set's pompous tone of voice. The hippos, it seemed, were not the least bit afraid of the god. Set looked utterly confused and at a loss for words.

The first hippo, after wiping a tear of laughter from his eye, got serious again. "Yeah, we know who you are. But, like I said, the prince isn't receiving visitors. Shouldn't you be out there figuring out what's going on? Go be a god and do god stuff." He shooed Set away with his pudgy fingers.

"Enough!" Set shouted. "Out of my way!" He began to push through them.

"Servants of the Prince," one of the hippos said, "you know what this calls for?"

In unison, they answered, "Bouncy balls!"

The hippos leaped in all directions. They tucked into ball-like shapes and ricocheted off the walls. They crashed through vases and knocked over statues. One smashed into the god's belly. Another thwacked him in the back. Another landed on his head and started tugging on his ears. Another knocked his legs out from under him. He went down and was soon pinned beneath a punching mass of angry, tiny hippos.

He didn't stay trapped long. Suddenly, Set wasn't Set anymore. He changed into a doglike creature. He squirmed out of their grasp, leaped away, and spun back to glare at them. He was slim, with a silky coat and long ears that hung down on either side of his snout. He was actually kind of graceful. It was a good look. But not for long.

He snapped back into his normal self. When the hippos came at him again, he was ready for them. Anger flared in his eyes. He was a god, after all. They were fast, but he was faster. As each hippo shot toward him, he grabbed them in midair and tossed them far into the distance, over the gardens and out of the palace grounds. He shook several off his legs. And he got a grip on the one who loved pulling on his ears. This one he drop-kicked farther than any of the rest. As the hippo sailed away, he shouted, "And don't come back. You're fired!"

Finally rid of them, he stood panting. "That," he snarled, "was deeply annoying. It's why I hate pets. Bouncy balls . . . Whoever heard of such a thing?"

36

A Water Break

"It's not as bad as it looks," Thea said. "The Night Barge isn't like a regular boat, and the air down here isn't regular air. It's like the barge pretends to float on the air like it's on water, and the air pretends to float the barge like it's on water. Neither thing is really true, but the rules down here are different. I saw Set patch the hull once. All he did was lay some sailcloth over it. He didn't use magic or anything. He just pretended it was a real patch and that was enough to get her floating again."

Gilli said, "This place is weird."

Jumpra gave one of his trills. I guess he agreed.

"Anyway, this is a good place to stop for a bit," Thea continued. "There's a spring down that tunnel." She pointed toward a black hole in the rock wall. "Set used to go to it sometimes for a drink. We can fill up a few urns from the cabin. Should be enough water to get us through to Apep."

Khufu spoke up. "If you all get water, Ash and I will stay to repair the barge."

Nobody objected, so Gilli, Iset, Seret, and Thea went to fetch water. Thea needed to show them the way, since there were a few intersections, and it would be easy to get lost. Thea led the way, using the wall for support. The others followed, carrying the empty urns. Khufu and I watched them slowly disappear into the dim tunnel. We stood there in silence.

"So," Khufu said, being the first one to speak, "no more daggers, huh?"

Ugh. Did he have to remind me? I resisted the urge to feel for their handles. I knew they weren't there and that reaching for them would make me feel parts of me were missing. I almost said something sharp. I hadn't thought about it since we'd climbed down into the Duat, but standing there alone with him reminded me that I was still mad about the way he'd been treating me. I wanted to give him an earful about it. I wasn't sure what to say, though. I chose to be moody and silent instead.

In the cabin we found what we hoped would work to make a patch: a sheet of papyrus, some nails, and a small hammer. I pulled the papyrus tight and held it in place so the air wouldn't flow through. Khufu placed the nails and hammered them in. It was a weird sort of repair, but it worked. The barge rose up and floated with the same buoyancy it had had before.

With the work done, we sat in silence. I did my best not to stare at the Winged Spirits that flew around above us, trying to attract our attention. Nor did I let my eyes follow the Glitter Fish, which swam beneath the barge. Sometimes they jumped into view next to the railing, like dolphins do beside boats on the River Nile.

Khufu cleared his throat. "Ash, I've been meaning to talk to you, but with all that's been happening . . . It's been too crazy. Until now."

I smoothed my hand over the patch as if I was checking that it was holding. Really, I just needed to do something and still didn't feel like talking.

"I think that . . ." He started, but his voice trailed away. He thought a moment and tried again. "Back at the caravan, after everyone had fallen asleep and the fire died down, I lay there looking up at the sky. I thought about my parents, wondering what they were thinking. I figured we'd be able to get to them the next day, but I knew they'd be up all night, miserable and worried. It was all my fault. I've been pushing. With the sunwings. With the skiff. With wanting Iset to cast her sunburst spell. With stopping at the caravan and then with riding Sweet Girl and losing track of time. Sudeen and the others were super nice, but what if they hadn't been? I really could've put us in danger."

I kept checking the patch. I held my hand above it like I was testing for leaks. I pressed on the nail heads with my fingers. Mostly, though, I listened.

"I've been acting like a jerk. You kept trying to tell me not to do risky things. I kept doing them anyway. And I didn't stop to think that it wasn't fair for you. So, I'm just trying to say I'm sorry."

I hadn't expected that. I'd assumed he'd never think of me. I thought I'd have to get angry and rant and tell him everything that was bothering me. And even then I wasn't sure he'd really hear me. I'd almost *wanted* to be mad. To say mean things. To hurt because I guess, deep down, I was hurt. But all that anger and all those words faded. Truth was, I didn't *want* to be mad. I wanted to be understood and valued. That's what Khufu just did.

"If I agree that you were a jerk," I said, "would you agree not to be one anymore?"

Khufu said, "Yeah. Definitely. When I asked about the daggers, I wasn't . . . being critical. I know they mean a lot to you. But it's okay. You've got skills without them. You did, after all, save us from the Wailing Goddesses!"

It meant a lot to hear him say that. I could feel the anger in me starting to loosen, to slip away. "Being mad isn't much fun," I said, "but once you are mad it's hard to let go of."

Khufu smiled and shook his head. "Yeah, I know."

"We've had really different lives, you and me," I said. "But I can understand that you'd want to have adventures and stuff."

"I did want to," Khufu said. "But boy did we get a bigger adventure than I expected. Hey." The prince piped up. "After all this is done, how about if you take me to your village? Show me your life. That would be a different sort of adventure."

For a moment I was going to protest. But I didn't. Why should I? There was nothing to be embarrassed about. The village was full of good, caring people.

Hard workers who loved their families and looked out for one another. If Khufu liked me, he'd also like where I came from.

"Okay," I said. "If we survive this it's a deal."

37

Meerkats of the Moon

The others returned with urns full of water. We drank and rested briefly.

"We're doing well," Thea said.

"Are we?" Gilli asked. "We almost sank. We almost got crushed by boulders. Almost got sliced and diced by Wailing Goddesses. Who, by the way, weren't really wailing. *Screeching* Goddesses is more like it. And there were those phantom fish and spirit bats Ash found so entrancing. Feels like one mistake and we'd—"

"Let's not make mistakes, then," Thea said crisply, like it was as easy as that. She took her position at the tiller, but paused a moment to adjust her Afro puffs, combing them with a pick and then squeezing them into shape. Once done, she exhaled, rolled her shoulders, and said, "Let's go. Next gate, the Meerkats of the Moon."

Meerkats. Those cute skinny guys who stand on their hind legs? They were the last creatures I'd expect to find in the Duat. But since this was the Duat, I had to ask, "How, exactly, are they going to try and kill us?"

I couldn't tell for sure, but it looked like the question made Thea blush. "This one is a bit different," she said. "You'll see. Just remember that when I say to close your eyes you have to close your eyes. I mean it. Close them!"

The Meerkats of the Moon were not like other gatekeepers. I realized this as we rowed toward them down a straight stretch in the cavern. They didn't have a gate. They spread out on small cliffs on the cavern walls. There were, according to Thea, a hundred of them. Each one occupied a small ledge. When they saw the barge approaching, they rose from sitting or kneeling or just lying about.

"You should close your eyes now," Thea said.

Jumpra perched at the front of the barge, looking very interested in the meerkats.

"Those are gate demons?" Khufu asked. "They don't seem like much to worry about."

As if to prove his point, the meerkats began . . . Well, they began dancing. There's no other way to describe it. They pounded out a rhythm with their feet and slapped out a beat on the stones with their hands. And they moved. They shifted. They shimmied. They rocked on their hips and twisted from the waist. They gesticulated with their arms, thrusting them out at sharp angles as they snapped their heads from side to side.

"This is the best," Khufu said. "It's like our own meerkats dance troupe!"

He might have spoken a bit too soon.

The meerkats stopped dancing. They turned around, suddenly moving with military efficiency. They faced the walls, straight backed, stern. The meerkats began to sway side to side, all of them perfectly timed with each other. At the same moment, they bent over and wiggled their bottoms in the air.

Khufu burst out laughing. I fought not to, but it was hard. I'd never seen anything quite so funny.

"That's it," Thea snapped. "Show's over. Close your eyes. No peeking."

Then it got weird. I mean, if this wasn't already weird. All the meerkats' bottoms began to glow. It wasn't a warm golden light like the sun. Instead, it was a cool light. It started out soft but got harsh fast.

"Eyes closed!" Thea shouted.

I slapped my hands over my eyes. Just in time, too. The blast of light hit us with a physical force. For a moment the world burned brilliantly white. It was so intense I could see it through my closed eyes and even through my hands. It was almost too much to bear. Fortunately, it didn't last long. The light faded, both the brightness of it and the intensity of the physical feeling. I didn't open my eyes until I was sure the others had already done so.

The meerkats had stopped dancing and weren't showing their behinds anymore. They just looked bored. Several yawned. Some scratched at fleas. A few lay down as best they could on their small ledges and fell asleep. Yep, the show was definitely over.

Jumpra, up in the front of the barge, turned around with large, stunned eyes. He looked dazed and dizzy, wandering in a zigzag over to Iset. I guess he might have seen a bit too much.

As Iset cuddled Jumpra, she said, "Wow. Who would've thought meerkats' butts could do that."

"Yeah," Thea said. "Thanks for listening this time.

You're lucky you didn't get blinded. That's what happens if you gaze into the power of the hundred meerkat moons!" She said that with such complete seriousness that it was hard not to snicker. "I'm not joking! Listen. If you had kept watching, those meerkat bottoms would've been the last thing you'd ever see. Down here everything is a trap. Beautiful bats. Lazy giants. Sword ladies. Dancing meerkats. No matter what, there's a trick involved—even if it's cute, even if it's funny. We can't trust anyone until we're out of here and back up in a sunlit world. Got it?"

We were silent. She was right, of course. She'd proved it several times. I knew we wouldn't be on this mission without her. But also, I realized how everything about what we were trying to do depended on her knowledge. Up above in normal times each of us had special skills. I had my daggers and fight training and even—when they let me—some strangely effective magic spells. Iset had proper magician skills. Gilli was super smart. Khufu was a prince. Seret—as a lioness— could do things none of the rest of us could.

But most of those strengths weren't working for us here. I *didn't* have my daggers. Iset's stylus was useless. Gilli may be smart, but he didn't know the dangers of the Duat. Being a prince in the world above didn't seem to mean anything to the creatures down here. Seret was still Seret, but Thea—she was the key to everything. Without her I wouldn't have made it past that first cute bat.

I said, "Yeah, I'm pretty sure we all got it. There's one thing I disagree on, though."

Thea squinted an eye at me. "What's that?"

"We can trust someone down here. We can trust each other."

She looked at me for a long moment, then smiled. "Okay. You're right. But nobody else! Especially not the One Who Asks Questions."

"The one who what?" Gilli asked.

"You'll see. He's up next."

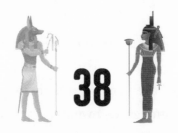

38

The One Who Asks Questions

Soon another gate was barring our way. This one was a real gate, closed tight and secured with a large lock. Thea brought the boat over beside a wide shelf of rock. She said, "We're getting out, so we need to tie up the boat again."

"But there's nobody here," Iset pointed out. "Just the locked gate."

"We have to get the key. It's up there." Thea pointed to a staircase that had been cut into the cavern wall. "Come on. The One Who Asks Questions will be waiting for us. He's always waiting."

"What scary thing does he do?" Khufu asked.

"He asks questions. You know, riddles."

Seret offered cautiously, "That doesn't sound so bad."

Thea lifted the glasses that hung from her necklace and looked through them for a moment. Hesitantly, she said, "It's not so bad. . . ." Her voice trailed off.

Gilli frowned. "Hang on a moment." He touched his nose in thought. "I've noticed something about you, Thea. When you touch your reading glasses, you're usually saying something that's not entirely true. You did it when you said piloting the barge through the Duat would be easy. And you just did it again."

Thea let her glasses drop back to rest on her chest. She looked sheepish. "Well, okay . . . The riddles aren't so bad so long as you answer correctly. If you get an answer wrong, then it's . . . probably pretty bad. I don't know for sure, though. I never went to the One Who Asks Questions before. I always just stayed in the boat. Anyway, there's a first time for everything. Let's go!"

Grumbling, we set out with Thea. I took my spear with me, the only weapon I had left.

It was a brief walk up the stairs, through a short tunnel, and out into a small, circular cave. In the center of the stone floor sat a rather strange-looking demon.

At least, I assumed he was a demon. His skin was a deep purple color—a dead giveaway that there was something supernatural about the guy. Other than that, he looked like a skinny, very human old man. He sat cross-legged on a woven mat, with a smile on his face. No claws. No knives. No fangs. Just thin shoulders and a birdlike chest. He looked like a peaceful village wise man. *Guess you can't judge a demon by his appearance*, I thought.

"Welcome, young travelers," the man called, his voice cordial and friendly.

"Are you the One Who Asks Questions?" Thea asked.

"I am," the demon said. With a wink, he added, "Aren't we all?"

I glanced at Khufu. I could tell by the look on his face that he was thinking the same thing I was. He couldn't be that bad. Could he?

"I trust you have come here because you need a key," the demon said. "That's convenient, because I have keys. Lots of them, as you can see."

He motioned behind him. Suddenly, there was a mound of keys at his back. Hundreds. Thousands of old, rusty keys.

Iset tried her luck. "May we have one?"

"Of course. That's what they're here for."

Pleased, Iset made a half step forward.

The demon snapped a finger into the air. "You have only to answer my questions correctly. That's all. Answer them correctly and you may have the key to unlock the gate and carry on. Answer incorrectly, you perish. You fall into the depths. Goodbye."

He pointed with one large, many-jointed finger, directing us to look down at our feet. We looked, then gasped and cried out in fright. Where there had been solid rock just a moment ago, there was nothing but air, only the depths, just as deep and dank and fathomless as the main cavern. Jumpra nearly leaped out of his skin. He jumped into the air clawing as if he was trying to swim away. When he landed again, his legs stretched out to all sides, and he looked mightily confused. Somehow, we stood as if on a solid base, but I had no doubt that we could all drop into an endless fall at any moment.

"You might want to explain to that little guy that he's *purr*fectly safe," the demon said. "You are in no danger—unless you answer incorrectly."

"We have to each answer a riddle?" Khufu asked.

"Yes," the demon said, grinning, "and so you fall one by one. Please don't take too long deciding who goes first. Such debates are so tiresome. I'm happy to pick for you, if you'd like."

I didn't like the idea of going first. I was pretty sure the others didn't either, though. It would be horrible to fall into the abyss, but it would be horrible to see any of the others fall also. Looking around from face to face, I realized we were a family of sorts—my family. I wouldn't want to see Iset, annoying as she'd been, fall to her end. And Thea, though I had only known her over these last crazy hours, seemed as important to me as anybody I'd ever known.

Fortunately, Thea spoke up then. "What if we answered together? You know, have one question that we all answer at once."

The demon seemed pleased by the idea. "You'll be happy to know that is within the realm of possibility. I could ask one question of all of you. One question. One answer. That answer would save you all if correct. If not—"

"We know," Gilli cut in, "we all perish. You don't have to sound so happy about it."

Thea continued, "It's something that my mom and

dad taught me. They work at the Great Library. I work there, too, sort of. I mean, I hang around and help them during the day. People always come in with questions. Whenever a difficult question comes in, my mom and dad and the other librarians all put their heads together to figure it out." She raised her eyebrows hopefully. "Maybe, if we work together, we can decide on the best answer together."

The others agreed, and the One Who Asks Questions exclaimed, "Splendid!" He cleared his throat and gave us the riddle.

39

A Riddle

The One Who Asks Questions intoned the following words:

> "The light that makes the dark,
> Calls it not dark but sun,
> Neither night,
> Nor day,
> The beginning,
> As well as the end."

His eyes lit up and he made a motion with his hands, flicking them out to either side as if pleased by the lovely thing he had just presented. "Spiffy one, isn't it? Feel free to talk amongst yourselves. You have the riddle. Speak next to me when you have your answer." He smiled and let his head tilt to one side.

During the next few minutes, we tied ourselves in knots. We recited the lines over and over, proposed different answers. Khufu thought it was about Lord Set. He had, after all, plunged the world into darkness, and he wanted an end to the pharaoh's rule and the beginning of his own. Seret proposed that it was all about the underworld itself: dark, filled with contradictions, and certainly being down here felt like the beginning of the end. Iset focused on *the light that makes the dark*. But what light makes dark? The two things were opposite.

The demon interrupted us. "Well, what's your answer?" He cracked his knuckles, clearly loosening them to gesture the command that would make the floor fall out from beneath us.

"We're still thinking," I said.

The demon looked aggravated. "Think faster."

I motioned for the others to huddle close. I spoke in a whisper. "I think I have something that might help. I'm not sure, but . . . maybe it's worth a try. Sudeen gave me something he called a memory pouch." I untied it from my belt, showed them, and told them about the vision of Yazen and Sudeen I'd had.

"Ahem." The demon cleared his throat. "Speed up the deliberation."

The group huddled even closer. Thea placed a hand on my shoulder. "That vision doesn't make much sense, but that doesn't mean it's not true in some way. I say Ash should try it again."

One by one, the others nodded agreement.

Breathing deeply, I turned away from the group and sat down. Setting my spear down, I made a point of not looking through the invisible floor. Jumpra brushed up against me, purring encouragement. I slipped my hand inside the pouch and concentrated. Just like before, the more I moved my fingers the more I felt the small, faint touches of the memories.

I felt one of them come to rest in my palm. Was it the right one? Was it even really a memory? I didn't know, but it was time to find out. I pulled my cupped hand out, placed it over my mouth, and inhaled. Like last time, the scene around me instantly changed.

I lay on my back, looking up at a blurry room. I waved my arms and legs in the air. I wasn't trying to do anything in particular with them. Just moving them was enough. The awareness that I had arms and legs that I could control was a new thing, one that pleased me. It pleased me so much that I cried out in joy.

In answer, a woman's face appeared. There. That was

another good thing! If I cried out, she looked down at me with moist eyes, with full lips and high cheekbones and dark brown eyes. It was the only face I had ever known. I thought it was very lovely. She spoke. The sounds didn't mean anything to me, but they were good to hear. It was the sound of her, and she was making them for me. I knew that much. She brushed her lips across my cheek and spoke some more, very softly. Her breath warmed my skin. Nothing had ever felt better. Nothing had ever been more right and comforting.

She lifted me up and hugged me. Looking over her shoulder through the window behind her, I saw the sun emerging from the horizon. It amazed me. I didn't know what it was, but I'd seen it before. I knew it was good. It brought the day, and I liked the day . . .

The memory vanished.

I sat just as before, hanging in the air above the precipice. Jumpra was still at my side, staring at me with his big green eyes, ears twitching. The demon watched me as well. The others breathlessly waited for my response. It took me a moment to produce it.

In the memory I had been a baby. That's why my thoughts were so simple, focused on small things like waving my arms. As a baby, I hadn't known that the woman was my mother. I hadn't known that word, and for me, she had been more than that. She had been the world, the beginning and the end of it, the first and only one sharing it with me. I also hadn't understood the words she spoke because at that point I hadn't learned to understand words.

But I could now. Sitting in the hush of the others waiting, I heard my mother's words again. She had said that people were coming for me soon. She wished they were not, but they were good people. They would raise me for great things. When she brushed her lips across the skin of my cheeks and whispered, what she had said was, "I am your mother, Ash. I love you more than anything in the world. But you are not safe. I must leave you. It's the only way to keep you safe. Do not forget me. Will you promise me that you won't forget me? No matter where I am in eternity, I will come back to you. I promise you, I will return, even if it takes a million lifetimes. Son, look for me with each rising sun."

"I need your final answer," the demon said.

I wasn't ready. I had just seen my mother's face. I had just learned things about myself and her that I had never thought I would learn. If she loved me, why did she have to leave? How did that keep me safe? What did she mean about eternity? About a million lifetimes? Who lives a million lifetimes? I wanted time to think about it, but I didn't have that time. If I was ever going to have it, I had to keep myself and my friends alive.

I closed my eyes, and there, on my dark eyelids, I saw the image of the rising sun again. The very thing she told me to look toward. And then I heard the words of the riddle again, with one thing changed.

"The light that makes the dark,
Calls it not dark but son,
Neither night,
Nor day,
The beginning,
As well as the end."

Suddenly, I saw the answer hidden within the tricks of the riddle's language. Before I lost courage and doubted myself, I said, "The answer is: the dawn."

40

Tricky, but Clever

"**T**he dawn?" the others all said at once.

"Are you crazy?" Khufu asked. "You're going to get us killed!"

Iset mused, "Hold on. There's something here. *'Neither night, nor day . . .'* Which is what dawn is, right?"

Gilli added, "*'The beginning, as well as the end . . .'* Dawn is the beginning of day and the end of night."

"But the most important part," I said, "is *'The light that makes the dark, calls it not dark but sun.'* The light is the sun at dawn. But it's also my mother. She's the light who made the dark—which means me, the shadow—but she called me not dark but . . . her son."

"Oh, that's clever," Thea said, smirking at the One Who Asks Questions. "Tricky, but clever."

"Is that your final answer?" the demon demanded.

I nodded.

The demon pressed his lips into two thin lines. "Your final, final answer?"

"Yes," I said. "The answer to your riddle is: the dawn."

"In that case . . ."

The demon gestured with his fingers. For a horrible moment, I thought that I'd been wrong. The vision was just some false imagining. The floor was about to drop out from under us. The rest of my life would be one long fall that would last . . .

"In that case you're free to go." The demon frowned, made a vague gesture that must have been a wave, and then tossed me one of the keys.

The floor, when I finally dared to look, was solid stone again. "You mean," I asked, "that's really the right answer?"

The demon didn't respond. He turned his skinny purple back and began sorting through his pile of keys. That was the last we got from the One Who

Asks Questions. He seemed to have forgotten us completely.

Seret put an arm around Thea's shoulder. "That was a great idea, Thea."

"Yeah," Gilli said, "but if you work in the library during the day and then work on the Night Barge at night, when do you ever sleep?"

Thea grinned. "Who wants to sleep when there's so much to learn? And what's better than being able to talk about it all with a god? Still . . ." She glanced at Seret. ". . . I take a catnap every now and then."

Still stunned by the emotion of my memory, I walked quietly behind the others as we returned to the main cavern. I heard Seret and Thea chattering animatedly, but I didn't follow what they were saying. I didn't even think about how scared I should be, considering we would soon be confronting Apep.

The image of my mother's face lingered in my mind. How incredible, I kept thinking. How incredible to finally know what she looks like. The strange thing was that as much of a surprise as it was, her face seemed completely right. Now that I had seen her again, it was as if I had known her features all along. I just hadn't known that I'd known.

Khufu fell in step beside me. "Why didn't you tell me about the memory pouch?"

"I didn't know if it was real. If it was, I wasn't sure you'd want me to have it."

"Why wouldn't I want you to?"

"I'm a shadow. My life is about protecting yours now. We aren't supposed to have our own lives, our own parents, or our own feelings. Not really. We're supposed to just be . . . shadows."

Khufu put a hand on my shoulder and slowed me to a halt. "That's absurd. It couldn't be true even if you wanted it to be true. You're not a shadow, Ash. You're a person, same as me. What's more, you're my friend. Got that? You know what that means? It means that I want the best for you, too. I'll make you a promise. If we survive this and get out of here, I'll help you find your mother. I don't care what my father says. We'll find out everything we can about her."

I didn't know what to say to that, but I certainly couldn't admit that I already had an agreement with his parents. "Thanks. I wish I could talk to Sudeen again. If the memory of my mother was real . . ."

". . . the one of him must be also. Wow. That's weird."

"You're telling me."

When we caught up with the others, they were clumped on the stairway that led down to the terrace. Jumpra was drawn up in a frightened curve, his body arched and fur bristling.

Khufu began, "Hey, what's gotten into—" The rest of his sentence never left his mouth. He was too surprised by something he saw. And then I saw it, too.

Someone waited for us at the barge. A very unwelcome someone.

41

An Offer?

Set kicked opened the prince's bedroom door, shattering it and sending shards of wood twirling into the room. He liked to make an entrance, and he hadn't kicked enough things recently. Doing so brought a spring to his step. This was turning out to be a blast of a night.

He found the prince huddled behind a large chest. "Prince Rami, just the royal personage I'm looking for."

"Lord Set?" the prince asked, peeking from behind the chest and looking flustered. "I thought you were a bandit or something. Who else dares burst in like . . ." The question trailed away. Apparently, too many other questions jostled in his mind. "What—what's happened? Everything is chaos! Where's the sun? Where are the other gods? Have you heard from my parents? Have you seen my sister? I can't find her. I'll be in trouble if anything happens to her."

"Well, you can be sure Princess Sia isn't hiding behind that chest with you." Set tapped one of his long fingers on Rami's nose. "Come out where I can see you properly."

Rami clumsily climbed over the chest. He stood, dusting off his tunic and adjusting his royal arm rings. Set studied him head to toe. Nothing terribly impressive going on here, *he thought.* Just a skinny kid with a bad attitude who spent too much time wrinkling his nose, frowning, and looking down on the world. *Much of the same could have been said about Set himself, but self-awareness wasn't a skill he had. All that mattered to him was that he had a figurehead, a royal to stand powerless and obedient beside him. For that, this prince would do.* Set threw an arm around his shoulder and walked him toward the large balcony with a view of the city.

"Dear boy," he said, "so many questions! Fortunately, I have the answers. I've come with an offer. It just might make your day." Set glanced out at the dark city below and corrected himself, "I mean, it might make your night."

Rami frowned, head cocked to the side suspiciously. "An offer? Last time you had an offer for me it didn't—"

"No use revisiting old history," the god said.

"Old history? It was a few weeks ago that—"

"Here's what you have to do," Set said. "I don't ask much. First, wash your feet. Second, get some of your servants to dress you up properly. You know, fancy-like. Look royal and distinguished." He paused after saying this, studying Rami with a skeptical gaze. "At least, try to look royal and distinguished. When my army arrives—"

"What?" Rami blurted. "An army? Are they coming to defend us? We're under attack? Who would dare attack Egypt?"

Set looked at him for a long moment. Then, just 'cause he thought it was cute, he let a tiny flame flare in one eye. A flame-wink.

The truth dawned on Rami. "What have you done?"

"Tossed his divine glowiness into the rubbish bin of history. That's what I've done." When Rami looked completely confused, Set clarified. "I speared Lord Ra and fed him to Apep. Fortune favors the bold, young prince. I'm nothing if not bold."

"Oh," he said.

"Yes, quite right. Oh. My army of demons—"

"Demons?"

"Yes, demons. Stop interrupting! We'll take the city. I'll then call you to my side and we'll officially take the throne.

Me on it. You beside—or slightly behind—me. We'll be the divine and human partnership always necessary to rule Egypt." He grinned. "I'm sure you'll grow to like it."

"But . . . my father and mother and Khufu. What about them?"

Set sniffed. "They've been dismissed."

"You haven't hurt them, have you?"

Now the boy gets squeamish? *Set thought.* He'll need a good bit of training if he's going to be the right hand of chaos. *What he said, however, was, "I've done nothing at all to them. They were off on their tour of Egypt, remember? I've no idea where they are. But worry not, prince, I wouldn't think of harming them! They'll just be rewarded with early retirement. Everyone loves early retirement! The pharaoh and queen can retreat to Buhen or something. Someplace quiet, out of the way, and far to the south. Let them relax and enjoy their twilight years. Write poetry. Find some hobbies. They'll thank us for it."*

Rami didn't look convinced. "I don't think that would suit them." Then another thought wrote itself across his face. "And what about Lord Horus and Lady Isis? Not to mention Lord Thoth and . . . well, all the gods."

Set exhaled a long, blubbery breath through his snout. "They've been taken care of. You know the Vault of Divine

Wisdom? I crammed them all in there and locked the door. They're stuck. They're completely powerless. Can't get out. Can't communicate."

"But, what will happen to them?"

"Nothing they don't deserve," Set said. "They'll stay trapped there together, huddled in the dark. Their immortality will become a curse as they live on through the ages. They'll come to regret the crimes they've done me." He grinned and made a sound like an animal growl low in his throat. His features shifted, as if he was starting to morph into some other creature entirely.

Rami backed away, horrified.

Noticing the movement, Set snapped back to his normally strange self. "Why so pale, prince? I suspect it's because you can't believe your good fortune. Your day—I mean night—has finally come. Call your servants and get spiffed up. Meet me at the Vault of Divine Wisdom. Make it snappy. I've got an invasion to attend to."

Set spun on his heel and strode away, leaving a very distraught prince of Egypt staring out over a dark city, smoldering with makeshift fires and clouds of smoke.

42

A Visit from an Old Friend

It was Ammut. The Devouress of the Dead. Her head and jaws of a Nile crocodile filled with hundreds of jagged teeth, her mane and torso of a lion with huge front paws with sharp claws, and her weighty rump and back legs of a hippopotamus. All that, and a very grumpy personality.

She stood upright, leaning against the bow of the Night Barge with one elbow propped up on it, looking bored. She used a slim reed to pick bits of food from her teeth. When she saw us, she grunted. She then flicked away the reed, flexed her claws, and fixed her eyes on me. They were large, bulbous, and intense—filled with hatred and a hunger for revenge. She thrust a paw toward me and beckoned.

No mistaking that, I thought. *A challenge.*

It wasn't one I wanted to accept. My fingers touched the skin just below my eye, itching to use the Eye of Isis to call for help. But this still wasn't the time. I'd have to handle Ammut on my own.

I stepped out from the stairway and in front of the others.

"Ash, don't!" Khufu called.

"I've fought her before," I said. "I'm not afraid of her." That was a bald-faced lie, but it felt important to not show my fear. "It's only Ammut. I could take her with my hands tied behind my back."

The demon obviously wasn't used to a future victim expressing such disdain. She stepped forward, smashing her heavy, thick hippo feet into the stone floor. She raked the air with her claws and opened her long, toothy snout, then snapped it shut with a thunderous clap.

Well, maybe not with my hands tied . . .

To the others, I said, "You guys take the key, unlock the gate, and keep going in the barge. We're too close for you to stop now."

With that, I rushed down the steps. I took them three and four at a time, barely in control. Ammut bellowed. She dropped to all fours and ran to meet me. Skinny, twelve-year-old boy clinging to a spear on one side; immortal demon with the body parts of three of Egypt's most deadly animals and a reputation for eating the hearts of the dead for fun on the other. Not exactly an evenly matched contest.

Truth is, at this point I didn't really imagine myself living through the battle that was about to begin. I couldn't think about that. I couldn't think about the life I wanted to lead, or finding my mother, or becoming a magician, or any of the other millions of things I might have had to look forward to. None of those things mattered more than my doing anything and everything I could to help my friends get away.

Unfortunately, that's why my attack failed so miserably. I put all my hope into the point of my spear, knowing it was the only weapon I had. I directed it right at Ammut, dead center of her hulking form. She saw my attack coming from a mile away and had all the time she needed to plan her defense.

As I shouted and thrust the spearpoint toward her, Ammut stood upright. She slipped to the side in a move that was as graceful as a professional dancer's. She grabbed the shaft of my spear, spun it away from me, and tripped me all at once. I sprawled across the stone, skidding, rolling, and coming to a halt at the very edge of the ledge, looking down into the depths. I sprang to my feet, sure Ammut was about to stomp on me.

She wasn't in that much of a hurry, though. She waved the spear around, taunting me. She pretended to offer it to me, only to pull it back suddenly. She imitated my attack, pretending to fall, making the goofiest of faces. She burst into rumbling laughter. Ammut was cracking herself up at my expense.

Then she got serious. She lifted the spear in a high, two-handed grip, and then she slammed it down on her thick hippo knee. It cracked in two. She tossed both ends over my head and sent them twirling into the abyss. With that, she dropped to all fours and surged toward me.

Seeing her coming, I wasn't scared anymore. I was mad. I jumped into a whirling roundhouse kick that caught the demon right on her snout. The impact knocked her crocodile head to the side. I landed on her shoulders. She tried to tear me off, but I climbed up her neck so that I could reach over to her face. With my two hands, I grabbed each of her eyelids, pulled them up from her eyes, and then let them go. The lids snapped back into place with an impact that left the demon dazed and stumbling about.

I leaped to the ground and moved away, increasing my distance from the barge. Ammut came at me with her claws shredding the air. It was all I could do to duck and dodge them. High and low, squatting and jumping and spinning. Every now and then I landed a punch or a kick or smacked her with my wrist guards, but the thud against her hippo thighs or lion chest or scaly face seemed to hurt me more than it hurt her. She was thick, muscly, scaly, and tough all at once. And she wasn't getting tired! The worst part was that I didn't have any plan. As far as I knew Ammut didn't have any weakness to exploit. She was as savage as they came, and there was nothing I could really do about it.

In a devious move, Ammut pretended to trip. When I moved in to give her a shove, she snapped out one of her stubby legs and knocked me off my feet. I landed on my back. Before I could do anything, the demon plopped down on me. Her jaws dangled over my face, nostrils flaring. A drop of drool slowly stretched toward me.

So now I knew which way Ammut was going to finish me off. A little bit of everything. Hippo bottom pressing me down. Claws holding me in place. Jaws about to snap shut and end me. With a little drool sauce for flavoring. I hoped that the others had used the time I'd provided them to get away. Maybe, just maybe, they'd still manage to save Lord Ra.

Ammut's jaws swung open.

43

A Crazy Idea

Thwack! The demon bellowed in pain.

Opening my eyes, I realized that something hard had smashed into the side of Ammut's head. She turned to see what had hit her. Bad move, because a second object smacked her right between the eyes. Another hit her back. She spun around, momentarily forgetting me in the process.

I scrabbled away, jumped to my feet, and took in the scene.

Khufu, Gilli, and Seret had the demon surrounded. They gave her a wide berth, but Khufu and Gilli had rocks clenched in their fists. Seret crouched with her paw ready to smack a stone sideways. Iset stood a few steps back from the others, her useless stylus clenched in her fist. Thea sat down by the cave entrance and seemed to be searching for something on the floor.

Seret said, "Let's get her! She can't fight all of us."

"If you pick on Ash," Khufu shouted, "you pick on us, too! Come on, Fish-Breath, let's fight!"

Ammut rushed at Khufu. Thea nailed her with a stone. The demon spun and charged her, but Seret scratched Ammut's hippo rump with a claw. Ammut roared and swung around, swiping Iset and drawing blood from her shoulder. She then swiftly changed directions so sneakily that her snapping jaws barely missed the tip of Seret's tail. She bounded for Gilli, but he escaped by diving for the ground and darting through her feet as she tried to stomp him to a pulp. I got in on it, too, grabbing up rocks and chucking them anytime the demon neared one of the others.

As grateful as I was that the others had joined the fight, I knew that throwing rocks wasn't going to defeat the Devouress of the Dead. By the look of her, it was just making her angrier—and hungrier. As we kept up the barrage, I tried to think of what to do next. There was the Spear of Vengeance in the barge, but I doubted I could get around Ammut and to it.

Another *whack!* This time a stone ricocheted off

one of the Winged Spirits that clung to the cavern walls. The giant bat-creature barked in protest. Its wings unfurled and it leaped into flight. In no time at all, others did the same. Soon, the air above us was all flapping, membranous wings, darting shapes, and high-pitched, screeching cries.

Jumpra couldn't resist. He crouched, wiggled his kitten behind, and then launched himself from the cavern wall toward a spirit.

"Jumpra!" I cried as he flew over the cavern. Thankfully, he landed right on top of a bat that flew beneath him. The bat sank under the weight, veered to one side, and then rose again, flying as if it didn't even notice the new passenger. Relief spread through me. Clever cat.

That gave me an idea. It was a crazy one, but . . .

The next time Ammut's back was turned to me I sprinted straight at her. She was exchanging furious claw swipes with Seret, so she didn't notice. I jumped as I reached her, ran up her back, placed a heel on her head, and leaped. She tilted her head up. Her jaws snapped at me, but they missed.

I reached up and grasped the leg of one of the Winged Spirits. It flew careening off to one side. For a few moments it was complete confusion. I flailed around, trying to grab on to something with my other hand. I finally caught hold of the spirit's other leg. As soon as I did, its flight evened out. When I saw the cavern wall heading right toward me, I pulled on one of the spirit's legs. Just as I hoped, it turned that direction. Suddenly, my crazy idea seemed a little less crazy. I had wings that could keep me above Ammut. That seemed a whole lot better than us all being down on the ground fighting her jaws, claws, and rump. The Winged Demons were dangerous, sure, but dangling beneath them I didn't risk looking in their eyes. Instead, I controlled them. The others could, too.

I circled back over the others. "Get wings!" I yelled. "Get wings!"

They did. Seret ran to Thea. The lioness tossed her onto her back and—with Thea clinging to her neck—leaped straight up. Her body stretched out, paws upraised. She caught hold of one of the bats' feet. It swerved to the side, but she hung on long enough for Thea to reach up and get a good hold on the bat's feet. Once Thea was secure, Seret dropped off and ran a few circles around Ammut. Khufu jumped from a boulder to catch a Winged Spirit.

Watching all this, the expression on Iset's face changed. She shook off her dismay, tucked her stylus beneath her tunic, and called out to Gilli. She interlocked her fingers, making a platform for him. He ran toward her, leaped onto her hands, and was boosted into the air just in time to catch a spirit. A moment later, Iset was in the air, too.

Ammut bellowed and hissed and stomped as all of us flew through the air, dangling and darting above her. I couldn't help myself. I started laughing. It just felt too good.

The feeling didn't last.

Seret leaped up to grab a winged spirit like the rest of us, but she couldn't get a good grip on the spirit's legs. Her claws just didn't grip like hands did. Her bat careened wildly around the cavern. When she passed too near to the demon, Ammut swatted the lioness's foot. It was just enough to make Seret lose her grip. The bat veered over the gaping chasm. Seret fell, her face frantic, her claws raking at the air as if she were trying to swim.

She plummeted out of sight.

44

Up from the Depths

"**S**eret!" I cried. "Noooooooooo!"

I yanked on one of my spirit bat's legs, making it carve down toward the abyss. Several large Glitter Fish rushed toward me, jaws open. I pulled up. I kept calling Seret's name. Tears bloomed in my eyes and blurred my vision. She was gone. She was really gone.

For a time, I let the spirit dart as it would, paying no attention, feeling only grief and guilt. It was my idea that had made Seret try to fly with the winged spirits. That meant it was my fault that she had fallen. If only they had left me to die fighting. I'd rather that than any of them perish.

Iset appeared next to me for long enough to say,

"Ash, I know it's horrible about Seret, but—" Her bat veered away before she could finish.

Khufu replaced her. "We're not done. Look! We have to stop Ammut!"

Thea careened by above me, shouting, "You're not to blame, Ash. Ammut is. Let's get her!"

That was enough to get me to find the demon. She was doing her best to tempt them back to the rock ledge. She raged up and down the cliff, roaring and stomping. When that didn't seem to work, she went over to the Night Barge and began to pound on it.

"She'll rip it apart!" Gilli yelled.

I would have to deal with the loss of Seret later. But for now, I was mad! I sliced down toward the demon. Before I reached her, Khufu cut in from the other side. He kicked her head. Nice one, prince! Ammut's head turned with the blow, and so was perfectly positioned for another kick. I slammed into her with both my heels.

Circling away, I realized we could get in aerial blows against Ammut. The problem was that we didn't have the power to really hurt her. I worried that she'd eventually get ahold of one of us. That couldn't happen. It would be too horrible.

Ammut jumped for Khufu. She missed. When she landed, she tripped over an uneven part of the floor. She stumbled but barely paid any attention. She was focused on the flying shapes above, desperate for one to come close enough to grab. That, I realized, was the weakness we needed.

As I swept past Khufu, I yelled, "Follow me! Do what I do!"

Khufu passed the message on to Thea. Together, we circled back toward Ammut. I carved them into a tight circle, flying low but just out of the demon's reach. She leaped and bellowed and ripped at the air with her claws. We circled. Ammut spun around and around beneath us. I steadily whirled us all toward the edge of the precipice. If I could just get her to step off into the chasm . . .

Just a little closer . . .

Ammut stopped spinning. She was just a step away from the edge, but she planted her feet and stood swaying. Dizzy, she shook her head side to side. Her arms drew circles in the air as she tried to keep her balance.

"No!" I whispered. "Keep spinning!"

Then something amazing happened.

A massive shape rose up out of the cavern's depths.

A neon Glitter Fish, the biggest one yet. It surged up higher than the ledge and higher than the floating Night Barge. Like a whale jumping out of the water, it crested and slowly began to tilt to one side. The sight of the giant was impressive enough that I almost lost grip on my winged spirit's legs. Then I saw her. "Seret!"

The lioness clung to the leviathan's back. The claws of all four of her paws were sunk deep into its thick skin. She wore a look of grim determination on her face. As the demon fish began to crash back down, Seret's muscles tensed. She leaped from the sinking giant and landed on the stone ledge. She then rounded back on Ammut, hurled herself at the demon, and shoved her toward the edge.

The demon's eyes bulged. She cartwheeled her arms in the air, and then tumbled backward. She fell into the depths. Down and down Ammut went, roaring the whole way. The sound grew fainter and fainter, until it faded completely.

Thea was the first to land. Her bat even seemed to set her down gently. The rest of us followed her. Gilli lay on the stone shelf as if he was hugging it. Jumpra climbed onto his back and stretched, clearly pleased with himself. We all breathed hard as it sank in that we'd succeeded. We'd beaten Ammut. Not *me*, but *we*. It was a good feeling.

Seret strolled over to us, acting cool. She licked her paw and began smoothing over her fur with it. "There," she said. "That went just as I'd planned."

For a moment I thought she was serious, but a grin tickled the edges of her mouth and made her whiskers tremble. She burst into laughter. Thea swatted her on the shoulder, and then changed the gesture by pulling her into an embrace. Khufu said, "You had us for a minute."

When the mirth died down, Seret admitted she had thought herself a goner. "I fell for so long. It just got darker and darker, and more horrible. There were demon fish all around, snapping at me. I batted them away as best I could. And then I saw the big one. I aimed for it and set my claws in deep when I landed. It wasn't happy about it, I tell you. It tried to bash me off against the cavern wall. But I held on, and it started rising fast."

"I'm glad it did," Thea said.

"Yeah, me too. I knew you could take Ammut without me, but I wanted to do my part."

We laughed and joked a little longer, making our way back to the barge.

Khufu exhaled a tired breath. "Let's focus. We've got unfinished business with Apep."

The others agreed, except for Thea. She looked thoughtful. She studied the locked gate. "We have the key to that gate. Once we're through, there's the Marsh of the Beginning of Time. It's a bit different than the cavern has been so far. If we get through that, we're at Apep's lair."

A long hush stretched as we considered what this meant. Somebody needed to say something, so I did my best to speak with more confidence than I actually felt. "Well, that's the point of all this, right? It's why we've come this far. Let's finish this."

Annoying Little Creatures

Lord Set wasted no time conscripting a group of human laborers to follow his orders. They weren't at all inclined to do so, but he pointed out that there were no other gods to be found, no pharaoh or queen. There were court officials and various nobles, sure, but the only god on hand was Set. It just followed that he was in charge of things. With the fire in his eyes and scorching touch of his gaze and his well-documented history of being rather horrible, the laborers didn't have much choice.

"Here's what you're to do," he told them. "Gather gold. Crates of it. Heaps of it. Mountains of it."

When the laborers' foreman asked where they were supposed to get this gold from, Set said, "Anyplace. Everyplace. Go to the royal treasury. Into people's homes.

Rob the rich. Melt down a statue or ten. I don't care where you get it. Just get it. Take it to the Vault of Divine Wisdom. We're going to cover the whole thing in molten gold . . . as a tribute to . . . well, divine wisdom."

When the foreman asked why they were going to do that, Set said, "Because doing so would please me."

The foreman pointed out that this would take a long time. Without the sun, they couldn't use solar barges to move the gold, or cranes to lift it, or the solar ovens to melt it down. They also couldn't see very well with just the starlight and glow from fires, and the smoke was making it hard to breathe and—

"I won't hear excuses," Set interrupted. "Has technology made you so soft? Just do it the old-fashioned way. Use your muscles. Bend your backs. Blood and sweat and tears. That sort of thing. Just get it done. And another thing . . ." Set paused. One of his ears stretched high and rotated, searching for something. ". . . in a moment the city will be overrun by demons. Things will get a little messy. But so long as you're working for me, you'll be left alone. Consider that a perk of the job."

Leaving them to it, Set strode away. "Humans!" he said. "Annoying little creatures. So many questions. So much complaining! I should do away with them entirely."

He didn't actually mean this, of course. Gods were nothing without humans to worship them. Demons were useful in a ravaging, monster-horde sort of way, but they weren't much good at building temples and saying prayers and erecting grand statues. In the ages to come, Set would need humans to do all those things.

They were also fun to boss around.

Set spotted an obelisk in honor of Ra. Narrow and tall, it stretched high above the city. He climbed it, reading bits of the long poem in praise of the sun god as he did. A lot of over-the-top drivel, in his opinion. He'd have the humans make modifications to it, adding his name, his deeds, praise of him instead. He perched atop the pyramid peak and scanned the dark horizon. There was movement out there. Shapes in the shadows, growing nearer. He heard his army approaching. It was an indistinct sound, a combination of grunts, snorts, stomping feet, and flapping wings. And farts. The farts were a dead giveaway of a demon army attempting a sneak attack.

Set inhaled an enormous breath. His chest billowed with it, going round as a ball. He held the inhalation a moment, and then blew it through his snout. The sound this produced was like a war horn, but sputtering and blubbery and a travesty to horn blowers everywhere. Set's tone was horrible. His ability to hold a note nonexistent. He had volume, though. The humans beneath him trembled, covered their ears, and rolled on the ground.

When he finally ran out of breath and fell silent, the demons answered him with howls and barks and growls and shouts. They gave up any pretense of stealth and rushed into the city. Some ran. Some leaped. Some slithered. Some flew. They came in all shapes and sizes. The cries of panicked citizens mixed with the bellows and roars and laughter of demons. Clouds of smoke billowed up into the night sky, illuminated with the orange glow of the fires that raged throughout the city.

"Such atmosphere!" Set said, taking it all in.

46

Is Somebody Afraid Of . . .

We hadn't gone far after our encounter with Ammut before the rocky tunnel began to change. The walls and ceiling faded into the distance, getting farther from the Night Barge. A thick fog tinted with green rose up around us, obscuring our view in every direction. The air grew warm and moist. This didn't seem at all like the cavern we'd navigated so far. When I went to dip my oar in for a stroke, I felt an odd resistance, different from before. I heard a splash. I peered over the side of the boat. The water looked thick and murky. Tufts of river reeds and water lilies poked from its surface.

"Um, guys," I said, "we're floating in actual water now."

"Yeah," Gilli said. "And you know what else? Our oar isn't working."

"Great," Iset said. "These oars work on air but not on water?"

"Yeah," Thea said. "It annoyed Lord Set, too. You have to get out here and tow the barge through. I'm pretty sure it'll take all of you working together to move us forward."

I looked down at the marshy water. Judging from the reeds it was shallow enough to stand in, but I didn't like the look of the viscous green and brown sludge covering much of its surface. "You want us to get into that?"

"It's the only way. You can use that rope up by the bow of the boat."

Reluctantly, we dropped from the side of the boat into the water. I sank in up to my hips at first, then up to my belly button as my feet pressed into the slimy mud floor.

"This is disgusting," Iset said.

Seret couldn't touch the bottom. She grabbed on to the rope with her mouth and swam with her head poking out. We formed a line and began to pull. It was slow going. We struggled for every step. We were wet, sweaty, and mud covered.

"Thea?" Gilli asked, grunting as he pulled. "You said this is a gate, right? That means there's some sort of challenge or danger we have to get past. So, what is it this time?"

"It's better if I don't say."

Seret stopped pulling and started treading water to look back at her. She tried to say something, but with the rope in her mouth it was muffled.

I glanced back at Thea on the barge. She looked nervous. Her eyes moved around the fog as if she was looking for something. Jumpra, sitting beside her, was doing the same. "How can it be better for us not to know?" I asked.

"You wouldn't want me to explain it," Thea said. "Just keep pulling. We still have a ways to go."

A high-pitched buzzing floated by my ear. I turned my head looking for the source, but the sound was gone as quickly as it had come. Maybe I'd imagined it?

"Gah!" Gilli exclaimed. He slapped at his neck. "These mosquitoes won't leave me alone! Figures that the underworld would have these little bloodsuckers."

As if on cue the buzzing by my ear came back. I felt a prick on the side of my face. I swatted it away. Now that he'd pointed them out, I noticed the little insects whirring all around us. They skimmed across the surface of the water and swarmed around our exposed bodies. In moments the air was a black buzzing haze.

"Is somebody afraid of mosquitoes?" Thea asked.

"Yeah, me!" Iset shouted. "I got eaten alive once when I visited the marshes of the Nile Delta. I had bad dreams for weeks. But those mosquitoes were nothing like these!"

She was right. What had seemed like normal mosquitoes a moment ago were now way bigger than any I'd seen before. Their eyes shone a dull red and their needle noses were nearly twice as long as their bodies.

"You have to ignore them!" Thea yelled over the deafening buzzing.

"How in the name of the gods are we meant to do that?" Iset screamed back. She thrashed her arms back and forth across her body knocking off the devilish insects.

"Act like they're not there. You don't see them. You don't hear them. If they bite you, you don't feel them."

"Ouch!" Gilli shouted as a big mosquito poked him in the shoulder. "But I do feel them!"

"No," Thea said, "you don't! These are like the Winged Demons. They're not real unless you believe they're real. If you ignore them they lose power and fade away."

I tried to imagine they weren't there. That I couldn't feel their long probing needle noses sucking greedily at my blood. Or see their round bodies growing into dark red bulbous lumps. I couldn't just stop believing in them, not when I could see them, hear their buzzing, and feel their relentless attack.

Seret's voice cut through the noise, "Get under the water!" I glanced over at her, and only the tip of her mouth was sticking out. "They can't get you under here."

I looked down at the muck, trying not to imagine the slimy, dirty green gunk on my face. I sucked in a huge gulp of air, plugged my nose, and dove underwater. I stayed down for as long as I could. *They aren't real. They aren't real,* I repeated over and over again in my head until my lungs were burning. *Nothing is going to be up there when you go back up.*

Someone tapped me on the shoulder. I surged up

to the surface, gasping for air and wiping slime off my face. Iset stood beside me, and everyone else was up from the water already. The mosquitoes were gone. I felt for the mountain of itchy lumps I was sure would be covering my body. But my skin was completely smooth.

"Wow, Ash, you can hold your breath for a long time," Khufu said, looking impressed.

Iset wrung her hands sheepishly. "Listen, I'm not sure, but . . . was that my fault? The marsh made me think of mosquitoes. Seemed like the kind of place they'd be. And then there were mosquitoes."

Thea frowned. Shrugged. "Yeah, that's the way it works."

We glared at her.

"Hey, what did you want me to say? Don't think about this specific thing? Of course, you'd think about it then. It'd be like pointing at something while telling someone not to look."

"You're right," Gilli replied. "So, now all we have to do to keep it from happening again is not think about our fears. That won't be . . ." Gilli trailed off, a distant look in his eyes.

"Gilli? What are you thinking about?" Seret asked.

"Um."

"Quickly, think of something, anything else!" Thea yelled.

Gilli said, "Too late."

47

Aunty?

A shape materialized in the mist, a short human form moving toward us. A small whimper wheezed out of Gilli. I braced myself.

"Here it comes," Iset warned.

The shape drew closer. It wore a dark brown tunic and shawl. Hands with wrinkles like canyons stuck out from the sleeves. In one of them it clutched a gnarled cane. A red headwrap covered the top of its head. Its face . . . Its face was normal. Soft eyes and deep laugh lines covered with dark freckles.

"Aunty?" Gilli whimpered.

"Aunty???" The rest of us asked in unison, turning to stare at Gilli. He'd sunk so low into the water he resembled a toad hiding in the muck.

"What," Iset asked, a look of disbelief on her face. "The thing you're most afraid of in the world is your aunty?"

"You don't know her."

"Gilli!" His aunty's voice was shrill and nasally. "It's cold down here! Bring me more blankets. Don't you know how to take care of your elders! Also get me a comb so I can untangle that knot on top of your head you call hair. And get that cat out of here!" She thrust an angry finger toward Jumpra, who was licking his paws at the bow of the barge. He looked up, surprised. "I've told you a million times. I'm allergic! Oh, and this one, too!" She waved her cane at Seret. "Filthy animals. Are you trying to kill your poor aunty?"

I couldn't help it. I broke out laughing.

Gilli's aunty turned on me. "What do you find so funny, young man? Think I'm here for your amusement? I'll show you what's amusing . . ." She rushed toward me, her cane raised high.

I tried to avoid her, but that's not easy in waist-deep water and muck. "I'm sorry. I didn't mean anything!"

"You think I don't know you?" she asked. "I see you, Shadow Prince. Hah! What a joke that is. Little village boy. Canal rat. Straw and twigs in your hair. Up to your elbows in goat poo. And an orphan at that! Your parents didn't even want you."

She swiped her hand and drenched me in water. She stepped close, eyed me up, and said, "Yeah, I know you."

She spun away and pointed at Iset. "And you, *magician*." She said it like it was a dirty word. "I know your secret. Top marks at the academy. Historically young. First in your class. But do these friends of yours know the truth?"

Iset stared at her. She shook her head, but she wasn't answering. It was more like she was trying to deny this moment was happening.

"You cheated," said Aunty. "Pure and simple. Slipped a little money to one of the testing judges in exchange for top marks. What do you call that if it's not cheating?"

Iset answered, "I . . . I . . ."

"I . . . I . . . One of these cats got your tongue?"

Iset looked ashamed. She moved her gaze around but wouldn't meet anyone's eyes.

"And you," Aunty said. "The Night Barge assistant. You think I don't know your secrets?"

"I . . . I don't have any secrets," Thea said, her voice shaky.

Aunty threw back her head and laughed. "That's rich. You think you're so smart. Always studying at the library with your parents or worshipping Lord Ra. You act so confident, but you know no one likes you. You don't have any actual friends. Do you?"

Thea was speechless. She shook her head slightly, desperately, hopelessly.

"But your parents aren't here, are they?" Aunty asked. "Lord Ra's not here, is he?" Aunty looked back at the rest of us. "There's not one of you who doesn't have something to be ashamed of."

"Thea," I said, "don't worry about her. Like you said, she's not real. She doesn't matter."

"I don't matter?" Aunty asked.

"No," Gilli said, "you don't." He crossed his arms. "Tell me I'm wrong, Aunty. Oh, actually, you're not my aunty. You're some imitation of her. You don't matter. Right guys? Tell *her* the truth."

"She doesn't matter," Seret said. "And I'm not a filthy animal. I'm quite clean." She looked down at her sopping wet fur. "Usually, I'm quite clean."

For the first time, Aunty looked unsure of herself.

"She doesn't matter," Iset said. "And I didn't cheat. My . . . my parents did. They didn't believe in me and bribed one of the testing supervisors. But it didn't matter." She drew herself upright and raised her chin. "I scored perfectly. They wasted their money."

Aunty's smug expression faded.

"She doesn't matter," I said. "And I'm not ashamed of where I came from. I was raised in that village. I love it and the people there. It's what made me who I am."

Aunty's face went a little green, like she'd eaten something that didn't agree with her.

"Thea," I said, "tell her."

Thea hesitated a moment, but then found her voice. "She doesn't matter. And . . . I do have friends. They're right here with me."

"That's right," Gilli said. "We're all Thea's friends! With all due respect, *imaginary* Aunty, you . . . don't . . . matter. We know who we are. None of us are perfect, but all of us are more real than you." He stepped nearer to her and pointed at her. "Tell me I'm wrong."

Gilli's aunty suddenly seemed like she'd misplaced something small and valuable. She began patting her tunic. "Well," she said, "if you put it that way."

And then poof! She was gone. Just like that.

"Yes!" Gilli shouted. "We did it!"

"Yeah, we did," Seret said. They high-fived.

"Is your aunty really like that?" Iset asked.

Gilli thought a moment. "Well, in person . . . she's scarier."

That got us laughing. It didn't matter that she'd just pulled fears and secrets and things we each worried about from our own subconscious. All of us have those things. What mattered was that we cared more about each other than any judgments she could make about us.

"Thea," Iset said, "I'm new to this group, too, but what you said was true. We are your friends. When we get through this and back to the world above, we will still be friends. All of us, right?"

We were all agreeing to that when Jumpra hissed. He stood arched on the barge railing, and with his fur bristling again, stared with round eyes at something.

Slowly, a figure emerged through the vaporous mist. Growing larger. Walking toward us. With dread in my stomach, I realized who it was—and that it was me who had summoned him.

48

The Spear of Vengeance

Lord Set walked out of the mist. With each step he grew more distinct. He was taller than I remembered him, broader across the chest, his arms longer. The easy strength of his swagger was more pronounced. The tufts on his head and his pointy ears higher than before. The grin that twisted his snout was as menacing as anything I had ever seen.

Seret growled. Jumpra hissed. Gilli and Khufu fanned out to either side of me. Iset pulled out her stylus. Probably just by instinct since it had no power down here. But there was no spear. No daggers. I crouched into a fighting position, fists raised.

"No!" Thea cried from the barge. "It can't be! He . . .

He's not down here. He's on the surface, being horrible."

Set threw back his head and laughed. He snorted through his snout and slapped his leg. When he got ahold of himself again, he said, "Surprised, little Thea? You shouldn't be. I knew you'd get up to mischief down here. I didn't, however, know that it would involve this little gang. This is absolutely delicious." He looked at me. "You and I have unfinished business, Shadow Boy."

"No!" Khufu shouted. "I command you to leave us alone. Remember, I'm a prince. If you harm Ash or any of us, you'll have to answer to my parents and Lord Horus and Lady Isis."

Set chuckled. "I've already taken care of Horus and Isis. They'll never trouble me again. And your parents . . . lost in the desert somewhere, I expect. I'm sure one of my demons will find them any time now."

"You lie!" Thea said.

"Frequently," Set said. "Not on this occasion, though."

"Don't listen to him," Thea continued. "Remember what I said. He only has power if—"

"Enough!" Set snapped. "If I wasn't the real Lord Set, would I be able to do this?"

He stretched his fingers and swept his hand before him. As he did so, all the others were blown back and vanished. All gone.

All except for Jumpra. He squatted, wide-eyed, looking around for the others.

Set smirked. "Disobedient kitten. Perhaps you'll respond to a more hands-on approach."

In a flash, Set disappeared. He reappeared at the barge, grasped Jumpra by the scruff of the neck, and tossed him high and far into the mist. His "mmeeeoooowwwww" faded into the distance and trailed away. I heard a faint, faraway splash.

The god said, "For the life of me I can't understand the Egyptian fascination with cats." He turned and began creeping toward me. "It's just you and me now, boy. I know what you were trying to do here. Save Lord Ra. I have to admit, you've got gumption. Your mentor would be proud."

I circled away from him until I had the barge at my back. I climbed in, wanting to put something, anything, between me and the god. I ran to the Spear of Vengeance. I knew it was unlikely, but maybe, just maybe, I could somehow lift it now.

Set clambered over the railing.

I grabbed the spear and inhaled a deep breath. I gritted my teeth, planted my feet, and heaved with all my might, with my whole body: back and legs and arms. And . . . nothing. The spear didn't so much as shift.

Set's feet crashed down onto the deck.

I tried again. Again, nothing. It wasn't going to budge.

Set strolled toward me. "That's a godspear, boy. Are you a god?"

I let go of the spear and circled away.

Set went over to the spear and traced his fingers down the long shaft of it. "What a glorious weapon," he said. "Many is the time I used this to defend Lord Blazing Annoyance. Isn't it glorious that in the end I used the same spear against him?" Set turned from the spear and looked at me. "But, as I said, it's a godspear. A worthy weapon against Apep. Or Ra. You, though . . . For you I'll need nothing but my bare hands."

I backed into something that almost tripped me. It was the handle to the tiller. Seeing it, I remembered Thea. What had she said? To listen to her. To believe her. She'd said that I wasn't facing Set, but every bone in my body was sure that I was. Even though it was hard to believe her, I could at least act like I did. That gave me an idea. My last hope.

"Wait!" I said. "Are you really Lord Set?"

Set raised his arms out to either side. "In all my glory. Your eyes do not deceive you."

"If that's true, prove it. Lift the Spear of Vengeance."

He lowered his arms, cleared his throat, and said, "I don't have to prove anything to you."

"Yes, you do. What are you scared of? Thea said you just loovveeedddd to brag about how strong you are." I did my best imitation of him. "'This is a god-spear, meant for the gods alone!' Right? 'Behold my might! See how I heft it!'"

Set clearly didn't like being mocked. He looked back at the spear. "I could totally lift this."

"Prove it. Lift it now."

He sniffed and said, "No." His voice was different from before. More like a grumpy child than an immortal god.

"If you don't," I said, "I will destroy you."

"And how are you going to do that?"

"By *not believing* in you."

"Not believing in me? How dare you. The impertinence!"

"Yeah," I said, feeling a bit more confident, "how about you just lift the spear?"

After pouting for a moment, he said, "Fine! I'll lift the stupid spear. See if I don't!" He turned back to the spear. He set his hands on it. He moved his hands around.

"Quit stalling," I said.

"I'm not stalling," he snapped. He cleared his throat. Moved his hips side to side. Did a knee bend.

"Still stalling," I said, using my best super-bored voice.

"Okay. Okay," Set said. "Here I go." With that, he heaved on the spear.

It stayed exactly where it had always been. Set's body stretched upright, and his arms went taut and his legs trembled.

Just then, behind him, I saw something amazing.

49

Jumpra to the Rescue

Jumpra appeared, flying through the mist and straight toward Set. His small paws were outstretched, claws bared, mouth opened in a long, high-pitched screech.

Set turned toward the sound but could only half-turn because he still clutched the spear. It didn't move at all, not one bit. That's when I knew. When I believed. I said, "Liar."

Set looked queasy. His eyes bulged and his snout went soft. "Oh . . ." was all he managed before he burst into a cloud of green vapor just as Jumpra hurtled through him. The caracal landed on the deck, spun across the floor, steadied himself, turned back, and watched the vapor disappear. He took it in for a moment, then sat, looking quite pleased with himself. He returned to licking his paws.

What a wonderfully disobedient kitten! I couldn't help it. I ran forward, scooped him up, and cuddled him. "We did it! We really did it!"

"Ash?" a voice called.

Still holding Jumpra, I ran to the railing. It was Seret! She crawled through the muck, dripping wet and not looking like her naturally impressive self. But it didn't matter. Seret was okay! She used her claws to scale the side of the barge and collapsed on the deck. Jumpra squirmed out of my arms and promptly began licking Seret's fur to dry her off.

I heard noise on the other side of the barge. Khufu this time. He waded through the water. "That was so weird!" he called. Sopping wet, he twisted the hair of his sidelock to squeeze out the water.

Thea's voice came from behind the barge. "Good trick with the spear." Gilli and Iset supported her on either side, and the three of them cut through the mist and climbed on board. "I was worried for a moment there," Thea continued, "but you remembered *not* to believe."

"Thanks to you," I said.

Everyone was wet and muddy, with bits of debris in their hair and on their tunics. But they were all okay. Once everyone was back in the boat, we talked about what we'd all experienced. Apparently, the others hadn't really vanished or even gone very far. They could all see me and Set the whole time. They just couldn't move and were trapped watching. I couldn't see or hear them, even though they'd all been shouting at me the whole time. What can I say? The Duat is a weird place.

"Hey, look," Iset said, pointing beyond the barge.

In the time that we'd stood talking, the landscape around us had changed. The misty, warm, and humid marsh had vanished. Instead, we were back in the cavern that felt comfortingly familiar. Again there were walls on either side of us. The barge floated in the ether, with the fathomless drop below. The shapes of Glitter Fish squirmed beneath us, and in the air around us Winged Demons did their slow flying dance.

"What's with him?" Gilli asked.

He meant Jumpra. The little caracal was sprawled on one of the barge's benches, purring as he preened himself. He looked like he was in his own world.

I leaned into Gilli and whispered, "He thinks his pounce is what made the fake Set vanish."

"Is he getting delusions of grandeur?" Iset asked.

"I think he already had them," Seret said. "He did name himself Jumpra . . ."

The kitten looked up at this. Watched us for a long moment, then squirmed on his back, batting the air with his paws.

"Oh," Gilli said. "Should we send him in first to deal with Apep?"

He meant it as a joke, but inside I thought, *Apep. Right.* The momentary joy faded. We still had the World Encircler to deal with. The real version. Not some figment of our imaginations.

"We should get going," Thea said. "It'll be a quick trip from here to the opening to Apep's lair."

None of us were that happy to hear this. Even having come through so much already, it was hard to fathom what it would mean to face Apep. It was even harder to imagine how we could defeat him and save Lord Ra.

Thea took the tiller again. The rest of us took position on the oars, and we began rowing. It was wonderful to fall into the rowing rhythm and feel the Night Barge slide forward with its easy, almost effortless tempo.

"So, what's our plan?" Iset asked. "We should have a plan, right? When we get to Apep, I mean."

Khufu answered. "This is where the Eye of Isis comes in. It's our secret weapon, right, Ash?"

"I guess," I said. "I've never used it before."

"One of the instructors at the magicians' academy had an Eye of Horus," Iset said. "He said that Horus could travel across great distances in a flash when summoned. If Isis can do that—"

"Then she'd literally appear here with us," Gilli said.

"You can stop rowing," Thea said, peering ahead. She looked a little confused, but then nodded. "This is it. It looks a little different from before, but the walls sometimes shift and change down here. Still, the entrance to Apep's lair is over there behind those boulders."

"Right over there, huh?" Gilli asked. "Are you sure we shouldn't just row ourselves out of here and get help that way?"

Thea shook her head. "I wish we could, but only Lord Ra can get us through the exit gates. It's a whole different thing. No riddles or fighting or anything. It's just Ra blasting through as he starts to become the sun. Without him we're stuck down here."

On that cheery note, we all climbed out of the barge onto a wide, flat shelf of rock. The walls around us seemed even more massive than before, strange folds and layers of rock, glistening and slick.

"Okay," Thea said, placing her arm around Iset for support. "Let's go over this one more time. We go in. We find him. As soon as we do, we use our secret weapon. And then, finally, we'll get out of this whole mess. Sound good?"

"Yeah, but . . . ," I said, "didn't you say after Apep there's another demon that's worse than Apep?"

Thea sighed. "The Keeper of Souls. Let's not think about her until we absolutely have to. Come on. Let's go."

Iset and Thea took the lead. We didn't get more than a few steps before what seemed like the entire cavern began to move, to slither. There was grinding stone and falling rock and earsplitting noise. The shelf of rock beneath us vibrated. It seemed like the entire cavern was going to collapse on us.

It didn't.

Instead, all the motion revealed itself as a slithering, serpentine mass of scales on an unimaginably large body. Out of all the confusion, two eyes opened, glowing, red, and massive. They could only belong to Apep.

50

The Thing About the Unwashed Masses

For Set, there was so much to see. Still perched atop the obelisk, he took it all in.

The demons arrived in a great horde. At first just grunting shadows with hideous shapes, they crept cautiously into the city. They were timid, unsure. With wide eyes, they took in the night sky and the fires and the frightened humans. Soon enough, they grew bold. They finally believed what Set had told them. There were no gods to stop them. No pharaoh or queen to judge them. No magicians' spells. Only . . . humans. They bellowed, roared, shouted, cackled, and then began to run through the streets, chasing their fleeing human prey.

A tentacled monster fought with a unit of soldiers, its long limbs snapping out to grab people.

All nine of the Jackal-Headed Demons ran through the streets, snapping at anyone they came near.

The Mistress of Anger—in the form of an enormous demon lizard—leaped from rooftop to rooftop. She sprayed torrents of liquid flame from her mouth.

Baboons and apes tore through the gardens, barking and grunting.

Winged creatures darted through the air, screeching and flexing their talons.

Royal soldiers did the best they could to form ranks against them, but the demons were fast, furious, emboldened.

Magicians were powerless against them. They fought just like other people, desperately, with whatever weapons they could find.

For Set, it was all terribly amusing.

As he watched, he caught sight of a small, flying thing. He wouldn't have noticed, save for the way it dipped and rose, weaving in a strange, loopy way that he recognized. Babbel. He flew up to the peak of the obelisk and hovered. Set ignored him for a moment, but finally said, "What?"

"Babbel reporting, Messenger Beetle Second Class," he said.

"I know that!" Set snapped. "What do you want?"

"Well . . ." Babbel looked around. "Have you noticed the endless night? The hordes of demons? Might you, perhaps . . . want to send a message of some sort? Call on other gods for help. That sort of thing? I'd ask someone else, but you're the only god in town, it seems."

Set sniffed and said, "Nah."

"Nah?" Babbel asked.

"That's right. Nah," Set repeated. "I'm good."

Babbel bowed his head, rubbed at his temples with two of his six legs. "Can you please send me somewhere with a message?"

"Just go. Do whatever you want. I don't care, beetle."

"I'm a messenger beetle, Set," Babbel said.

"That's Lord Set to you."

"Fine," Babbel said, annoyed sarcasm in his voice. "Loooord Set, I can't just go somewhere. I need a message to carry to a particular recipient. It's in the handbook."

"Set!" somebody called. "This is madness! Call this off, please!"

It was Prince Rami shouting from the courtyard below. Set sighed and said to Babbel, "You're dismissed." He climbed down the obelisk.

As Set leaped down to the ground, a flying demon vulture dropped from the sky. It landed in the panicked crowd a little distance away. The monstrous, grotesquely feathered bird snapped at people. It knocked others away with its flapping wings. One brave soldier ran at it with his spear raised. The demon fixed him in its black eyes. It pinched the spear in its beak, snapped it, and then lunged at the soldier, chasing him behind a building and out of sight behind the Vault of Divine Wisdom. The man let out a high-pitched scream. Then he went silent.

"Lord Set," Rami said, "that man just . . . he just . . ."

". . . met a gruesome end," Set finished. "It's his own fault, you know? If these humans would just submit, they'd be well taken care of."

"Taken care of? Do you think that vulture-thing would stop to chat even if the soldier wanted to?"

Set sniffed. "No, I suppose not. That's the thing with the unwashed masses of demons. You can rile them to action easily enough; controlling them is a different matter."

If Rami had looked pale before, he was positively ashen now. His eyes darted from monstrous sight to monstrous sight. His lower lip quivered. His arms shook so much that his armbands tinkled like soft music. This kid is useless, Set thought, shaking his head. Noticing some *laborers taking a water break, Set strode over to berate them.*

The prince jolted when a sharp, high voice whispered, "Rami!"

Turning, he saw a sight that, at first, he didn't comprehend. A young girl strode toward him, like the tip of an arrow point with others of similar height trailing behind. She wore chest armor, wrist guards, and a battle helmet. Her upper arms were ringed with gold bracelets engraved with royal hieroglyphs. She carried a bow, and there was a quiver of arrows strapped to her back.

Blinking to believe his eyes, Rami realized who it was. Princess Sia.

The Serpent with Many Names

Apep's head swung down from its resting place on the craggy wall. It bobbed in a slow, lazy motion in front of the boat. His jaws were wider across than the barge. He could have chomped down on the front half of the ship and then slowly consumed the whole thing. I'd seen small snakes in the village do that to mice and tiny lizards. Apep, though, was no desert snake.

His tongue flicked out, slapping the front of the barge. His eyes were dead things. When he moved them, they ground against his eye sockets like boulders. Worse than that. When they moved, they turned toward us.

What we'd thought had been the walls of the cave were actually Apep's long, sinewy body. The coils moved, a sound like an earthquake, drawing tighter around us until we were surrounded by a curving barrier of massive, scaly demon-serpent. He blew a breath of dark, foul smoke through his nostrils. It smelled of rotten eggs and burnt bone. It felt ancient, immortal, and deeply, deeply wicked. This wasn't a demon like the other ones we'd faced. This was a god, but a god of destruction and misery.

"What's this?" he asked, his voice so loud it made the real cavern walls shake. "Creatures from up above?" His eyes slid lazily across us. Lingering on Thea, he said, "You I recognize. Lord Ra's apprentice, right?"

"Ye-ye-yes," Thea stammered.

"What are you doing here? We both know you're out of a job."

"We were just . . . um, piloting the barge through to . . . uh, return it to . . . um . . . to return it to you?"

Apep grunted, sounding skeptical. "And who did you bring with you?"

"Oh, let me introduce them," Thea said, and began doing so.

I managed to stop staring at Apep long enough to glance at my friends. Seret was crouched low, all her hair standing on end, with a low animal yowl emanating out of her bared teeth. Jumpra was a mirror image of her. Only smaller. Gilli and Khufu were still as stone. I could see the sweat running down Gilli's face and soaking his tunic. Iset's whole body was shaking. Her stylus slipped from her limp hands and clattered to the stones, forgotten.

Thea was the only one who seemed to have retained any of her senses. When Apep leaned in to study Khufu, she whispered, "Ash, it's time for the plan. I'll distract him while you use the Eye of Isis." She stepped toward the serpent. Raising her voice, she said, "Mighty Apep. Many is the night I've marveled at your power."

The serpent squinted one eye. "Is that right?"

"Absolutely. It didn't seem fair that Lord Set should attack you with the Spear of Vengeance each and every night. What an ordeal for you!"

I backed away. I couldn't go far. Apep's surrounding coils made that impossible, but I moved off so that I was out of his direct gaze. I reached up and touched the spot where Isis had placed her eye on my face. I felt heat bloom, almost hot to the point of discomfort, but not quite. I saw a blue light emanating out and realized my face must be glowing. I turned away so that Apep wouldn't see it.

A part of my consciousness snapped out of my body, rose up to the surface, and zoomed across the desert. It was exhilarating. I had escaped the Duat. I was in the air, crossing a great expanse at an unimaginable speed. I closed my eyes, ready to commune with Isis and bring the power of the gods to bear. Then the small part of my brain that had flown away bumped into a wall. Stopped. Waited. There was a short silence followed by a low-frequency buzzing and then a click.

A familiar voice said, "Hello?"

It was Isis! Relief and excitement flooded through me. Keeping my voice low but talking fast, I began, "Lady Isis. It's Ash. Please help us. We're in the Duat, trying to save Lord Ra from Apep. We need your help. Fly here to me and—"

"You have attempted to contact me, Lady Isis, through magical means," her voice said. "I'm sorry for the inconvenience, but if you are hearing this message, I am not currently able to accept any communication. I will be notified of your attempt and get back to you at my earliest convenience. Goodbye. And long live the glory of Egypt."

There was another click and then my mind snapped back into the cave. "You've got to be kidding me!" I muttered. "What in the world was that?" I touched the Eye again, but this time nothing happened.

I glanced at Apep. He was watching me, giving me a puzzled look. Fortunately, something Thea said got him talking again. I moved back toward the others. Noticing Iset had dropped her stylus, I picked it up and tucked it into my tunic to give her later.

When I rejoined the others, Gilli whispered, "Please tell me an army of gods and goddesses are on the way."

"She wasn't available."

"Not available?" Seret asked. "Isn't that part of the gods' job? To be available?"

"Something must be wrong," I said.

"Yes," Apep said. His entire body slithered, every inch of him grinding across the stone as he moved suddenly. His head pressed forward toward me. "Something is wrong."

Thea stepped in front of me. "Lord Apep," she said, speaking fast. "You don't mind if I call you *Lord* Apep, do you? You've been too long denied your full status as a god and—"

"You're a rescue party! A group of kids and a couple of cats . . ." Apep's body began to rumble, a horrible, loud, terrifying sound. Only as it faded did I realize it was his version of laughter. "Thought you'd call for help, but there's nobody there!"

"Lord Apep," Thea said, speaking fast, "that's not it at all. We—"

He rolled over, which meant that the long, encircling coils all around us moved. "He's given me a stomachache. What I need is something sweet and soothing for the belly. Dessert. That'll do the trick."

Apep's head turned toward me. His eyes pinned me. "You want to save Ra?" he asked me. "Come and get him. He's right here . . ."

Quick as lightning, his head snapped toward me, mouth open, fangs bared. His jaws slammed shut and that was it. I'd been swallowed.

PRAYERS FOR THE DAWN

52

The Belly of the Beast

The inside of the serpent was nothing like I would've expected—if, that is, I'd ever stopped to imagine what the inside of a demon snake would be like. It wasn't cramped. I wasn't pressed between slimy walls. I wasn't being dissolved or melting away. Actually, it was quite roomy, more like a long, living, breathing tunnel. The air was smoky, but breathable. It was dim, but the longer I looked the better I could see in the murky reddish light.

Standing, I looked up and down the tunnel. On one side was the shut trap that led to Apep's mouth. Looking the other way, the serpent's body curved out of sight. I began walking. My sandals squelched with each step. Every now and then the walls flexed and shifted. Rumbling shudders rolled by in waves. The first few knocked me down, but I learned to anticipate them and kept on my feet.

The tunnel of Apep's long belly turned and squirmed, squirmed and turned. I couldn't see too far ahead or too far back. It didn't take long for me to find evidence that things swallowed by Apep do eventually die. Bones. All shapes and sizes of them. I saw rib cages and leg bones. I stepped on a skeletal hand and heard it crack. "Sorry," I said, and hurried on. There were skulls, too. They were the creepiest. Some of them looked human, some looked like various animals. Some could only be the horned or tusked enormous heads of demons. Apep, apparently, wasn't a picky eater.

This wasn't a regular belly, I realized. It was a living prison. I sighed, more dejected than I'd ever been before. Who would've thought that being swallowed by a giant serpent wasn't a quick and painful death? Instead of that, it seemed that I was going to spend ages trapped inside the beast, with a collection of bones for company. I'd probably die of starvation. Or thirst. That gets you first.

Or, worse yet, I'd die after having days and days of thinking about all the things I was losing, fearing the whole time that I had failed to save Khufu or the others.

Had I done enough to ensure that Khufu could become the great ruler the prophecy said he could become? No. That much was clear. Not with Lord Ra swallowed and Set and Apep on the verge of ruling Egypt.

When another of the rolling tremors caught me off guard, I pitched backward. I landed on my butt and didn't get up. This tremor had been different. It rumbled in a cadence I recognized. It was the sound of Apep talking. I couldn't make out his words, muffled as they were inside him. If he was talking, maybe my friends were still safe. Maybe there was still a chance. But how?

I exhaled an exasperated breath. Sitting there, I recited the words of the prophecy in my head, trying to find good news in them, some sense that what we'd been through had fulfilled the requirements for success. Each time I ended with the final phrases ringing in my head.

Shadowless lies ruin. Demon darkness. Evermore.

Wasn't Khufu shadowless without me? If so, I'd failed. The more I thought it through, the more I came to believe that conclusion. I leaned back against the slimy stomach wall, my thoughts getting darker and darker.

"Or maybe I'll die of boredom," I said. "Miserable, failed boredom."

I shook my head, trying to clear it. I wasn't doing myself any favors by dwelling on failure. I needed to think of other things. I reached down and untied the memory pouch. Maybe, if this was to be the long, slow end of my life, I should spend some of it rediscovering some more lost memories.

This time the memory settled into my palm like it had been waiting for me. I pulled it out, breathed it in, and was transported.

The vision began with pain. Agony radiated from the ball of my left shoulder, shooting from there through every inch of my body. I hung dangling from the back of a wagon. A moment before I'd been riding on the bundles of supplies Yazen was bringing home from a trade fair. In a careless moment, I got jarred by a bump in the road. It sent me toppling toward the ground. The fall would've been bad enough, but my left arm got caught in one of the straps that bound the supplies. The weight of my body pulled the trapped arm out of my shoulder socket and left me hanging there, screaming.

Yazen freed me and lowered me to the ground. He tried to soothe me, but I was too engulfed in misery to listen. I pleaded for Yazen to make the hurting stop. Instead, he left me and dashed away. He came back with the village healer, a man who had always terrified me.

Not him! *I thought.* Not him!

He was an old, dour man who walked with a limp. The other boys told tales of the horrible things he did to his patients, the things he made them drink, the ways he twisted and pinched and prodded them. His cures were always worse than the ailment that needed treating. I panicked. I thrashed and shouted, more scared than I'd ever been before.

Yazen held me down while the healer took hold of my arm. The man moved the arm slowly, drawing a circle with it. Tears poured from my eyes. This was the worst thing that had ever happened to me, and it was going to go on forever and . . .

The shoulder slid back into place with a gentle pop. The torment vanished in an instant. Relief washed over me. I lay panting, amazed, grateful. The healer said something. He smiled and patted me on the head. He rose and turned away and . . .

The vision ended there. I blinked, the memory of the pain still physically in my body. Instinctively, I grabbed for my left shoulder. It was fine, of course. It was an older, more muscled version of the shoulder in the vision. Again, I had just relived a moment in my life before my memory began. Why that moment? One of pain and fright? What was the logic behind seeing the moments I did? Perhaps it was all just random.

I pulled the drawstrings on the pouch tight. It might be a while before I ventured another exploration of my past. As I tucked the pouch away, something jabbed me in the side. Iset's stylus. I pulled it out and stared at it. So strange, looking at this slim strip of gently curving metal. A tool that helps humans channel the power of the gods. But, like Iset when she dropped it, I couldn't help but want to toss it away.

In fact, that's what I did. It twirled away, drawing silver circles in the air as it fell.

53

A Spark of Magic

"**W**hat!?"

I looked at the stylus. It lay on the tunnel floor, an ornate sliver of metal. Motionless now. But I could have sworn I saw . . .

Carefully, I picked it up. I held it for a moment, wondering if it felt more alive than before. It just might. I drew with it in the air. The point flared into life, glowing bright yellow. I stopped and stared as the line shimmered in front of me. Energy crackled off it.

Magic! I thought. *That was magic. But how is it possible?* Magic came from the power of the sun, and I was about as far away from the sun as you could get. Then it hit me. I was far away from the sun, but I might be very near . . .

"Lord Ra!" I exclaimed. That was the only explanation. He must be near enough that some of his energy could power the stylus. And if that was true, it meant that he was still alive.

I jumped to my feet. Turning around a few times, I got my bearings, and then carried on down the tunnel. Ra was in this beast; I was going to find him.

It didn't take long. When I saw the body, the first thing that struck me was that it *was* a body. Not a skeleton. It was still a shape of flesh and blood. The second thing I noticed was the ram's head. The horns that curved up from it were treacherous, like something a fierce demon would sport. I had to remind myself that Ra was only a falcon-headed god on the surface of the world. Down here, he looked much more menacing.

"Lord Ra?"

Moving closer, I noticed other things. Even lying on his back the god was impressively tall, strongly muscled, and regal. His eyes were closed. He looked like he was just sleeping. But there was the wound. A dreadful, ragged puncture. His abdomen was a mass of torn skin and blood. Set's spear had done serious damage. It was a death wound, the type no human could survive.

"Lord Ra? Are you all right?" It was a silly question and I knew it. Of course he wasn't all right! Ra might be a god, but Egyptian gods could die if they were hurt horribly enough.

Cautiously, I picked up the god's arm by the wrist. Deadweight, completely limp. He wasn't cold to the touch, but maybe nothing inside Apep's belly would be cold. Asking the god's forgiveness, I leaned close to his face. I touched my ear to his ram's head muzzle and held still a long time, trying to feel any breath of air. I wanted to believe I felt something, but I couldn't be sure.

But the stylus, I thought. That has to mean he's alive. There was still enough life in the god to radiate magic. And if Ra made it, I could use it.

Standing up, I tried to think of what to do first, what sort of spell to try. I wanted to get Ra out of Apep's belly, but the god was in no condition to travel anywhere. I spent a while trying to formulate a spell to help him. Nothing seemed quite right. It was too complicated to fix such a horrible injury. I just didn't know how to do it. It would be a hard job for even a skilled physician. "A physician!"

Back with the One Who Asks Questions, I'd found

the answer by drawing a memory from the pouch Sudeen had given me. Maybe this memory was also a solution. I took a deep breath, and then I drew the glyph for healer.

Or . . . well, that's a bit of a simplification. I didn't know the glyph for healer. So, hoping that my magic was smarter than I was, I drew the pictures that symbolized these four things: memory, pain, fright, relief, and . . . an old person. Basically, I did the best I could to put the memory of the healer fixing my shoulder into a glyph.

I surrounded the spell in an oblong. That completed the cartouche. I stared at it a moment, putting all my hopes into it. Before it faded, I slashed it into life.

54

A Persistent Beetle

"**S**ia?" Rami asked. "Is that you?"

The princess strode up to her brother, looking none too pleased with him. "Yes, it's me!"

"But . . . you're wearing armor?"

Sia scrunched up more than eight years' worth of disdain on her face. "I've been getting military training since I was seven," she said. She gestured toward the armed kids standing behind her. "We all have. If you paid more attention to me, you'd have noticed."

"Do Mom and Dad know?"

"Of course. They agreed to it so long as Lady Sekhmet oversaw my training."

Dumbfounded, Rami asked, "You've been training with Lady Sekhmet?"

"Yeah. They said if I was going to learn about war I should also learn about healing. Sekhmet's the goddess of both, so . . ." She snapped back to focus. "Enough about that! What were you doing talking with Set?"

Flustered, Rami stumbled on his words. "I . . . well . . . we were . . . just . . ."

"What's he up to?" Sia demanded. "I know you know. Tell me."

Rami hesitated a moment longer. Then he went limp as wilting lettuce. "It wasn't my idea. It was all Set's. I didn't do anything."

Sia grabbed her brother's tunic and pulled him down so their noses were almost touching. "What is the anything that you didn't do?"

"Apep has swallowed Ra," he said, barely more than a whiny whisper. "Set has trapped the other gods in the Vault of Divine Wisdom. The demons have risen. We are doomed to a world of eternal darkness!"

Sia frowned. She looked past Rami toward Set, who was towering over the laborers and lecturing them. "Yeah, that's what we figured."

This confused Rami. "Really? You . . . figured?"

"Isn't it obvious!"

Just then, Babbel flew down and landed beside them.

He spoke his usual line. "Babbel reporting, Messenger Beetle Second Class. Prince, Princess, any chance you have a message for anyone?"

Sia answered before Rami could. "Could you get a message to our parents?"

Babbel shrugged. "Dunno if I could find them, but I could try. What should I tell them?"

"Tell them that Lord Set has completely lost whatever sanity he may once have had," Sia said. Then, quickly, she passed on what Rami had just told her. "Tell them that . . ." Again, she shot a glance at Set. ". . . that we won't let him get away with it."

Babbel's eyebrows raised. "Oh. I like the sound of that!" He straightened, clicked his heels, and said, "Babbel, Messenger Beetle Second Class, will deliver this message." His wings whirred to life, and he flew away in his weaving, meandering style.

A cry went up on the other side of the courtyard. A four-armed demon had a family cornered and was lurching closer, cackling with anticipation of a meal. Seeing them, Sia slung her bow over her shoulder. Instead, she loosened the battle-club that was tied to her waist. Her friends did the same. She said, "Team . . . with me!"

She and her small patrol sprinted toward the family

and demon, weapons drawn. They surrounded the demon, all the kids fighting like old pros, darting in to smack him on the back, the side, the legs, the arms. Finally, Sia launched into a flying kick right into the demon's belly. At the same time, she whacked him on the head with her club. That did it.

Poof! The demon vanished in a cloud of putrid green smoke. Demons didn't truly die in battle. Instead, they got transported back to whatever foul region of the Duat they'd come from. Whoever the demon was, he wouldn't be back in this fight any time soon.

Sia was back on her feet in no time. She and her group helped the family get to safety. Rami stared after them, slack-jawed and wide-eyed.

Set swaggered back. He eyed the princess and her troops with squinty disdain. "Was that the princess? Feisty one, she is. I suspect she'll meet a tragic end quite soon, though." To Rami, he said, "I gave those laborers an earful. It's tiring business driving workers to exhaustion. We need to keep a constant eye on them. Let's get a better view of things."

He pinched his snout in a particular way and blew a high-pitched whistle through it. It was loud enough that Rami covered his ears. And loud enough that the demon *bird heard it. It rose up from the other side of the Vault of Divine Wisdom. Its head craned around until it spotted Set and flapped toward him. It landed with enough force to crack a few paving stones and make the earth shake. It looked right at them and squawked, blowing hot, foul air into their faces.*

Set didn't seem to mind. "It's good to see you, too, my dear. Rami, meet the Rejector of Rebels."

Without warning, the god reached out and grabbed Rami by the scruff of his neck. Holding him off the ground, he strode toward the demon bird. Rami screeched and screamed and begged not to be fed to it. Set leaped onto its back, taking Rami with him. They landed behind the bird's massive head, which didn't stop Rami's screaming.

"Oh, hush," Set said. "Nobody is eating you. Yet. We're just going for a ride."

The Rejector of Rebels jumped into the air and rose through the smoke. In a few beats of its wings, it was high above the city, circling. From there, Set took in all that he had created. The endless night. The demons still rushing into the city. The people running through the streets. His workers pushing, carrying, and dragging gold toward the Vault of Divine Wisdom. It was all going gloriously to plan.

And then Rami threw up his dinner.

Set considered tossing him to splat on the city below, but he still needed him. And nothing, at this point, was going to disturb his good mood. Certainly not a little bit of sick.

55

Spells in the Darkness

The glyph symbols blended together and reformed as the outline of a small, glowing man. I could see through him, but I could also see his features clearly, drawn in fine lines of light. It was the healer from my memory; a foot-tall, glowing red version of him, at least.

The healer looked around a moment, studied the unconscious god, and then found me. He gestured toward the god, his head tilted to the side as if asking a question.

"Yes," I said, "he's the reason I called you. Can you help him?"

The healer strode over to the god and climbed up onto his muscular chest. Perched atop his pectorals, he studied the damage gravely. He examined the wound so long that I began to fear he couldn't do anything.

"Well, can you heal him?"

A palm shot up, shushing me.

Hey, I thought, *I created you. Don't go shushing me.*

The healer rubbed his hands together, did a series of stretches, and then did something completely unexpected. He dove, headfirst, into Ra's injured abdomen. I gasped and almost turned away, but the result wasn't as gross as I feared. The healer lost his shape as he touched the damaged flesh. He became a swirling, pulsing, weaving ribbon of light. He rippled and curved through the torn flesh, rebuilding Ra's internal organs from the inside out. Slowly but surely, the death wound vanished before my eyes.

When smooth flesh covered where the gaping hole had been, the light shifted back into the healer's shape again. He paced in a circle over the ribbed compartments of the god's abdominal muscles, bending down to inspect his work. He straightened, wiped his hands together, and looked up at me. In an elaborate gesture, he motioned toward the work he'd just completed. Before the sweep of his arm was complete, he began to fade.

Remembering my manners, I called, "Thank you!"

The physician nodded as he vanished.

"Wow," I said, "I'm good." I glanced to one side and pretended to be speaking to someone. "What's that? You say you need some cognitive magic? Let me introduce myself. Ash, cognitive magician at your service!"

I bent over Lord Ra and spoke to him. He wasn't conscious yet, but his chest rose and fell with breaths. It might take some time yet, but I was sure he was recovering. As if to prove it, the point of Iset's stylus pulsed with more and more energy.

Now that he was getting better, I put my mind to getting us out of here. I tried to imagine what another magician would do, but I hadn't really ever seen other magicians at work. There was the spell version of Teket, but in the testing he'd only ever tried his best to kill me, not save anyone. I'd only ever seen one magician do something right before my eyes, but it wasn't something I could use, just a casual trick. Nothing that could help me. Or . . . was it?

I doubted very much that the idea that came to me would've been what Iset came up with, even though, in a way, she had given me the idea. It would take a bit of thought. And the right timing. And a spell like none I'd ever tried before. But it was worth a try.

I set a hand on the sleeping god's chest, feeling the growing heat within him. Yes, he really was getting better. The stylus hummed with more energy as he grew stronger. Maybe this would work. I said, "Keep healing, Lord Ra. I'm going to try something. Wish me luck."

Walking as quickly as I could, I made my way back toward Apep's head. I tried to remember just what glyphs Iset had used at the banquet that night. No, I wasn't going to make iced cream, but there was something about the cold. I thought of the feeling of being high in the sky when the sunburst took us to where it was hard to breathe. It had been so frigid there. I was sure there was something in that I could use. I searched for ways to translate that feeling of incredible cold into glyphs that I could string together to do what I had in mind.

As I walked, my hand sketched glyphs. Apep's body still moved at times, and as I got nearer to his head the booming of his laughter and voice got louder and clearer.

"Let me get this straight, Prince," Apep rumbled.

"In the name of your parents you're offering the deal of a lifetime. Is that right?"

I could hear Khufu responding, but not clearly enough to know what he was saying. I waited, hoping the prince could find some way to talk Apep around. I didn't have to wait long to have that hope squashed. Khufu didn't get far before Apep interrupted him.

"I've no interest in your offer," the serpent said. "You see, I already have everything I want. As soon as I've digested Lord Ra—and taken a nap afterward—I'll head to the surface to assume my new role as a god of Egypt. I'm to have my own city, you know. It will be a whole new age, and I'll feed much better up there than I have down here. I had my doubts, I assure you, but old Wobbly-Snout has finally managed to pull off one of his crazy plots."

Several voices spoke in protest.

"ENOUGHHHHH!" Apep roared. "You're giving me a headache to go along with my bellyache. There's only one thing to remedy it. Another snack!" His body moved. His coils, I realized, were tightening around them. He hissed with pleasure and said, "The lot of you will do quite nicely."

With that, I was done waiting. I didn't really feel

ready, but that didn't matter. I ran. My sketching turned into full-on spell writing. I drew glyph after glyph, even as I crashed through them as I ran forward. Any and everything I could think of that was cold, frozen, icy, teeth-chattering, shivering, sniffling. Anything that was the opposite of basking in the Egyptian sun on a clear, hot day.

Apep's head rose. He opened his mouth, and I knew he was about to strike my friends. I was out of time. I drew one last glyph. It was a small one—the one Iset had used back at the banquet to freeze the dessert cream. Then—hoping, praying, that all the pieces I'd written would bind together into something greater than any one piece by itself—I ignited the spell.

56

Iced . . . Serpent?

A strange web of silver threads spread across Apep's body. The serpent's soft flesh—which had squished under my feet—went hard, crunchy, and slick beneath me. For a moment the serpent's body twisted. It was as if he was trying to shake off the spell. But then he shuddered to a stop. He exhaled one long, cold breath, and then all was stillness and frigid cold.

I climbed up Apep's frozen throat. Where his head tilted downward, I slid down his tongue and grabbed on to one of his fangs to keep from falling all the way out of his mouth. Clinging there, I looked down. I was greeted by the most wonderful sight I'd ever seen.

Khufu and Gilli and Seret and Iset and Thea and Jumpra were all there, paused in postures somewhere between fear and confusion. Apep's tongue was a curving ribbon that hung just above them. They stared up at Apep as if wondering if this was some trick, each of them looking like they still expected the serpent to swallow them all in one gulp. I wanted to make sure they knew that wasn't going to happen.

"Hey guys!" I shouted, waving.

"Ah . . . ," Gilli said, ". . . this is weird."

"Ash?" Khufu asked. "What . . . what happened?"

"I worked a little spell," I said.

"A spell?" Iset asked.

I grinned ear to ear. "Yep, one that you inspired, actually. I modified it a bit."

"How is that possible?" Seret said.

"I'll explain later," I said.

"Lord Ra!" Thea exclaimed. "He's alive?"

"Yes. He's getting better by the minute."

"What . . ." Iset seemed at a loss for words. "What did you do to Apep?"

"Froze him. A little bit of this. A little bit of that. Put it all together and this is the result. It's sort of an iced cream–inspired spell, if you want to know the truth."

Iset shook her head. "I never would've thought of that."

"An iced cream–inspired spell . . . ," Gilli said, thoughtfully. "You know that ice melts, right?"

Oh. I hadn't thought of that.

Thea said, "I'll go back to the boat and get it ready."

"I'll help you," Khufu said.

Apep's tongue twitched. Only a small tremor, but enough to worry me.

"Ah," I said, "we should hurry. Let's get Ra out of here."

"How?" Seret asked.

"Climb up his tongue and follow me. We'll need a few hands to get Ra moving."

Jumpra didn't hesitate. True to his name, he jumped. He sank his claws into the serpent's frozen tongue and scaled it. Cautiously, Gilli, Seret, and Iset followed.

"We need to get him out and fast," I said, as I led them back to Lord Ra. "It's crazy cold in here."

We blew clouds of white vapor when we breathed. Gilli marveled at the little bumps bristling on his bare arms. Seret puffed out her lion fur, looking amusingly fluffy in the process. I had the strangest numb sensation in my fingers and toes. All of it made me think I didn't care much for the cold. Bring back the Egyptian sun, I thought, which was exactly what we were all about to do . . . hopefully.

When we reached him, the god was still sleeping. I assured the others that he was looking better and better. His body radiated warmth now, and his skin had regained its dark coloration.

"He's breathing all right," Iset said. "I can see it. But where's his wound? Thea said Set impaled him with the spear."

"Oh, I fixed that." I told them about the healer vision and the spell I'd thought up afterward.

Iset stared at me. "Wow. You've got skills, kid. Not sure I would've thought of that, either. Sorry if . . . if I doubted your magical abilities before. I was . . . just . . . well, I'm embarrassed by how I acted back at the banquet."

Laughing, I pulled her stylus out and offered it to her.

She hesitated. "Maybe you should keep it."

"No, it's yours," I said. I pressed it into her hand and then folded her fingers closed around it. I smiled. "Now, let's get out of here."

57

The Fight Ahead

After a lot of tugging and grunting and straining—gods are *really* heavy—we got Ra upright and started shuffling forward. It was great feeling the heat of his body. It fought back the cold of Apep himself. Before long I was actually hot, sweating. Each step we took began to squelch, and water started to drip from above.

"Apep is starting to thaw," I said. "Let's move faster!"

Lord Ra began to mumble unintelligible words. His eyes fluttered open. He looked at us, clearly confused, and then closed his eyes again. He at least seemed to understand that we were helping him. He took some of his weight onto his legs and stumbled forward. By the time we reached Apep's open mouth, Ra was awake enough to slide down the serpent's tongue by himself. When he landed, he walked away from us, gaining strength with each step.

Jumpra went with him, darting around his legs, speaking with the strange chirruping sounds that made up caracal speech.

Ra went straight to the barge, where he saw Thea and hugged her. Khufu walked over to join the rest of us. He said, "I've never heard Jumpra talk so much. Couldn't understand a word, but he's got a lot to say, apparently."

We waited a little distance away, letting Thea, Ra, and Jumpra talk.

"You know," Gilli said, "if we get out of here somebody should give Thea a medal."

Khufu corrected him: "*When* we get out of here, that's the first thing I'm going to tell my parents."

That sounded great, but I noticed that Apep's tongue had started to sway a little. Looking back at him, I couldn't help but feel he was watching us. Did his eye just twitch? "Guys, I think—"

"Hey, look," Khufu said.

In the barge, Thea beamed. She motioned us over and said, "Lord Ra powered up my leg braces. Look."

Thea stood and danced. She jumped and twirled, nimble and fast.

"I'm glad to have helped," Ra said. "We could all use a little help sometimes. Even me, apparently." He studied us, looking at each of us in turn. "What a wonderful thing," he said. "A god who is taught to walk by children. A god who is snatched from the belly of Apep by ones so young. Thea has told me what you went through to rescue me. Thank you. Your bravery will soon be sung all across Egypt. But tell me, Shadow of the Prince, did you not use your Eye of Isis to call on Lady Isis for aid?"

"I did," I said, "but she didn't answer."

Ra frowned. "That's troubling. You should be able to reach her anywhere in Egypt. She wouldn't fail to respond." He paused, his frown deepening. "Unless . . . After I didn't rise on time, the gods would surely have gathered in the capital to figure out what had happened and to plan a response. There's one place they'd do that—the Vault of Divine Wisdom. And that is the one place a message wouldn't be able to reach Isis. If Set has somehow trapped the gods within . . . Oh, this is urgent. We still have a fight ahead of us. Or, I should say that *you* still have a fight ahead of you."

"What do you mean?" Thea asked. "You're coming with us, right?"

"We will get out of the Duat together, but once in the world above I must become the sun and provide light and magic to all of Egypt." He paused, looking us over one by one. "It will be on you to go to the capital, confront Set, and—if I'm right about what he's done to the gods—to free them."

"Oh," Gilli mumbled, "and here I was thinking we'd already done the hard part."

Ra raised his voice. "Ready the barge for departure! Thea, take the tiller. If you piloted the Night Barge as far as this, you can surely steer us straight and true during what's to come.

"Stow the oars and find something to hold on to," Ra said.

With Thea shouting instructions at the rest of us, we worked as fast as we could. We stowed the oars. We threw off the docking ropes and hunkered down.

I looked back at Apep. Had his head moved? It wasn't at quite the same angle I thought it had been. And he was . . . closer. He was closer and moving slowly toward us. His eyes definitely were fixed on us. On *me* actually! "Hey, guys . . ."

Lord Ra stood at the very tip of the barge. He planted his feet widely. He inhaled a deep breath, and then held out his arms to either side.

He looked forward again. His horns were even longer than before. Suddenly, the brilliant glow of a sun disk appeared, framed between his horns. With his hands clenched into fists, the god roared words that I couldn't understand. They sounded ancient, dense, and complicated. His whole body began to glow. Something tall and straight rose up from the deck of the barge. A mast! A sail unfurled from it and glowed with energy.

"Has he ever done this before?" Iset asked Thea.

"No, never," she answered. "He's usually asleep in this part of the cavern and the Night Barge only transforms into *The Boat of a Million Years* outside the Duat. This is a first!"

Turning to glance over his shoulder, Ra's ram head said, "Hold on tight."

58

The Keeper of Souls

Thea shouted, "Everybody hold on! I have a feeling this is going to be epic!"

I wedged myself in between two benches. Khufu used a section of rope to tie himself to the railing. Thea and Gilli huddled inside the cabin, both of them staring out the front windows. Seret flexed her paws, unsheathed her claws, and sank them deep into the deck boards. Only Jumpra didn't seem worried. Like a house cat waiting to be fed, he whipped his body around Ra's legs.

I was so in awe of the god that I was caught totally off guard by what happened next. Jumpra leaped into the air. It was the highest, craziest somersaulting jump

I'd ever seen a cat do. He soared up and over Lord Ra. As he passed above him, he twirled like he was doing a midair cartwheel. His kitten face was enraptured. Upside down, he stretched out one paw and touched Ra's sun disk as he passed above it. He carried on and landed, perfectly, on the other side of Ra. He looked instantly calm, like nothing had happened at all, except I could tell he was pleased with himself. It only took me a moment to realize why.

Jumpra had just *jumped over Ra*! He'd done the one thing he'd named himself for. He was still a kitten, but he'd just accomplished his life goal! He'd jumped over the sun!

If Lord Ra noticed any of this he didn't show it.

The sunsail filled with his energy. The barge leaped forward. We all shouted in excitement. Really loudly. Like, really, really loudly. The entire cavern trembled with it, which was strange, because I was pretty sure none of us had the vocal cords to make that happen. As if to confirm this, a tremendous roar reverberated through the cavern. It shook the walls on either side of it. It knocked loose stones from the ceiling. They fell all around us, tumbling down into the void below.

I climbed out from between the benches, looked behind me, and said, "Oh, no . . ."

It was Apep! He had thawed. He was not only moving, he was in a rage. His body looked even more massive than usual. He squirmed at incredible speed. He belched black smoke and spat flames, his eyes fixed on us with determined focus. He gained on the barge, roaring his anger as he did so.

I shouted to the others, "It's Apep! Go faster!! Must go faster!!!"

The cavern walls rushed by on either side of the barge. Demon fish, excited by the speed, leaped along beside us for a time, until even they couldn't keep up. Try as she might, the curves sometimes caught Thea off guard. On occasion she skimmed the stone. Winged Spirits jumped into flight, protesting and dodging away.

Thea carved the barge through the bend just ahead of us. Her knuckles were white from gripping the tiller so hard. Side to side, she threw her whole body into each new turn. She was amazing, but Apep still gained on us.

At the front of the barge, Ra kept up his incantations. He still held his arms out to either side and shone so brilliantly it seemed he was made entirely of light and energy. He gave no sign that he was aware of the serpent closing in behind us. As if all this wasn't enough, it got worse.

"There's another gate!" Seret cried.

"What? It's closed?" Thea asked. "It's the Keeper of Souls! Usually, the gate is open. She's almost never here. Why tonight?!"

The Keeper of Souls was a monster to rival even Apep. A massive, tentacled monstrosity with more arms than I could count spread out across the gate she held shut behind her. She had an enormous bulbous head and bloodred eyes. When she saw the barge, her numerous tentacles squirmed in anticipation. Her head shifted, exposing a hooked beak of a mouth that she pointed at us. We headed right toward her.

For a moment, I felt everything slipping away. All the hope and excitement and the feeling that we were finally going to escape the Duat and see the living world again . . . it all seemed impossible. The Keeper of Souls and the gate she clung to made an impassable barrier. Behind us, near enough that bellows of smoke clouded the air now, was Apep. At the very least, we'd be smashed between the two of them and crushed by both of their monstrous bodies.

At least, that's how it looked to me. Lord Ra had other plans.

The god kept right on, sails straining with the energy filling them. His voice boomed, "DEMON, MOVE ASIDE!" He slashed the air with one arm. The demon was torn away from the gate and thrown to the side. She smashed against the cavern wall. Ra punched the air with his other fist and the gate splintered, boards and stone and metal supports shattering. The barge shot through the crumbling gate. Pieces of debris swirled all around us, but Thea swerved and dodged the biggest obstacles.

Behind us, Apep squirmed through the debris, still roaring toward us. He thrust his neck forward, stretching his body. His eyes were fixed on me. His mouth was open, fangs bared, about to clamp down on the back of the barge.

"Hang on!" I shouted, sure that he was about to pin us in his jaws.

That didn't happen. Instead, the serpent suddenly jolted back. His mouth clamped shut, bit nothing but air. For a moment, Apep looked as confused as I was. But then we both realized what had happened. The Keeper of Souls had him. The two giant demons became a mass of writhing serpent curls and squiggling tentacles.

We started to pull away. "Yes!" I yelled. "We're going to make it!"

Have I mentioned that sometimes I speak too soon?

Just when I was sure we were safe, one of the Keeper of Souls's tentacles snapped out at us like an enormous whip. The very tip of it wrapped around Lord Ra, squeezed, and plucked him off the barge.

We all yelled, "Noooo!!!!!"

The barge pulled away. Behind us, Ra receded, his arms outstretched toward us.

I watched as Ra pulled his arms in tight to his chest. He bloomed into a bright light and shot a beam of it right at us. He bellowed, "Go! FREE THE GODS!" His words and the beam of light shoved us forward. My last glimpse of Lord Ra was seeing him turn from us and start his struggle with both monstrous demons.

We rushed toward the mouth of the cavern, going faster and faster as the opening grew nearer. We surged out of the cavern mouth and into the world above. Every line and shape of the ship glowed brilliantly.

Every part of it hummed with energy. The Night Barge was now fully *The Boat of a Million Years*! Ra's energy stayed with the ship, propelling us forward.

The sensation of the fresh air caressing my face was amazing, as was the feeling of space expanding out in all directions, so different from the cramped, stifling underworld. As we rose, the desert all around came into view. Looking down from on high in a ship made of light, we flew over the barren, empty desert. We were silent, all of us afraid that Lord Ra might not have been saved after all. All of us aware that we were rushing headlong into a world still owned by demon darkness. Who knew what we would find?

59

Second Thoughts

Set and Rami stood on a raised platform near the Vault of Divine Wisdom, where the Rejector of Rebels had dropped them off. Human laborers worked in long lines, bringing in basket after basket full of gold things: necklaces and bracelets, bowls and goblets, door knockers, vases and small plaques. Still others hefted statues. Some just carried sacks or pushed wagons piled high with gold nuggets. There were great heaps of golden things surrounding the vault. Large vats had been hung above wood fires, and the workers were tossing in the gold to be melted down. Once enough of it was liquid, Set would have it poured over each and every part of the vault. It would cool and harden, further sealing the trapped gods inside.

"Quite impressive for a night's work, wouldn't you

say?" Set asked the prince. "Right now, scenes of chaos and demon rule are playing out in cities and towns all up and down Egypt. My minions are innumerable." The god glanced at Rami and clarified, "That means there are too many of them to count."

Rami didn't respond. He just stared, dejected, at the miserable scene.

Set carried on. "Here's the agenda. We cover the vault with molten gold and watch it harden. Order workers to buff and polish it. Then you and I will go to the throne room and officially become the divine and human rulers of Egypt. We'll have to get some priests to bless it and make it official, but I'm sure we can convince them. Then, it's off on a whirlwind tour of my new domain!"

He slapped Rami on the back, with a bit too much force. The boy stumbled forward and nearly fell off the platform. Rami took a few steps back from the edge. "Wh-what's going to happen to all these people?"

"They'll live lives of constant toil and fear, slaves to their rightful master."

Rami frowned. "What about making Egypt... greater? Isn't that part of what we should do?" He watched the workers strain under their heavy loads for a moment, then said, "You know, all this work would have been *accomplished by now if we had the light of day, with the sun powering the hovering barges and cranes to shift the gold, and with a solar-powered furnace to melt it down. Those poor people wouldn't have to work so hard, either."*

"What's the fun in that?" Set asked, honestly perplexed.

Rami hesitated. "I don't know. I used to think I wanted power, but if it's all about making other people miserable . . . well, that doesn't seem right. I've been thinking about something my brother—"

"That sniveling little do-gooder?" Set snapped a hand up and stopped Rami by showing him his palm. "Forget about him. Just learn to look on the dark side. The masses are here to suffer and toil. They sweat and labor day and night. They live desperate lives of fear and hopelessness as they serve masters who enjoy their misery. See? That's the old-fashioned way. You'll get used to it."

He went to pat Rami on the back again, but the prince dodged him.

Set stiffened. In a tight, low voice, he asked, "Did you deliberately dodge?"

Rami shook his head. "No. I wouldn't do that. I'm no dodger. I just . . ." His eyes darted around until they found something to focus on. "I just wanted to see that better."

He pointed and Set followed his finger. The first

cauldron of molten gold was being cranked slowly up from the ground with a tall, awkward-looking crane. A crew of workers strained at the levers and cranks to make it move.

"Put your backs into it!" Set called.

The workers tried, but still the crane moved slowly.

"They look tired," Rami said. "Maybe we should call it a day? Let them finish up later?"

"Are you mad?" Set asked. "This is the capstone that will assure my rule. All the gods forever trapped. Why would I possibly want to delay that? Really, Rami, you'd do well to toughen up a bit. And don't you dare start having second thoughts. If you're to be my right hand you've got to be merciless."

The cauldron began to pour the molten gold. It spread, glistening in the torchlight. Behind the first crane came another. And another. All poured more and more gold onto the Vault of Divine Wisdom. It covered the whole flat roof and began to drip down the walls, soon covering it completely.

Set said, "From now on we'll call that the Prison of Divine Wisdom. Isn't that great?" He threw back his head and laughed his odd, snorting version of laughter.

Rami looked away. He spotted the messenger beetle wheeling drunkenly above the city as it flew away, carrying his message. With all his weaving, he hadn't gotten very far. Because Rami's gaze was looking into the distance, he was the first to notice a bloom of light far, far away. It was the only bright spot in the entire night sky. "Is that . . . is that Lord Ra?"

Set saw it, too. "No," he said, "that's not possible. He's . . . he's . . . dead. Surely, he's dead!" He leaned forward, his face a tight mask of concentration. He squinted. His eyes quivered as he channeled his godly powers through them, spanning the distance. "Blast it!" he said. "The Boat of a Million Years. *I should've sunk the thing.*"

The light grew brighter, larger. Enough so that the demons also noticed it. They pointed at the light, murmuring, grunting, and grumbling as their slow brains processed what they were seeing. One of them stammered, "Rrrr-rrr-rr-r . . ." He finally managed, "Ra?" The mention of Lord Ra's name struck them all with hushed, murmuring fear. Other voices took up the god's name. Some spoke it. Some grunted it. Some growled it. Some burped it. All feared it.

Set had to think fast. "Everybody calm down!" he shouted. He pulled himself up to an exaggerated version of his natural height. Snout held high, he projected his voice with an air of authority. "Friends, demons, twisted creatures of the foul regions of the Duat, lend me your ears." That got their attention. Many ears swiveled in his direction. "We stand at the cusp of victory." That confused them. Set clarified, "I mean we've almost won this. What we must do now is stand together. This could be our finest hour! All great battles come down to one moment—a moment that requires our bravery. Ra is but a single god. Believe me, if he somehow escaped mighty Apep's belly he'll still be weakened. I pierced him with the Spear of Vengeance. He's weak. Look for yourselves. If he had his full power he'd be blazing up into the sky to light the whole world. What chance does a wounded god have against all of us? Now is the moment for us to hold together and fight as one. Am I right?"

The demons weren't sure. They glanced around, each needing to check with the others before answering.

"You can still have all that I promised you. Let us rally and stand against the tyranny of the light!"

Several demons piped up in agreement. Soon others joined. With that, Set had them. They roared. They shouted in each other's faces. They stomped on the ground. They howled and beat their chests.

It was just the response Set wanted, but quietly and

to himself, he mumbled, "So close. I was so close. I wonder how the old bird escaped." He contemplated that for a moment, then shrugged and turned to the prince. Lowering his voice, he said, "Here's what we do. When Ra gets here and the horde attacks, I'll transform us both into demons. In disguise, we'll hightail it out of here."

"What?" Rami asked. "What about all the stuff you just said?"

"You didn't fall for that, did you? That little speech was just for the dimwitted. Got them riled up. But let's be real. When the Glowy One gets here this horde will be toast. You and I, though, we'll be long gone."

"You tricked them?"

"Of course I did." Set grinned. "It's my one true gift. Okay. Here he comes. Be ready. When I snap my fingers, we'll go out demon style. Horns or a tail? Which do you prefer?"

The Boat of a Million Years *arrived. It was too bright to look at directly. The ship's brilliance slowly faded, changing from shimmering lines of light to its physical, earthly form of wood and canvas and metal. It floated to a stop and several figures were revealed on the deck: Ash and Khufu, Gilli and Seret, Thea and Iset, and a very excited-looking caracal kitten.*

60

Feeding Time

When the barge came to rest in the capital, we finally knew what faced us. It wasn't pretty. A throng of boisterous demons crowding a smoky, shadowy city beneath an endless night sky. A malevolent god sneering at us. No good gods to be seen. In a way, none of that was surprising. We'd known this was all a plot of Set's. And we knew he must have done something to the other gods. What was surprising?

"Rami?" Khufu said. "What are you doing with . . . with . . . him?"

Set's sneer turned into a smile. He draped an arm over Rami's shoulders. "The prince and I have become great friends. Been hard at work all night. As you can see . . ." He swung his other arm out theatrically, indicating the whole foul, dark, smoky scene. "Yes, yes, we've been having a grand time, haven't we, Prince Rami?" Rami tried to pull away from him, but Set tightened his grip and continued before the prince could respond. "He's been a big hit with the demons."

On hearing themselves mentioned, the demons surrounded the barge. They howled and barked and bellowed. One of them croaked out, "Can we eat them now?"

"Yessss, eat them!" another cried.

Others picked up the call and made it into a chant, "Eat them! Eat them! Eat them!"

Some demons clawed at the hull. A few started to climb on board. When one got a grip on the deck, I stomped on his fingers and he dropped away, yowling. Seret scratched another one, and Gilli used a boat hook to threaten a third until he backed away.

During all the commotion, I caught a glimpse of a vibrant color amid the muted black and brown horns and fur and scales. Blue. A lovely iridescent shade of light blue. I saw it for just a second, before it disappeared behind the screen of demon bodies.

"Just a moment!" Set bellowed. "Silence! I said SILENCE!" He didn't get complete silence, but the demons calmed down enough for Set to carry on talking. "Little Thea, I must say I am surprised. Didn't expect to see you again, and in such distinguished company! So kind of you to deliver Khufu, his shadow, and these others to me. I'm sure you have quite a tale to tell. Alas, as you can see, you've not arrived at a happy ending. Haha! It's perfect, though. Now Prince Khufu gets to see the downfall of his family's rule and the rise of the demons! Such fun, eh, Rami?"

Rami struggled to shape an answer but couldn't put more than two words together. "It's not . . . I didn't . . . I'm not . . ."

"He's so excited he's at a loss for words," Set said.

Something touched my toe. Thinking it was a demon, I yanked my foot away and got ready to kick, but I froze instead. The hand reaching through the railing was blue. Pudgy. I looked over and down onto the small, round face of a miniature blue hippo. I opened my mouth in surprise.

And then something even more surprising happened. Another face appeared beside the hippo. A girl in armor and a helmet, with large brown eyes and a face I recognized. I almost shouted, *Princess Sia!*

Almost, but Sia put a finger to her lips before I

could get the words out. I shut my mouth. With quick hand gestures, she pointed in different directions, using her fingers to indicate creeping forward. Understanding, I nodded. She and the hippo sank down into hiding, and I straightened. We had a plan. Delay as the rest of the hippos got into position.

Loudly, I said, "You won't get away with this."

"Won't I?" Set asked, twisting his face into a puzzled expression. "Let me count the ways you are mistaken."

I whispered to the others, "Keep him talking."

Set pushed Rami away so as to have both hands free. He used one hand to count his points on the other's fingers. "One, Lord Ra is serpent food. Two, with him gone humans have no magic. Three, I've imprisoned all the other gods in the *Prison* of Divine Wisdom. I've just renamed it." He motioned toward the now gold-encased chamber. "Four, demons now rule the everlasting night. And five, Egypt is now mine to rule as I please." He grinned maliciously. "So, you see, I've already gotten away with it."

I spotted a hippo as he climbed up a nearby obelisk. He moved with stealth, like a cat sneaking up on a mouse.

In a flat, determined voice, Thea said, "We saved Lord Ra."

For a moment, Set's face drooped with genuine puzzlement. But he shook it off. "Nice bluff, but that's impossible."

Another flash of blue as one of the demons near the barge said, "Who is stepping on my toes?"

"We did save him," Thea continued.

"That's right," Khufu added. "Ash froze Apep and we all helped get Ra out."

"He's still alive," Seret said.

"And he's way more powerful than you are!" Iset spat.

Set sniffed and asked simply, "Where is he, then?"

That was one question we weren't ready to answer.

Glancing over the railing again, I saw that two more hippos had snuck in. They crouched low, ready. Another one slipped through a large demon's legs, holding his nose as he did so.

"I asked a simple question," Set said. "Why won't you answer it? If Ra is alive, why isn't he with you? Why isn't he soaring up into the sky right now?"

"He will," Thea said. "He's coming. He just . . . um . . . got tangled up with something."

"He sent us to warn you," Gilli added. He puffed out his chest, his usually humorous, round face looking sharp and fierce instead. "It's your last chance. Call off this attack before he gets here. If you do, the gods may go easy on you."

Set glanced at Rami. "Can you believe these kids? You have to admit they've got gumption. Lying right to my face. I almost admire them." He turned back to us. "*Almost*. But not quite as much as I loathe them. Demons, you've been patient. And now it's time for your reward. You may feed now."

61

A Princess, a Few Friends, and an Eruption of Hippos

That line had a familiar ring to it, one that sent a chill running up my spine.

For a brief moment, the demons stared at us, licking their chops and seeming amazed that they were being given permission to devour us. The hesitation didn't last long, though. One demon—with the head of a warthog—squealed and dashed forward. With that, the other demons scrambled to get on board the ship.

But the first figure to land on the deck wasn't a demon. It was Princess Sia. Several armed and armored kids her age flanked her. She shouted, "Servants of the Prince, bounce the demons!"

The eruption of hippo power that call unleashed

was immediate. From their hiding spaces beneath the barge, blue balls of fury shot out into the demons. They smashed into demon bellies, knocked demon legs out from under them, sent some twirling into the air. Still others attacked from behind the demons, hurtling in with cocked fists and little legs kicking.

The one perched atop the obelisk had a special target. He leaped from the vault and shot like a pudgy arrow. He slammed into Lord Set's back with enough force to knock a breath of foul air out of the god's lungs. Set was thrown off the platform and fell down into the brawling chaos of the demon horde.

On the barge, we had our hands full fighting off the monsters who managed to clamber aboard. We did our best to beat them back, using anything we could: fists and feet, claws and jaws. Gilli and Iset bonked demons on the head with the boat's oars, getting a few so good that they vanished in a haze of foul-smelling vapor. Gone back to the Duat. That was great, but as one disappeared another stepped in to take its place.

Thea unfurled the sunsail on top of a hyena-shaped demon, tangling it up so that Seret could shove it overboard—squashing a bunch of other demons in the process. More clouds of demon vapor. When one particularly large, six-armed creature got on board, Sia and her friends surrounded it, fighting hand to hand with speed and skill that stunned me.

For once, it was all too much for Jumpra. He scaled the mast and perched at the top, a ball of puffed-up fur and large, frightened eyes.

Human soldiers rallied and ran into the fight, spears and daggers drawn. Laborers joined them, fighting with shovels and axes, waving torches. Crane operators turned the cranes into weapons, sweeping their heavy cauldrons through the demons and knocking them twirling into the air.

The more time passed without the sun rising, the more I feared that Lord Ra had perished for real this time, defeated by both Apep and the Keeper of Souls. Things were just too frantic. I was always moving, always a split second away from death.

I caught a glimpse of Rami. He was still on the platform, his eyes jumping from thing to thing frantically. "Rami!" I shouted. "Don't just stand there! Do something! Help us!"

His gaze locked on me. His cheeks trembled, his eyes full of fear. He mouthed something, but if he actually said anything I couldn't hear it. I looked away from him, so mad I couldn't stand it. He really was betraying us.

A figure rose from the center of the demon throng. Set. In all the motion, there was something frightening in the slow, steady way he kept growing. He grew past his normal height. To twice his size. His arms stretched grotesquely long, his fingers curving into thin, sharp claws. His snout stretched, and the tufts on his head sprouted into twisted horns. He was Set, but a ghastly, monstrous version of himself.

Once transformed, he looked directly at me. The touch of his gaze made my skin burn. I was instantly sweaty, trembling, unable to do anything but stare at him. Around me, the others fought on. They didn't seem to notice Set. He strode toward me, knocking demons out of his path. He stretched out one of his clawed hands and grasped me, pinning my arms to my sides. He lifted me off the barge and brought me close to his face.

"Shadow," he hissed, "how I've wanted to devour you. Now there's nobody who can stop me. Yours will be a slow, painful death."

He opened his mouth. The foul stink brought tears to my eyes. I knew for a certainty that being swallowed by him would be even worse than by Apep. It would be the beginning of ages of suffering. Set, I realized, carried within himself a roaring chaos of pain and discord and misery. There was a vast, hellish realm inside him that took my breath away. I'd glimpsed it once before, but that time I'd been saved by Khufu and Yazen arriving. This time, nobody could save me.

I craned my head around to look at my friends. They were below me on the deck, staring up at me even as they kept fighting the demons. All of them looked as miserable and desperate as I felt. I closed my eyes, not able to bear the sight of either them or of Set's maw as it opened to consume me.

The Radiance of Ra

It was strange then that instead of falling into darkness, a sudden light shone through my eyelids. Warmth washed over me. Rather than exhaling another horrible breath, Set inhaled suddenly, as if surprised. I didn't go down his throat. His jaws didn't close around me. I just dangled there, in a grip that had gone slack.

I opened my eyes to a world suddenly bathed in light. Glorious, radiant light. It was so bright that I blinked as my eyes adjusted. What a scene! Demons all around struck dumb, frozen in violent postures, all of them with their eyes tilted to the sky and terror on their monstrous faces. The sun. Lord Ra! He soared up into the sky and hung above us, midday bright in a blue sky. He'd made it! He was alive!

Set dropped me. I fell screaming down to earth. I was lucky—if you can call it that—to land on a chubby, furry demon who felt like a plush cushion. I scrambled off him and leaped up to the barge. The others swarmed me, relieved and smiling, patting me looking for injuries.

The demons were still near at hand, but they seemed to have forgotten about us. They mumbled and grumbled among themselves. Some gnashed their teeth. Some cried. All stared up at the sun in horror. Considering all the noise and motion and darkness of just moments ago, it was a really weird change of scene. We stood on the barge, sweaty and panting from all the fighting, fists raised and ready if any of them attacked us. But nobody paid us any attention.

"Look!" Thea called, pointing.

Set was shrinking slowly back into his normal form. It was sort of like he was wilting, going soft and dejected, looking like a wet puppy version of himself. He exhaled through his blubbery snout and said, "So close. I was so close to having it all. But . . ." He paused a moment, looking around at all of the now frightened demons. ". . . I'm out of here."

He turned and ran, shoving demons out of the

way. He leaped up onto the platform, grabbed Rami by the wrist, and pulled him as he jumped into the air. Rami craned his head around toward us, mouth open, surprise and regret on his face. Set's free hand came up. His fingers snapped. By the time he and Rami hit the ground they'd been transformed into two hideous demons. They were instantly lost within the throng.

Seeing Set flee did it for the demons. They fell into complete mayhem. They ran in all directions, pushing and shoving, tripping over one another in their haste to get away.

"Rami!" Khufu shouted. "Rami!"

He lurched forward as if he was going to run after him, but I caught him and held him back. "No, Prince! You can't."

"I have to." Khufu tried to twist out of my grip. "He's my brother!"

"He betrayed us," I said. "You saw it."

"We all saw it," Seret said.

Iset added sadly, "Your brother is in league with Set."

Khufu sobbed. Faintly he said, "But he's my brother. Why would he . . ." He walked a few steps away, put his hands on the railing, and stood there.

One by one, the Servants of the Prince left the fighting and jumped onto the ship. They gathered around Khufu protectively, but even they knew to give the prince a moment.

From up on the mast, Jumpra meowed. He wasn't having fun climbing down. Claws deep in the wood, he wiggled, shifted, scooched down a bit, wiggled some more. Apparently, climbing down was the one thing he *wasn't* good at. Eventually, he gave up and just jumped. He landed on the deck, stretched, and licked his paw. His fur settled back to normal. He looked at us as if saying, *What are you looking at?* Then he leaped onto the railing, hissed at a passing demon, and seemed pleased with himself as it ran away.

"Wow," Gilli whispered, "did you see what Set did to Rami? Is it just me, or is Set scary when he gets angry?"

"That," Seret agreed, "wins the contest for the scariest thing I've ever seen."

Thea said, "Yeah, but even he's afraid of Lord Ra."

"Are you all right, Ash?" Iset asked. "You were almost—"

"I'm fine," I said, cutting her off. I was sore, scraped

here and there, but I was alive. I was a lot better off than if Set had swallowed me. That's what mattered. I picked up Jumpra. He started purring, which went a long way toward making me feel better.

Sia walked over to her brother and put a hand on his shoulder. Khufu turned and, seeing her up close after so long, tears pooled in his eyes. They hugged.

"I'm so glad you're here," Khufu said. "When did you become such a fighter?"

"We'll talk about that later," Sia said. "About Rami, though, it's not as simple as it looked." She pulled away from him and turned to face all of us. "I don't think Rami truly betrayed us. I'll explain, but first we have to finish with all of this." She gestured to the demons still chaotically running around the barge. "My crew will help finish the fight. You all, try to free the gods. They're in the Vault of Divine Wisdom."

With that, Sia jumped over the railing, landed on a passing demon's shoulders, and bonked him on the head. The demon vanished beneath her, and she fell through the smoke, landing on her feet and drawing her bow. Her friends did the same. They formed a half circle and began picking off demons with arrows, firing fast and accurately. Clouds of demon smog floated thicker and thicker in the air. Whoever had trained them really knew what they were doing!

"My sister is right," Khufu said. "We still have things to do. Ra said to free the gods." He turned and looked at the massive, gleaming gold cube that had been the Vault of Divine Wisdom. "Let's do it!"

63

Breaking the Vault

The Vault of Divine Wisdom was an enormous rectangular structure, with a single entrance. Or, it once had a single entrance. Now the entire building had been covered in molten gold. It had even flowed down over the door, sealing it closed. Hesitantly, I touched the gold and traced the outline of the door. It was still warm, but it had cooled enough to become solid again.

The workers who had poured the molten gold over it came to us, apologizing to Khufu and explaining that Set had forced them to do it. Khufu assured them that nobody would blame them. "We know that this was all Set's doing," he said.

"But how do we undo it?" Seret asked. "How are we going to get this open?"

"We could chisel away at it," one of the laborers offered.

Another said, "Or build a great fire close to the door to melt it."

"That will take too long," Khufu said. "We need something faster."

Seret pointed to the sun. "Lord Ra is back in the sky. There's magic on our side again."

"Okay," I said. "So what we need is a skilled magician. Luckily, we've got one of the best right here."

Gilli smirked. "You're not talking about yourself, are you? I mean, you're good with giant slugs and things like that, but—"

"No, not me!" I said. "Iset, do you think a spell could melt it?"

"Well, maybe. But are you sure?" she asked. "The last time I did magic it put us all in danger."

Seret scratched her chin with one of her claws. It was one of her thinking gestures. "You could say that. You could also say that the last time you did magic it put us in the one place in the world where we could meet Thea, learn what happened, climb down into the

Duat, and . . ." She pointed to the sky. ". . . bring Ra back to the world."

"He's right," Thea said. She placed a hand on Iset's shoulder. "I wouldn't be here if it weren't for you."

Reluctantly, Iset said, "Okay. I'll try."

She pulled out her stylus. She held it pinched gently in her fingertips as if remembering the weight and feel of it. And then, like the skilled magician she is, she sparked it to life. She began to draw. She was fast, real fast. The spell took shape, her glyphs crackling as they hung in the air. Out here with the bright light of the sun powering them, they looked different from the glyphs I'd cast in the Duat. I tried to read them, but I'd barely started when she'd circled the spell in a cartouche. She slashed in the closing stroke, releasing it.

We all stepped back. The hippos—normally so fearless—slipped behind our legs and peeked out to watch.

The glyphs pulled into a tight ball, pulsing with the energy of a tiny sun. And then it flew into the vault, hitting the center of the door and spreading like liquid flame that sketched out the outline of the door. The gold covering melted away, revealing the door beneath.

And revealing the twisted metal bar that had held it shut. *That* didn't melt. Someone pressed against the door from the inside, but the bar held the door closed. Shouts and entreaties came from inside, but that was all.

Iset looked at me. In the daylight, her eyes were again strikingly silver. "The bar is too strong," she said. "I don't think my magic is powerful enough to melt it. I'm sorry. I can't do it."

"You mean you can't do it alone, but what if we helped?" I asked.

"Oh, that's brilliant!" Gilli said. "Like we did during the shadow testing!"

"For that we'd need more styluses," Seret added.

Khufu knelt to speak to the hippos. "Servants of the Prince, here is your mission. Search the city. Find styluses. Bring them here. Fast."

The hippos nodded gravely. They consulted with one another for a moment, then shot off in all directions, blue blurs moving as fast as bouncy balls. They'd hardly been gone a minute before the first of them zoomed back. Then another. And another. In no time at all they had returned, each of them holding up a stylus gripped in their small fist.

Seeing our surprise, the hippos said in unison, "We know this city like the back of our fists."

"Thank you," I said, "though we didn't need quite this many."

Once Gilli, Seret, and I had chosen styluses, Khufu gave the hippos another mission—to take the rest of the styluses back to the magicians who could also use them. The hippos shot away again.

"Wow," Iset said, "those little guys are pretty great." She raised her stylus. "Okay. We have styluses. What exactly do you have in mind?"

"On the last day of the shadow testing we all made a spell together," I explained. "We each drew our own piece of it. Whatever we thought of. Then we closed it in one big cartouche and the spell became not a bunch of separate spells but one big one. It was more complex than what any of us could have done on our own."

Iset raised her eyebrows skeptically. "That's not something I ever learned about in the academy. But . . . it worked?"

"Not exactly," Gilli said. "This other candidate, Sutekh, added a glyph that made the spell explode on whoever ignited it. That should've been Ash, but then another candidate, Kiya, shoved us away and ignited it herself. She got blown up by it. Big crater in the ground and everything."

Iset stared at us, confused. "So . . . it didn't work? And you want to do that again?"

"We'll do it better. Let's really work together this time. Okay?"

Once they agreed, Khufu and Thea stepped back. Gilli, Seret, Iset, and I raised our styluses. I said, "Let's do this."

We began drawing.

I drew the first thing that came to mind—an image of the strongman back in the village I was raised in. I drew him as I'd thought of him as a kid. To me, he'd seemed stronger than anybody in the world. He worked as a blacksmith. I'd often watch him pounding metal glowing hot from the fire in his forge, shaping it into the tools the villagers needed. I added the symbols for strength and an image of the bar cracking into two.

That's all I had time for. I didn't even read what the others had drawn. With all our glyphs hanging in the air before us, I enclosed them in a big cartouche. I concentrated on binding them with cognitive magic, with making them a thinking spell that would use all of what we'd put into it to do what we wanted. I thought of what I'd done in the Duat to heal Lord Ra. Then, before any of it could fade, I slashed in the strongest closing stroke I'd ever made.

I wish I could describe the spell in a way that really captures it, but it was so much more than any one thing. One spell made the twisted metal come alive, like a wriggling snake that began to eat its tail. Another spell made two horned figures that pulled the knotted spear shaft in opposite directions. A burly, muscled, and glimmering spell-figure strode toward the door, brought up a massive ax, and slammed it down on the twisted spear shaft. That was my part of the spell. And then flames engulfed the door, so hot it felt like I was on fire. The spell contained all these things at once, all working to break the spear.

But also, maybe it was a bit too much because then . . .

Well, then it exploded.

64

Why the Crown Sits Heavy

I have no memory of what happened after that. For the second time in my life, my use of magic had drained me. It knocked me out, into a sleep I was to learn was quite long. I didn't wake on my own but was gently coaxed back into consciousness. A voice beckoned me. In my semi-dreaming state, I thought it was my mother, and that I was still the babe I'd once been in her arms. But when my eyes finally fluttered open there were two faces above me. Neither of them was my mother.

Queen Heta and Lady Isis looked down at me, both of them smiling. The queen said, "Ash, there you are! So good to see you awake."

The goddess added, "You had us worried for a time, but Lord Thoth wove healing and sleep spells so that you could have the rest that you deserved. Come. Sit up."

They helped me to rise and propped a pillow behind me. Not for the first time, I realized I was in the palace infirmary. A small private room that looked exactly like it had when I woke up after my battle with the spell-magician Teket on the final day of the shadow testing. But that was before. What had brought me here this time was different.

"What . . . what happened?" I asked.

"Oh, many things," Isis said. "That spell you children cast created quite a blast. It freed the gods from the prison that the Vault of Divine Wisdom had become. There's much work to be done to clean up the damage Lord Set and the demons created, but you saved us from a very dark time. The gods fanned out across Egypt, each traveling by their fastest method and going to the place where they were needed most. We've returned order. The demons have retreated to their deep lairs. Apep has vanished. As has Set."

"And Rami also," Heta added.

Oh. Rami. The memories came flooding back. Did they know that Rami had been working with Lord Set? It was such a betrayal that I was afraid to ask the question. Instead, I asked the one I could. "My friends. Is everyone all right?"

Isis nodded. "They too were knocked unconscious by the blast. They didn't sleep as long, though. Because you put in the closing stroke most of the spell's energy reverberated back at you. The prince and your friends have been awake and are well. You'll see them soon."

That was a relief. "And Lord Ra?"

Heta gestured toward the open window and the bright day outside it. "He lives, as you can see. He fought a mighty battle with the Keeper of Souls, but he prevailed. And he was only able to do that thanks to you children. You've done extraordinary things since last we spoke."

Oh, boy, was that ever true! It all came rushing back. Sunbursting in the skiff. Finding Sudeen and the caravanners. The unending darkness and Thea. The journey in the Duat, fighting demons, solving riddles, coming face-to-face with Apep, being swallowed, finding Lord Ra, the escape from the cavern, the battle with Lord Set and the demon horde, and finally, the spells that opened the vault. Yes, so much had happened! I could barely believe it all. There was one thing hanging over all of it.

"The prophecy," I said.

"Yes," Heta said. "*When Ra to darkness is consumed* . . . Little did we know that line would so soon become reality."

"Does that mean the other lines are true, too? That those things will happen?"

Isis nodded. "Yes, but what exactly any of those lines mean we cannot say. With prophecy, one only understands it after it's happened. But you are at least armed and ready. You know things will be coming. That will keep you ever vigilant." She smiled and reached out and traced where she'd drawn the Eye of Isis on my face. With her touch, I felt the symbol tingling with life for a moment. "And, hopefully, next time you call for me via my Eye I'll be there to see you and to help. Set's plan to trap us in the vault really was devious. If only he would put that mind of his to work on good instead of mischief. But"—she shook her head—"we all have our role in the drama of life. Set's role is no less important than any other god's.

"Indeed, out of all Set's chaos something positive has been born. We've realized that—as much as we can count on Lord Ra—we must do even better to harness solar power to aid humanity. Lord Thoth has set his other work aside to develop storage methods so that we can harvest the energy of the sun and then save it for use through the night. Light beetles were nice, but he's finding ways to keep many other tools, vehicles, and machines working whether Ra is in the sky or not. Thanks to what you and the other children accomplished there will never be another night as long as the one we just lived through. Or as dark."

That was good to hear! I wouldn't exactly say the whole adventure had made me afraid of the dark, but . . . well, okay. Honestly, I guess I was a little nervous about the dark and probably would be for a while.

Queen Heta cleared her throat. "I'm sure you want to see your friends. There's just one other thing I must ask you about. It's this . . ." She drew something from a fold in her tunic and held it out. The memory pouch that Sudeen had given me. "The other children told us how you used this to access memories you didn't even know you had. Is that so?"

I nodded.

"And it was given to you by a caravanner that you met in the desert? You did not recognize him until you saw him again in the memory from the pouch?"

I nodded again.

"And in one of the memories you saw that this man knew you and Yazen when you were still a baby?"

"Yeah, that's what I saw."

"But Yazen never mentioned this Sudeen before?"

They had a lot of questions, but my answers were simple enough. I shook my head.

The two women shared a solemn look, and the silence lasted long enough to make me nervous. I said, "I don't know if it's even a real memory. Maybe I just—"

"No, it's clear there is substance to this," Heta said. "It's no trick. No false memory. If it was, you wouldn't have been able to answer the One Who Asks Questions correctly."

Oh. Yeah, there was that.

Lady Isis pinched her chin as she thought. "There is a mystery in this that I don't yet grasp. I will speak with Lord Thoth about it. He may have answers that I don't. But that is not a thing to be dealt with just now. This Sudeen appears to have helped you, but not everything is as it appears. And not everyone will want to help you. Ash, if ever you see Sudeen again, you must call me through the Eye of Isis."

"I will, but . . . why? Sudeen helped me."

"So it seems," Isis said. "He may have helped you. Or he may have other motives we don't know yet."

I wanted to ask a bunch of questions, but nothing about the grave look on her face made me think it was time for that.

The goddess turned to the queen. "I think for the time being Ash should keep his pouch of memories. It was given to him for a reason."

I watched what looked like a number of different thoughts pass across the queen's face. How many things was she considering? How many secrets and dangers? I didn't know, but I was relieved when she finally nodded and said, "So be it. But on one condition. Keep the pouch safe, Ash, but let the secrets remaining inside stay secret. Leave your memories in the past for now. Do you agree?"

I nodded, and she held the pouch out to me. I grasped it, but before letting go she added, "Ash, be vigilant. Trust no one except those who are closest to you. This is the life I—and you, it seems—were born to. It's why the crown sits heavy on our heads, and why we worry more than we rejoice." She said this sadly, but then a slight grin lifted one side of her lips. "Perhaps, though, in time you will learn and tell me even more things than I'm able to tell you."

With that, she left the pouch on my raised palm.

65

As Bright as the Sun

When Queen Heta and Lady Isis left, I climbed out of bed and got dressed. A new linen tunic had been laid out for me. It wasn't fancy, but it was comfortable, soft and light on the skin. I cinched it with a leather belt with a turquoise scarab buckle. There was a pair of sandals as well, highlighted with gold thread work. I slipped them on and stood studying myself in the long mirror. Royal casual. That's what this was. And the boy wearing it?

Maybe I was a little taller, a little wider in the shoulders, with more than a few bruises and scratches as evidence of what we'd been through. But beneath all that I was still just me. If anything, I was even more me. I mean, I was all the old things I'd been: a villager raised by a strict but kindly mentor, an orphan who longed to know his parents, a boy who had found the friends he'd always wished for.

But on top of that were the new things. I was part of a prophecy, a player in the fate of Egyptian history, a protector as well as a friend. I'd seen the depths of the Duat and returned from it. I'd brought a god back from the brink of death. And I'd been gifted memories from my earliest days. Because of them I knew my mother's face and could hear her voice. And because of that I knew that I'd been loved. Whatever drove my parents to leave me in Yazen's care wasn't abandonment. It was part of a greater purpose. One way or another, I was going to find out what that purpose was. If I could, I'd play a part in it. I would see my mother again. I'd look for her in each rising sun. Someday, she'd find me. Or I'd find her. And perhaps when I could look into other memories from the pouch I'd see and hear my father as well.

Yes, I was different, but the differences were mostly on the inside.

Something else had been set out for me. Several

belts with jeweled daggers. They were beautiful and well-crafted. Also, a spear leaned against the wall, longer and stouter than the one Ammut had snapped over her knee. I ran my fingers over it, but I didn't pick it up. Nor the daggers. I would strap them on soon, I knew, and I'd be the Shadow Prince again. Today, though, I just wanted to see my friends, and for things to be calm, peaceful. And brightly lit!

A knock on the door pulled me away from the mirror. I opened it and was surprised to find Princess Sia waiting for me. This version of Sia looked more like the shy girl I'd remembered meeting during the shadow testing. She had the same large brown eyes and thoughtful expression. It was a quiet energy that was very different from that of the warrior girl who had fought Set and his demons. Like me, she wasn't wearing armor or carrying any weapons.

"If you're ready, Ash," she said, "I'll take you to Khufu and the others. They're waiting for you in the Great Plaza."

We didn't speak as we weaved through the corridors of the infirmary, past rooms in which I caught glimpses of other patients. Clearly, many had been injured during the demon uprising. Healers and even magicians attended them. I was glad for that. I knew they'd get the best care possible, which was exactly what they deserved.

When we stepped outside, I asked, "How is everyone? Khufu and the others. Everyone's really all right?"

Sia dipped her head. "They've been through a lot. You know that, of course. But yes, they're all right. They've had a few days to recover. There's a lot to catch you up on."

"Like what?"

"For one, Khufu is going to train with me and my friends—to learn fighting techniques from Lady Sekhmet. Seret, too. Sekhmet can teach her special lioness claw-and-jaw skills. We hope that you will join us."

Wow. Train with Lady Sekhmet? That would be amazing. And terrifying! She was known as the Powerful One, the Mistress of Dread, and other equally frightening titles. Thankfully, she was one of Egypt's fiercest protectors. Yazen had taught me a lot of things. I couldn't even imagine what a *lioness* warrior goddess could teach me.

"I'd like that," I said. "It terrifies me, but . . ."

"Don't worry. She's only scary when she needs to be." Sia smiled. "Sekhmet has a soft side, too. You'll see."

She led me through a tunnel, up a flight of stairs, and onto the Avenue of the Gods. It was awe-inspiring walking beneath the massive statues of gods like Sekhmet, Ra, Horus, and Bastet. In the bright and warm sunlight, I blinked as I looked up at them. The child in me had always thought the gods were enormous beings like their statues. Seeing Bes's and Taweret's towering and impressive sculptures here, it was funny to think how down-to-earth they seemed in person. Bes's cranky demeanor. Taweret's earnest devotion to protecting young children. I guess seeing and hearing them made them feel more . . . well, more human, even though I knew they were much more than that, too.

"Iset is still going to train Gilli," Sia said as we continued walking, "but they're also going to work with Lord Thoth to find the best ways to harness the sun so that we can have power night and day."

"What about Thea?" I asked. "With Lord Set hiding, who is going to pilot the Night Barge?"

"Thea has officially become the pilot," Sia said. "The first human ever to have that rank aboard the Night Barge. She won't be alone, though. The other gods have agreed to take turns on the nightly voyage with her. Apep is also in hiding and the other gods are ensuring Lord Ra will always have a protector to keep him from being attacked."

Again, I was stunned. That meant that Thea was going to spend night after night with different gods, getting to know them, hearing their stories, learning from them. "That's amazing," I said.

"And last but not least there's Babbel."

"Who?" I asked.

Sia suddenly looked serious. She stood straight, clicked her heels, and saluted. "Babbel, Messenger Beetle First Class!" At my perplexed face, Sia hunched over, laughing. "I guess you don't know him. You'll meet him. He's a good beetle. He was trying his best to help during the uprising. I vouched for him and he's been promoted. I think he's pretty happy."

We reached a high balcony that looked over the Great Plaza toward the Vault of Divine Wisdom. With the gardens and pools, tall obelisks, and colorful patterns in the paving stones, it was beautiful. Bathed in the bright light of the sun. Bustling with people. It was a wonderful sight.

"Do you see what they're doing on the vault?" Sia asked. On one side of it, there was scaffolding set up from bottom to top. Workers were doing something there. "They've decided to leave the gold covering as a reminder of what happened. Those artists are carving hieroglyphs of your deeds into the gold. All who come and gaze upon it can read the tale of the children who voyaged through the underworld—through the dangers of the Duat—to save a god, to fight demons, and to bring sun and life back to Egypt. It's sure to be a tourist attraction for years to come. That's your story, Ash, and it will be written in gold for all time."

"What about your story?" I asked. "You played a part in the fight, too."

"It's all right. My time will come. My story is just getting started." She smiled, but then grew more serious. "But Ash, I came and got you because I wanted to talk about something with you. It's about my brother. Rami, I mean."

I groaned and shook my head. "I can't believe he betrayed us all and joined Set."

Sia stopped walking, turned toward me, and pinned me with her eyes. "You *shouldn't* believe it. I know everyone does. I know how it looked. I know that Rami has made many mistakes. He's not evil, though. He's . . . unsure of himself. He's worried about how he fits in to the family and what his role is now that Khufu has you—and possibly the throne in time. Being afraid can make people do the wrong thing. But I believe in him. I'm going to find a way to bring him back to the family."

"'Being afraid can make people do the wrong thing' sounds like something my mentor, Yazen, would say during one of his lessons," I said. "Have you been talking to him?"

"Not yet. But I'll get to. He's here, waiting for you."

"Hey Ash!" someone called.

A figure waved from near the vault. Several figures. It was Khufu, Gilli, Seret, Iset, Thea, Jumpra, and a beetle who looked to be hovering in the air in excitement. And also Yazen! He really was here!

"We shouldn't keep them waiting," Sia said.

We started down the long sloping ramp to the Great Plaza and the Vault of Divine Wisdom. Before long, I was jogging. Then running. My friends did the same, running toward me.

And behind them Yazen waited with a smile on his face that was as bright as the sun.

Glossary of the Gods in the Shadow Prince Series

APEP was a giant serpent deity of evil, destruction, and chaos. He was the archenemy of the sun god, Ra. Every night, as the sun traveled through the under-world, he would launch his attack. It was Set's job to fight him. Apep was a powerful force who could never be entirely defeated. He was not worshipped like other gods; instead, he was feared.

BES was one of the most popular Egyptian gods. He protected women and children, fended off evil, and could be fierce when fighting for peace and justice. He was featured on lots of everyday items such as furniture, mirrors, and knife handles. Bes is depicted as a bearded dwarf with large ears, bowlegs, and some lion facial characteristics.

HORUS was the son of Osiris and Isis, the divine child of the holy family triad. He is one of many gods associated with the falcon. His name means "he who is above" and "he who is distant." The falcon had been worshipped from earliest times as a cosmic deity whose body represents the heavens and whose eyes represent the sun and the moon. Horus is depicted as a falcon wearing a crown with a cobra or the Double Crown of Egypt.

ISIS represented the power of love to overcome death. She brought her husband, Osiris, back to life and saved her son, Horus, from certain death. She was portrayed wearing the hieroglyph for "throne" on her head, and she sometimes wore a solar disk between cow horns. She was also often depicted mourning the death of her husband and nursing their son.

MAFDET was a goddess of justice who pronounced judgment and meted out execution swiftly. Her name means "She Who Runs" for the speed with which she dispensed justice. The earliest feline deity in Egypt, she protected people from venomous bites, especially from scorpions. Mafdet is also the protector of the pharaoh, his chambers, his tomb, and other sacred places.

NEKHBET, portrayed as a vulture, was the principal goddess of Upper Egypt, whose king she protected. Her northern counterpart was the cobra goddess Wadjet. The two are referred to as "the Two Ladies." She was also a protector of royal children and, in later periods, of all young children and expectant mothers.

RA was the sun god and was considered the central and original power of creation. The daily rising and setting sun offered tangible evidence of the sun's power to fall into the western sky and be reborn each morning in the eastern sky. Ra brought Maat, the principle of truth and balanced justice, to the Egyptians. This became the cornerstone of Egyptian civilization.

SET was the god of darkness, drought, and chaos. He was the opponent of everything good and life-giving. He was an animal-headed deity with a curved head, tall square-topped ears, and an erect arrow-like tail. The animal he represents has not been identified.

SOBEK was a god of the Nile who brought fertility to the land. As the "Lord of the Waters" he was thought to have risen from the primordial waters of Nun to create the world and to have made the Nile from his sweat. One creation myth states that Sobek laid eggs on the bank of the waters of Nun, thus creating the world.

TAWERET was a hippopotamus goddess, though she also has the limbs and paws of a lion, and the back and tail of a Nile crocodile. She was a protector of women and children and helped with childbirth. She was nurturing but could be ferocious when she needed to be. Like Bes, Taweret was featured on household items such as furniture, cosmetic cases, pots, and spoons, and in fertility images.

THOTH was the ibis-headed moon god and the patron of the arts, hieroglyphics, science, speech, and wisdom. He was the author of the Book of the Dead and delivered the final verdicts at the trials of dead souls. Thoth organized the government and religion, as well as being the protector of scribes. Considered a great magician, he knew "all that is hidden under the heavenly vault."

Acknowledgments

My heartfelt thanks to my editor, Elise McMullen-Ciotti, to Stacy Whitman, and to everyone at Tu Books and Lee & Low. Thank you for believing in these novels and for making *The Shadow Prince* into a series!

About the Author

DAVID ANTHONY DURHAM is the award-winning author of the Acacia fantasy trilogy: *The War with the Mein*, *The Other Lands*, and *The Sacred Band*, as well as the historical novels *The Risen*, *Pride of Carthage*, *Walk Through Darkness*, and *Gabriel's Story*. His middle grade solarpunk fantasy novel, *The Shadow Prince*, was his first book for young readers and the beginning of this series. His novels have been published in the UK and in French, German, Italian, Polish, Portuguese, Romanian, Russian, Spanish, and Swedish. When he isn't authoring books, Durham teaches creative writing at the Stonecoast MFA Program. You can find him at davidanthonydurham.com.

RESOURCES FOR EDUCATORS

Visit our website, leeandlow.com, for a complete Teacher's Guide for *The Longest Night in Egypt* as well as discussion questions, author interviews, and more!

Our *Teacher's Guides* are developed by professional educators and offer extensive teaching ideas, curricular connections, and activities that can be adapted to many different educational settings.

How Lee & Low Books Supports Educators:

Lee & Low Books is the largest children's book publisher in the country focused exclusively on diverse books. We publish award-winning books for beginning readers through young adults, along with free, high-quality educational resources to support our titles.

Browse our website to discover Teacher's Guides for 600+ books along with book trailers, interviews, and more.

We are honored to support educators in preparing the next generation of readers, thinkers, and global citizens.

LEE & LOW BOOKS
ABOUT EVERYONE • FOR EVERYONE